TESSERACT

INFINITY ENGINES BOOK V

ANDREW HASTIE

There are more things in heaven and earth, Horatio,
Than are dreamt of in your philosophy.

Other books in the Infinity Engines universe.

The Infinity Engines

1. Anachronist

2. Maelstrom

3. Eschaton

4. Aeons

5. Tesseract

Infinity Engines Origins

Chimæra

Changeling

Infinity Engines Missions

1776

1888

1

REWIND

[Exposition Universelle, Paris. Date: 1889]

The world around Josh drained of colour, the noise of the circus fading into the background as his mind tried to deal with the realisation that Zack was gone.

Caitlin turned towards him, her eyes wide with fear and brimming with tears. Instinctively, he reached inside his jacket for the tachyon, his fingers finding the rewind button before it came out of his pocket.

Praying that two minutes would be enough, he pushed it.

Nothing happened.

Rufius held up his own watch. 'They're useless, the entire circus is surrounded by some kind of stasis field — something to do with the ticketing system.'

Josh squinted in the half-light, anxiously scanning across the rows of seats, searching the sea of happy faces for any sign of a baby. Suddenly it seemed as if the entire audience was made up of families, children of all ages squealing with delight at the antics of the clowns.

'What's the matter?' asked Alixia, getting up from her chair.

'Someone's taken Zachary,' shouted Rufius, his deep voice carrying over the noise. 'We need to search the marquee.'

Her eyes hardened and her mouth set into a tight, thin line. She gestured to the rest of her family to get up, much to the displeasure of the people behind them.

With her usual efficiency, Alixia organised them into pairs and sent them off in different directions.

'They won't have gone far,' she tried to reassure Caitlin. 'No one can leave the tent during the show. I've sent Rufius to talk to Cuvier's security team, he'll have men covering all of the exits.'

'What if they get out into the park?'

'They won't,' Alixia said calmly. 'Don't worry.'

Those were two of the hardest words Caitlin had ever heard.

Josh wrapped his arms around her as the others left.

'Why would someone take him?' she asked between sobs. The sense of loss was so intense, it felt like someone was ripping her heart out.

'I don't know,' was all Josh could manage through gritted teeth. He wanted to be out there searching for him, he could feel the anger building inside, like a coiled spring, his body tensing for action.

In an effort to calm himself, Josh closed his eyes, letting his mind replay the events of the last ten minutes. It began with the distraction by the harlequin, for some reason he'd been convinced it was Dalton Eckhart — which made absolutely no sense. The arrogant bully who'd nearly destroyed the timeline hadn't existed in any of the last fifty iterations of the timeline — no one should even know who he was. But Josh could still see him, waving from the stalls with that stupid leering grin on his face.

'Do you think it was because he's a seer?' Caitlin whispered into his ear, breaking his concentration.

Josh opened his eyes and sighed. 'I doubt it. Hardly anyone knew.'

She pulled away from him, wiping her cheeks with her sleeves. Her eyes burned with a dark intensity as she tried to make sense of what had happened.

'Who was it you saw?' she asked, as if sensing Josh's thoughts.

'No one you know. You've never met him. Anyway it couldn't have been him.'

Desperate for answers, he could see she wasn't about to be so easily put off. Caitlin put her hands on either side of his face and glared into his eyes. 'Tell me!'

'His name was Dalton Eckhart. I used to know him, in another life.'

Part of him was relieved when there was no flicker of recognition at the sound of his name, he didn't want to have to explain who Dalton was. 'I thought he was dead,' he added.

She scowled. 'And was it him?'

Josh shrugged. 'I don't know. I lost him in the crowd.'

She let go of his face. 'I should have stayed—'

'Don't do that to yourself.' Josh cut her off. 'You didn't do anything wrong. We can't be with him twenty-four seven and I'd trust Rufius with my life.'

She bit her bottom lip and crossed her arms over her chest. 'I know, so would I. But why did he think it was me?'

'No idea, maybe you'll find a way to come back and get him?'

Caitlin shook her head. 'Unlikely, the circus is time-bound. It only exists in the now, you can't weave in here.'

The latest act finished and the crowd around them rose to their feet, giving a rapturous round of applause.

'How long before the show finishes?' asked Josh, watching the performers take a bow.

'One more I think.'

Caitlin caught Lyra's eye as she paraded around the edge of the ring. She stepped down and walked over to them.

Lyra was stunning in her shimmering sequinned costume. A plume of white feathers were woven into her hair and another set swept behind her like a peacock's tail.

'Where are the others?' she asked, looking at the empty seats.

Caitlin took her hand; it was something they had done since they were children, a quick way of conveying a lot of information without the need for words. The smile rapidly faded from Lyra's face as she read the events directly from her touch.

'Have you called the Protectorate?'

Caitlin shook her head. 'Your mother thinks they're still in the tent.'

Lyra's eyes rolled back, their whites shining in the semi-darkness of the stalls. Her brow furrowed as she turned her head blindly one way, then another. 'I can feel his presence, but something is obscuring his location,' she added in a wistful voice.

The band struck up once more, signalling the start of the final act, and the audience began taking their seats.

Lyra's eyes returned to normal. 'I need to tell Uncle Georges not to let anyone leave. The temporal stasis will be released after the next act.' She turned on her heels and ran down the stairs towards Benoir who was surrounded by prowling sabre-tooth cats.

Alixia and Methuselah returned a moment later. The expressions on their faces told Josh everything he needed to know.

'I need to go,' he began. 'I can't just sit around and wait for something to happen.'

Alixia grasped Caitlin's hand and nodded. 'We'll take care of her.'

Josh bounded up the staircase towards the higher ranks of bleachers. Half way up there was an exit, he ducked through the heavy velvet curtains and found himself on a wide corridor running around the inside of the tent wall. A ramshackle line of stalls were selling hot food, drinks and other merchandise to passers-by. There were hardly any visitors out here, most were inside watching the show, but a few stragglers were perusing the wares or hurrying back from the toilets.

Josh spotted the colonel coming towards him, his face flushed pink beneath his beard and there was a sense of purpose to his stride that told Josh it wasn't his first circuit of the perimeter.

'Nothing,' muttered Rufius when he reached Josh. 'The guards have been briefed at every exit, but there's not much we can do once the temporal stasis field drops. Most of them will simply return to their own timeline.'

'Can we keep them here?'

Rufius blew out his cheeks. 'That's up to Cuvier. I've not been able to find him as yet.'

'Lyra's gone to talk to him.'

'Good.' He clapped Josh on the shoulder. 'Don't worry my boy, we'll have the little fellow back in no time.'

'Lyra thinks we should call in the Protectorate.'

Rufius grimaced. 'Wouldn't be my first choice, but it's your decision.'

Josh knew exactly what he meant. Chief Inquisitor Mallaron had already tried to have him redacted, and he wasn't going to forget the stay in Bedlam courtesy of the Raven either.

Simeon De Freis joined them, slightly breathless from running. 'No sign of him in the Southern quadrant.'

'So they're still in the crowd,' said Rufius. 'Hiding in plain sight.'

'Have you thought about calling the Protectorate?' asked Sim.

'Yes,' replied Josh and Rufius in unison.

Sim held up his hands in surrender. 'Okay, just a suggestion.' He fished his almanac out of his coat. 'Any idea who might have taken him?'

'No,' replied Josh, trying to ignore the terrible visions of what might be happening to his son, his over-active imagination was making it difficult to think clearly.

Sim made a quick note with the stub of a pencil and wedged it back into the spine of the book.

'It's just that they say the first twenty-four hours are the most crucial.'

'Who does?'

'We do,' came the voice of a stranger.

The three turned as one to find a tall, dark haired man in a long leather coat standing behind them.

'Inspector Sabien,' he said with a strong Irish accent. 'I believe you have lost a child.'

2

PROTECTORATE

[Exposition Universelle, Paris. Date: 1889]

Protectorate officers were standing at strategic points around the main ring when Josh walked back into the arena. Their faces were obscured by dark lensed masks, watching over the crowds like predatory birds.

Benoir and Lyra were working with the other performers to keep the animals calm while Sabien's officers were taking down the names of every member of the audience before letting them leave.

There was a tense atmosphere amongst the crowd; no one was especially keen on the Protectorate, whose heavy handed approach had ended the last act before the finale could be completed. Men and women were still hanging from ropes above their heads as the technicians hastily worked on the rigging to bring them down safely.

Uncle Georges sat despondently on one of the small podiums kicking mounds of sawdust with his velvet shoes.

'If the perpetrators are still here we'll find them,' reassured Sabien as they passed Caitlin and Alixia.

'Where else are they going to be?' snapped Caitlin.

The inspector ignored her and went over to talk to Cuvier.

'Who called them in?' asked Rufius once Sabien was out of earshot.

'Benoir,' said Caitlin. 'When they couldn't find Uncle Georges he had no choice.'

'Where was the old bugger?'

'Indisposed,' Alixia explained politely, 'with one of the seamstresses.'

'So what happens now?' asked Josh, watching the slow procession of families filing past the various officers before disappearing back to their own time.

'They're taking names, checking identities and then letting them go,' explained Alixia.

Caitlin scoffed. 'Shouldn't they just be looking for babies?'

'I'm sure they are.'

An hour later the arena was virtually empty.

Sabien had ordered his officers to begin a sweep of the benches, moving slowly, checking beneath the ranks for abandoned bags or bundles of clothes.

'This will take a few hours,' the inspector explained, climbing the stairs to where they were sitting. Caitlin refused to leave their seats in case they found some way to rewind once the stasis field was dropped.

'We're not leaving,' she protested, her eyes glowering.

'I think you would be better off at the station. We need to ask you some questions and there's nothing else you can do here.'

Josh took her hand. 'You need to eat something at least,' he pleaded with her.

'How did they escape?'

The inspector adjusted one of his gloves. 'That is what we intend to find out. My officers tend to work better when they're not being observed.'

There were always rumours about what kinds of special ability the Protectorate looked for in a recruit. They were said to be picked from the darkest parts of the Order and many believed that the division had more than a few eccentricities amongst their agents.

'Lyra says someone is hiding him,' Caitlin muttered under her breath.

Sabien took out his almanac and thumbed through a few dog-eared pages. 'That would be Lyra Cousineau?'

Her married name still sounded odd to Caitlin, and her brain took a few seconds to process it. She nodded. 'Yes, she's a seer.'

The inspector made a note against her name, put his book away and adjusted a series of dials on a bracer strapped to his wrist.

'So if you would like to accompany me,' he said, holding out his hands to Josh and Caitlin.

Caitlin shook her head.

'I don't want to.'

'It wasn't a request.'

A shimmering bubble expanded around the three of them and the others stood back as the field hardened into a mirror field and then disappeared altogether.

[Ministry of Justice, Chrysler Building, New York. Date: 1930]

Sabien's tenth-floor office was a small, minimally furnished corner room overlooking Central Park that smelled strongly of coffee and old leather. As he took off his overcoat, Josh spotted a large pistol holstered under his jacket. He pulled out the gun, a .38 Special, and locked it in a drawer in his desk.

Whether it was from shock or the technology he used to pull them out of the circus, they were both feeling exhausted. Caitlin grudgingly accepted the espresso that Sabien poured from a small metal percolator, which looked strangely out of place in his gloved hand.

She shifted awkwardly in her chair, like a child being made to sit still against her will. Josh tried to take her hand, but she refused, glaring at him with a wild look, like a feral cat.

'I promise this won't take long,' Sabien assured them, sitting down in his seat and dropping a cube of sugar into his cup. 'The sooner we have all of the facts the sooner we'll have your child—'

'Zachary,' snarled Caitlin, 'call him by his name.'

The inspector held up his hands in surrender. 'My apologies, Miss Makepiece. The sooner we'll have Zachary back with you. Am I right in thinking he was only a month old?'

'Seven weeks,' she corrected him.

He nodded and took out a pencil, correcting something in his almanac.

'And you left him with —' He consulted his notes. 'Rufius Westinghouse, while you went to get popcorn.'

'Is that a crime?' asked Caitlin.

Sabien sighed and put down his notebook. He looked tired, his jaw clenching under a three-day-old beard. There were dark circles beneath his eyes, which looked haunted, like a man who'd seen too much.

'No, I'm just trying to understand the sequence of events. To build up a picture of what really happened.'

It was Josh's turn to snap. 'Why can't you just go back and check? I thought that's what you guys did?'

The corner of the inspector's mouth twitched. 'Usually it is, but the circus has some rather interesting temporal shielding that my technicians believe may not be strictly legal.'

'Meanwhile someone runs off with our son?'

Sabien ignored the question and went back to reading from his notes. 'Westinghouse believes that it was you that came back to take Zachary to the toilet. Now, why would he think that?' he asked, looking up at Caitlin.

She gripped Josh's hand, her nails digging into his palm. 'I've no idea, I was with Josh buying popcorn. Don't you think I would remember taking my own son to the bathroom?'

'So he was mistaken?'

'Obviously.'

He turned the page, his eyes scanning slowly across the notes that were scrolling across its surface. Josh guessed they were reports from other members of his team.

'Is it true you only returned from the Maelstrom seven weeks ago?'

Caitlin sat back in her chair and folded her arms. 'I did. Zachary was born as I re-entered the continuum. I'm not sure how that's relevant.'

'May I ask why you were out there?'

'No, that's none of your business,' she said, shaking her head.

Sabien shrugged nonchalantly and took a sip of his coffee. There was something of a seer about him, Caitlin couldn't put her finger on it, as the colour of his eyes changed slightly.

'Can you think of any reason why someone would want to take your child?'

Caitlin bit her bottom lip, tears streaming down her cheeks. 'He was a perfectly normal baby.'

'Healthy,' Sabien corrected her, his eyes narrowing. 'Most people say healthy baby.'

Josh stepped in, changing the subject. 'Don't you think we've asked ourselves the same question? What we want to know is what you're going to do about finding him!'

Sabien stood up and went over to the window. The sky was darkening outside and the lights of New York's skyline twinkled in the dusk. He was wearing a three-piece suit that had seen better days and Josh wondered exactly how senior this investigator really was.

'The standard procedure for an abduction generally involves a site wide search of the area and a memory probe of all witnesses. Are you willing to undergo a reading?'

'Whatever it takes,' said Caitlin, wiping her eyes with her sleeve.

Josh was less enthusiastic, the last thing he needed was a redactor digging around inside his head. 'We weren't actually there. Shouldn't you start with Rufius?'

Caitlin glared at him.

Sabien turned back from the view. 'We already have Westinghouse downstairs. We're just awaiting the arrival of the Grand Seer.'

3

QUESTIONS

[Ministry of Justice, Chrysler Building, New York. Date: 1930]

R ufius paced around the small interview room feeling like a caged bear at the zoo.

Muttering to himself as he walked, he tried to ignore the presence of the Protectorate guard who was standing like a statue in one corner of the room. The black mask hid any sign of humanity.

They'd taken away his almanac and his tachyon, so there was no way to know what was going on with the search. It was quite obvious from the way they were treating him that they thought he was a suspect.

'If only that fool Benoir had just given him a little more time,' he said under his breath. 'I'm sure I could have found the baby, but now the bloody crows are involved everything's about to get way more complicated.'

And now they'd lost the advantage of time. *Damn Cuvier and his stupid temporal tricks.*

For the hundredth time, Rufius went over the last

moments in his mind: Caitlin came back to her seat. She'd smiled and taken Zachary out of his arms, telling him that he needed changing, but the crowd had been so loud and the bright lights of the show so dazzling, maybe it wasn't her?

No, it had definitely been her.

He shook his head, trying to rattle the memories into something that made sense, but it just made his head ache. It was a waste of time, he had a good memory for detail, you had to in his line of work.

When Kelly arrived they would know for sure.

Rufius remembered Inspector Sabien, he was a good man. They had met once before, a long time ago, when Marcus Makepiece murdered the men who'd imprisoned him. Caitlin found her uncle, trapped in a mirror dimension, he'd been in a terrible accident that was hushed up by his commanding officer, Colonel Jaeger. The Xenos called him a 'Chimaera', his body had been merged with a creature from the Maelstrom. She'd saved his life, but she wouldn't remember any of that — Kelly had redacted her.

Sabien was a bloodhound, the kind of cop that didn't give up, no matter what. He was working homicide back then and Rufius wasn't sure who he'd pissed off to get moved to missing children cases — the man was obviously not destined for promotion.

Much like himself.

The door swung open and the Grand Seer entered with his usual theatrical finesse, a trail of black feathers sweeping in behind him.

'Westinghouse you old fool! What on earth have you got

yourself into now?' Kelly asked, handing Rufius a silver hip flask.

Rufius opened the flask and took a long drink.

'Well, that's what you're here to find out,' he said, handing it back.

This wasn't the first time the Grand Seer had gone rummaging around in Rufius's mind, but it was no less annoying. The man was a skilful redactor, able to tiptoe through someone's memories without leaving a trace. Yet, there was something terribly humiliating about letting him into your most private thoughts, like being made to stand naked in front of your peers.

Kelly took off his feathered cloak and handed it to the Protectorate guard as if he were his personal valet which made Rufius smile - if nothing else, the man knew how to make someone look ridiculous.

Sitting on the opposite side of the table, the seer took a crystal ball out of his black robes and rolled up his left sleeve, revealing an elaborate array of scars, the markings of his profession.

Kelly's eyes darkened as he waggled his fingers in the air like an old woman tuning an invisible harp — most of the ritual was just for show. He had known the man long enough to have learned the old fool's tricks.

Focusing on the small scrying globe, Rufius watched the inverted face of the seer going through the 'gobbledegook' phase of his mantra.

His voice grew deep, like a Shakespearean actor delivering a monologue.

'If circumstances lead me, I will find where truth is hid, though it were hid indeed within the centre.'

The glass sphere filled with swirling smoke and Rufius could feel the seer's mind reaching into his. With tiny, gentle movements of unseen fingers, his memories parted like a deck of cards spread across a table. As the seer shuffled the moments into order, he began to hear the sounds of the circus and catch fleeting glimpses of the show, pulling him back into that moment.

And suddenly there he was, sitting with the baby nestled in his arms, watching Lyra on the back of a mastodon as she rode it around the ring. Just as the first time, he caught the whiff of something dreadful emanating from Zack's nappy and looked up to find Caitlin walking along the row of seats towards him, smiling with her arms outstretched to take Zachary.

'He needs to be changed,' he said to her as she approached.

She nodded and took him, then turned and made her way up the stairs. Rufius could feel the sense of relief that came with not having to deal with it himself.

'I see no falsehood here,' said Kelly, the memory dissolving away.

'I thought she spoke, but it was me,' Rufius said to himself. 'I could have sworn she had.'

Kelly picked up the glass and held it up to magnify one of his eyes. 'Sometimes the mind can play tricks.'

As he spoke the sphere disappeared.

The Grand Seer stood and took his cloak back from the guard. 'You may release him, he speaks the truth.'

The man nodded and unlocked the door.

Kelly walked out of the room and along the corridor. Rufius followed a few steps behind.

Once they were out of earshot of the guard he turned to face him. 'So did you notice the faint smell?' he asked, lowering his voice to a hoarse whisper.

'You mean the nappy? I'd hardly call that faint.'

The seer tapped the side of his long nose. 'Not the child, the other smell. There was an odour about the memory that sent this old beak a-twitching.'

'What was it?'

'Electrickery. No mistaking it.'

Rufius tried to mask his confusion and failed.

'The thing that took the child was heavily dosed in it. Like a sailor's strumpet on shore leave.'

'An electromagnetic field?'

Kelly waggled a finger. 'Exactly.'

'And you think it was using some kind of cloaking device?'

The seer shrugged, wrapping his own cloak about him. 'I've no idea, but it might explain why these fools can find no trace of the charlatan.'

They reached the outer door, which looked more like something that belonged in a bank vault.

'So how are we supposed to find him?' said Rufius, hammering on the metal hatch.

Kelly took out a small key and placed it in the lock, which was much larger. 'Lyra formed a powerful bond with young Zachary. It wouldn't surprise me if she could find him, given enough time and a small pinch of luck. I will call a Conclave of the Seers Guild.'

Giving the key a delicate twist, they heard the locking mechanism begin to grind into motion.

'I don't think we have the luxury of time and we may need more than luck,' protested Rufius, standing back as the door swung aside.

'Indeed. My nose tells me we may need a time-*ship*,' Kelly said, stepping through the round opening on tiptoes like a cat on a hot tin roof.

'The *Nautilus*? But she's back in the Maelstrom.'

'Then I suggest you look at ways to contact the adventurous Madame Makepiece.'

He plucked a black feather from his cloak, wrote something in the air with its nib and disappeared.

4

SHAPESHIFTER

[Regent's Park Zoo, London. Date: Present Day]

'Hello stranger,' Kaori greeted Sabien as he stepped through the pressure door into her lab.

She was standing over the grotesque remains of a creature which lay disembowelled on the table. The diminutive Japanese doctor was covered from head to toe in what the inspector assumed was its last meal.

'Lesson for today,' she said, waving a metal wand. 'Never puncture a gaseous perigoar's stomach with a laser scalpel.'

His face screwed up at the smell, it was like it had eaten something from the bottom of a sewer.

She sighed. 'Guess, you'll not be wanting a kiss then?'

He laughed, it was a deep, honest sound that she adored. 'No, this is business.'

She put down the surgical device and pulled off her latex gloves. 'Wow, okay. Give me a sec. I'll just go and hose myself down.'

He watched her walk into the decontamination chamber and slip out of her scrubs. She knew he was watching and the sight of her bare bottom was nearly enough to forget what he came for.

'You can come and scrub my back if you like,' she said over the sound of the shower.

'Working,' he reminded her.

'Never stopped you before.'

He wandered around the table, trying to imagine what the creature would have looked like before she'd taken it apart. There were at least eight limbs, two that could have been arms and another three pairs of various lengths that he assumed it walked on.

Sabien was used to autopsies, in his twenty years on the force he'd spent many hours poring over dead bodies. His talent with organic materials meant that he'd had to read the memories of more than one dead man in his time.

The sound of the shower stopped and Kaori walked out in a fresh new jumpsuit, towelling her hair dry.

He bent down to kiss her, tasting the soap on her lips.

'So Mr Policeman, what's so important?'

'How are you on shapeshifters?'

She smiled. 'Are we talking mythical or corporeal?'

'Real ones.'

Kaori went over to one of the large touchscreen displays and tapped on a series of icons. Random images of unusual creatures flickered across the screen as she searched the xenobiology database.

'There are a number of xenotypes that can manipulate their physiology to match their environment, kind of like a chameleon.'

'Can any of them mimic humans?'

She turned towards him, her eyes widening. 'Really? You mean like a doppelgänger?'

'Is that in your database?'

'Er no, because they don't exist.'

Sabien sighed. 'Then I've no clue what took her baby.'

'Whose baby?'

'Caitlin Makepiece, someone who looked remarkably like her just walked up and took him.'

Kaori punched him hard in the arm. 'Why didn't you say! God she must be in a terrible state. When was this? Where?'

'Paris 1889. I've just come from taking their statements. Rufius Westinghouse gave the child to someone who he claims was Caitlin, but it wasn't her. So we had his memory verified by the Grand Seer and it appears he's telling the truth.'

Kaori's eyes widened and she dropped the towel. 'I came across something like that a month back.' She went over to her console. 'Someone broke into the secure vault and tampered with one of my specimens. The system logs reported that it was me, which is pretty hard considering it has a retinal scan verification system and I've still got both my eyes.'

She brought up a series of images, grainy still frames from a security camera.

'Whoever did this knew what they were doing, they dropped a virus into the network that took down every one of our security protocols and let out the entire collection.'

'And you never thought to mention that?

'We don't bring work home, remember. Anyway, we got it under control in forty-eight hours.'

'Was that around the time we started getting ghost-shark sightings in the park? About a month ago?'

She smirked. 'Sorry, that's restricted information.'

The images on screen were going through some kind of

digital reconstruction, lines of finer detail were being revealed with every pass.

'When we finally got the systems back up and running, we found that the virus had scrambled every one of the feeds. I wrote a routine to try and clean up what was left, it's been running for weeks now.'

They watched the pixels sharpen on the images, a woman standing in front of the Hazardous Containment unit, a woman who looked very much like Kaori.

'Well, she's definitely got your arse,' observed Sabien.

'More than that,' Kaori said, swiping to one of the other images which showed the door open and the figure halfway into the chamber.

'What was in that room?'

'An Aeon.'

'Like the parasite you found in the Ripper?'

She nodded. 'Symbiotic life form, we found an entire cluster of them. They'd been infecting members of the royal houses of Europe all over the nineteenth century.'

'Why?'

'That was what I was trying to find out when the break-in occurred. All the samples we had were destroyed or lost.'

'Did Joshua Jones or Caitlin Makepiece have anything to do with this?' he asked, taking out his almanac.

Kaori drew in a sharp breath. 'Josh was infected. It was a miracle he survived to be honest. Caitlin found some ancient extraction device and managed to pull it out of him.'

Sabien scribbled something down on the page.

'So who do you think broke into your lab?'

She shrugged. 'Either a long lost twin sister I never knew or something that can change its physical appearance at will, unless of course they cloned me.'

He wrote that down.

'That wasn't supposed to be an official statement.'

'Second doppelgänger in a month, sounds like too much of a coincidence.'

'Agreed, but don't call it that, it sounds like something out of the Twilight Zone.'

He looked over to the table. 'Honey, I think you live in the Twilight Zone.'

5

CHAPTER HOUSE

[Chapter House]

They sat at one end of the Viking long table, their food growing cold as it sat untouched on their plates.

After the Protectorate had finished taking their statements, the *Cirque d'Histoire* was sealed off. No one was allowed back into the marquee while their specialists examined every inch of it for evidence.

An awkward silence lay over the dining hall like a thunder cloud, filled with unspoken frustration and disbelief. No one could find the right words and the lack of conversation left a deafening void of sighs. At the beginning, Rufius had apologised so many times that Caitlin eventually told him to shut up, and then hugged him.

It was the first time Josh had ever seen the big man cry.

Benoir turned up later, explaining how the investigators kept him behind to demonstrate how the control systems worked for the temporal ticketing system. Uncle Georges was too devastated to come himself, but sent his apologies.

Lyra went to the Conclave with Kelly. No one knew

exactly what that entailed, but Sim thought it was some kind of secret ceremony that involved every member of the Seer's Guild.

Alixia and Methuselah did their best to keep everybody fed and watered even though both of them were struggling to put on a brave face.

Everyone was on edge, waiting for the smallest piece of news. It felt like a wake, Caitlin thought, it felt as if Zachary was already dead.

'I need to do something! I can't just sit around and wait for the bloody crows!' bellowed Rufius, getting to his feet. 'Kelly thought the abductor was using some kind of cloaking device.'

'How did he know that?' asked Josh.

Everyone turned to look at Rufius who was looking slightly embarrassed.

He cleared his throat, wishing that it didn't sound so crazy. 'He said he could smell the electricity on them.'

Josh tried to stay calm. 'And you didn't think to mention it earlier? How did he manage to dig that out of your memory when you couldn't?'

Rufius raised his hands. 'I've no idea. The man's a total mystery.'

'A cloaking device,' repeated Caitlin, turning to Sim. 'Do we have anything like that?'

Sim took out his almanac. 'Not that I know of, but you never know what the Outlier Department is up to these days.'

'Why would they be working on a cloaking device,' added Josh, looking over Sim's shoulder.

'I don't think they are, but those guys are always trying

out wacky things. They built a gun that actually catches bullets last week,' said Sim, leafing through the pages of his book.

Rufius sat back down. 'Kelly also thinks we're going to need the *Nautilus*.'

'The *Nautilus* is in the Maelstrom. There's no way to reach her,' Caitlin added despondently.

'But it would be good to have it back, just in case, don't you think?' said Alixia, trying to make Rufius feel less uncomfortable.

'In case of what?' Caitlin snapped. 'In case they've taken him back to the Ice Age?'

Everyone fell silent once more, forks scraping plates as they went back to their food.

'What about Marcus?' suggested Sim. 'He's a ranger, surely he should be able to track them down?'

It troubled Josh that he hadn't thought of Marcus Makepiece before. If anyone could find Zack it would be Caitlin's uncle. Obviously the shock of the kidnapping was making it hard to focus, his head was filled with doubts and stopping him from thinking straight.

'Where is he now?'

Caitlin threw her hands in the air. 'Wandering around the past trying to find the Anunnaki.'

'I found him once, I can find him again,' offered Rufius, getting to his feet once more.

'Fine, but bring him back here,' ordered Caitlin. 'Don't go off on some wild goose chase.'

Rufius nodded, turning to Methuselah. 'Do you still have that parabolic chamber?'

Alixia's husband nodded, looking relieved to finally have something to do and took Rufius off to his study.

Caitlin turned to Josh and took hold of his hand. 'We need to talk — alone.'

He followed her out of the room and up the stairs to her old bedroom.

'I've been thinking,' she said calmly, sitting on the bed, 'on what Lyra told us about Zack. If he is such a powerful seer, don't you think someone might want to steal him?'

'Like who?'

She sighed, running her hand through her hair, curling strands of it around her fingers. 'I don't know, but if Lyra's right, he's too valuable to lose. They'd take care of him wouldn't they? No one would go to all that trouble just to kill him?'

He could hear the doubt creeping into her voice. She was trying so hard to find hope in all the smallest details. Anything that would keep her world from collapsing into despair.

Josh sat down on the bed and put his arm around her, but she shrugged it off.

'Don't. I need to think clearly right now. Getting emotional just complicates things.'

'You're allowed to be emotional.'

'No, not until we find him. We need to focus on that, nothing else.'

She had that steely look in her eyes, one that he'd seen so many times before. When she resolved to do something, there was no changing her mind and it felt better trying to find him than reliving the moment when they discovered he was gone.

'Who else knew he was a seer?'

He shrugged. 'Other than Kelly, Lyra and Benoir. No one.'

'Think, Josh. There must have been someone else.'

Closing his eyes, he tried to recall everyone they'd met since he'd woken up, but there were blanks, the extraction of the Aeon had left yawning gaps in his memory. He felt the grief welling up inside of him and his throat tightened as he tried to hold it back. 'I wasn't there when you found out.'

Caitlin touched his cheek gently, wiping the tears away. 'Sorry, I keep forgetting. There was a dinner here, a celebration I suppose. Lyra did this thing with one of her rings. It's a kind of test. I'm sure other people saw it too.'

He opened his eyes. 'But they're all friends.'

She nodded and got up from the bed. 'There's got to be something we're missing. Whatever it is, we need to work together. We don't tell anyone about his abilities, especially not that inspector.'

'Okay,' Josh agreed. 'So now what?'

'Now we stop waiting for someone else to fix this and we start working it out for ourselves.'

6

EDDINGTON AND SIM

[Map Room, Copernicus Hall]

Sim studied the lines of possibility spreading like veins of fire, branching out from the events leading up to Zack's abduction. Thousands of tiny threads wove in front of his eyes, the paths of destiny pulsing through the historical model of the Infinity Engine.

'Two hundred thousand and counting,' intoned Professor Eddington, who was measuring the exponential growth as they moved further along the timeline.

'It's impossible,' whispered Sim.

'Highly improbable,' corrected the professor. 'Although with a few refinements to the search parameters we might be able to reduce the scope.'

There are too many variables, Sim thought, careful to keep his doubts to himself. With over a thousand people at the circus that day, each one a time traveller, and even with the data from the Protectorate, there were too many iterations after one hour — let alone twenty-four.

Every day that passed would increase the chances of never finding him by a power of ten.

Sim's head was beginning to ache. Sixteen hours spent running continuous scenarios was beginning to take its toll, but he wasn't about to stop. He couldn't go back to Caitlin without an answer, this was the raison d'être for the Copernican Guild. If he couldn't tell her where her son had gone, what was the point?

The professor took the news of the abduction with his usual impassive detachment, as though it were just another problem to be resolved. He began by resetting the engine, which took over an hour, and then insisted that Sim initiate the search three days prior to the event.

Focusing on Zack's timeline, Sim minimised the interaction parameters to all but the closest contacts until a series of golden strands of light twisted and branched across his vision. Tiny temporal markers and notations slipped under his fingers as he carefully manipulated the chronology back and forth, looking for patterns.

He knew he must be missing something. Random strangers didn't just walk up and steal babies, at least not ones that looked so similar to his step-sister that Rufius couldn't tell them apart.

One of his initial theories was a type of temporal closed loop; that a future version of Caitlin returned to take her son. It was the most logical route, but there were no signs of a deviation and according to Uncle Georges, the temporal shielding at the circus wouldn't have allowed her to enter the continuum.

That and the fact it would break the prime directive that forbade anyone from interfering in their own timeline.

It also didn't explain the presence of the electrical field that the Grand Seer had detected.

As far as Sim knew, the only other source of electricity in the vicinity of the circus would have been Edison's exhibits in the *Galerie des Machines*, which produced hardly enough to power an electric lightbulb let alone a cloaking device.

He discounted the theory and moved further back.

Zachary's timeline encircled his mother like a vine around the trunk of a tree. They were inseparable. His bright, incandescent line followed her every moment. During Josh's recovery, they spent most of their time in the vicinity of the Chapter House, taking short walks around the local park, or visiting Caitlin's office at the Great Library.

There was a comforting normality to their daily routine, nothing out of the ordinary and virtually no interactions with any random actor.

Sim went back even further.

'Where are you going Master Simeon?' asked Eddington, looking up from his own branch of the holographic timeline.

'I wondered if there was something in the previous months that might trigger the event.'

'Prior to the birth?'

Sim nodded, pointing to a large knot of chaos in Caitlin's timeline. 'During the Aeon disruption. There are several areas of uncharted activity towards the latter part of the sequence.'

'Indeed there are,' agreed the professor. 'I have three correlation departments working on the consequences of those particular interactions at this very moment.'

'Has Doctor Shika managed to identify the point of origin for the Aeon?' Sim wondered aloud.

Eddington shook his head, waving his hand over his work to dismiss it. 'She has not. We have been charged with that particular task. Our primary objective is to calculate the entry vector of the species into the continuum.'

'You believe they were introduced rather than evolved?'

'Of that I have no doubt.'

Sim could see the chaos the Aeons had caused, during the previous months, to Josh's timeline. It was as if someone deliberately erased weeks of time leaving large gaping spaces in his life. In truth it was nothing more than missing data in the model, times when he'd not been carrying an almanac or a tachyon. They could use statistical algorithms to predict what occurred during that time, but the professor preferred not to make assumptions.

Sim moved his hands apart, changing the scale, zooming out to look at the overall pattern that Josh and Caitlin's lives made when looked at from afar.

Caitlin's timeline was relatively normal for a member of the Order: the loops and twists of her travel into the past made for a flower-like pattern around a central trunk, which still tended towards a straight line.

Josh, on the other hand, was unreadable. His travels seemed to form no recognisable pattern whatsoever, resembling a large ball of string that had been pulled in multiple directions as if someone were trying to unravel a large and complex knot.

The only element of stability within his chaos was Caitlin, and more recently Zack. Sim could see what a positive effect the son was having on his father, even more so than Caitlin. But nothing about their lives showed any evidence to help explain why he'd been taken.

As Sim shifted the perspective again, the lines faded and died.

'That is enough for today,' said Eddington, removing his

glasses and rubbing his eyes. 'There is only so much one can do without rest.'

Sim had never seen his mentor take off his spectacles. It was as if he suddenly became more human, more vulnerable. There were dark circles under each eye that were hidden by the metal frames. He suddenly looked tired and very old.

'I could do with a few hours sleep,' agreed Sim, stretching his arms and feeling the strain in his shoulders. 'Just to rest my eyes.'

The professor nodded. 'Four hours should be sufficient.'

Sim went over to one of the cots that the others had prepared for him and curled up under the blanket. He was asleep before Eddington left the room.

7

LYRA AND THE SEERS

[Seers Meeting Place]

Despite the reason for being there, Lyra was finding it hard to contain her excitement.

She'd never witnessed a Conclave before and the sight of so many seers in one place was exhilarating. Having never really felt as if she belonged to anything, other than her immediate family, to be suddenly standing in a hall filled with people who knew exactly how she felt was a new sensation entirely.

Seers didn't tend to have too many friends. Their abilities generally scared other people away or made them paranoiacally suspicious. There was a rumour that you could never really lie to a seer, that they were truth-sayers, and that tended to lead to very difficult conversations in the early stages of any relationship.

And then there were the 'fakalists', those people who befriended seers because they wanted to be read by them. Like a fortune teller at a sideshow, wanting to know about a lover, their life, or something equally dangerous.

Seeing people's destinies was a difficult burden — some would say a curse. Telling someone what was to come might not only change their future, but often led to the seer being blamed for not meeting their expectations.

Lyra learned quickly to avoid such people, it made life a lot less complicated.

She knew that the Grand Seer convened the meeting for her. Since their guild didn't use almanacs, his invitation had appeared in their minds as a single thought: *Lyra requires assistance.*

And they had come. All of them.

The entire seers' guild watched as she walked towards the front of the hall where Edward Kelly stood waiting, dressed like the high priest of a bird cult.

There were over a hundred seers, of all ages and eras. Some had donned the Delphic white robes of the guild, but most were dressed in more eccentric outfits, the kind that gave seers a bad name.

Sim would have called it a freak show but Lyra had never felt more at home than she was now, surrounded by her own kind, even if most of them were trying very hard not to stare at her.

Kelly waved at her and she quickened her step.

He cleared his throat as she climbed up onto the small stage at the front of the auditorium.

'Welcome one and all,' he began in a deep, resonant voice. 'I have called you together for one purpose. One of our own has been taken. A seer child stolen from his mother's arms.'

There was a collective intake of breath, and some of the

older members shook their heads and began to chatter amongst themselves.

The Grand Seer held up one of his long fingers and raised his voice over the babble. 'Not all is lost however, Lyra here has managed to form a sympathetic bond with the infant, and with your help we may be able to enhance the empathy and clarify it into a locus.'

A locus was a type of scrying ball, one that could be used to help find something. It was a tool that sensed the presence of whatever it had been infused with, like a dowsing rod, normally for finding lost artefacts, Lyra had never heard it used on a person.

Kelly turned to her. 'Would you like to say something before we begin?'

She'd never been asked to talk in public, let alone to a room full of people who were presently glaring at her with big moon-like eyes.

'His name is Zachary,' she said quietly.

'Speak up!' shouted one of the white-haired gentlemen in the back row.

'His name is Zachary,' she repeated, trying not to shout. 'He's one of the most powerful seers I've ever met. He's seven weeks old and someone took him from the *Cirque d'Histoire* less than twenty-four hours ago.'

Lyra could feel tears stinging her cheeks as she recalled what happened. Somehow telling them about it felt natural, they listened intently, no interruptions or questions.

When she was finished, someone in the front row brought forward the small glass sphere and handed it to her. She was a little old lady with kind eyes and a round, pink face.

The locus was cold in the palm of her hand, its surface

blacker than a thunder cloud on a dark night. It was the first one she had ever held.

'Show us,' the old lady said kindly, 'with your mind.'

Lyra closed her eyes and retreated into the quiet place inside her head.

For as long as she could remember, she'd been able to isolate her mind from reality. There was a still space inside her thoughts where Lyra could shelter from the constant bombardment of voices that generally plagued all seers. The background noise of humanity, it was a coping mechanism that kept her sane.

But it was also where she stored some of her most precious memories, and one of them was the day she named Zachary.

She would never forget the day his mind had touched hers. It was like a shining star, filled with wonder and awe at the new world he'd entered. Lyra had never encountered such an innocent mind, nor felt so much power in one so young.

Opening the memory was like taking an exquisite jewel from its velvet box. Lyra could feel the other minds gathering around her, gentle ghosts hovering on the borders of her consciousness, willing her to share the experience with them.

And so she did.

She heard the collective sigh as each of the seers immersed themselves in the moment, immediately understanding what she saw in him. It took less than a heartbeat for everyone to realise how important Zachary was.

'Reach out to him,' the Grand Seer whispered into her mind, his words twisting like leaves in the wind. 'Find his essence.'

Lyra felt the power of their unified minds lifting her as she followed the memory, leaving her physical body and transcending linear time. She was no longer standing on the stage in the auditorium, but floating inside the nexus of the continuum surrounded by an infinitely complex web of destinies.

Somehow their combined abilities allowed her to delve deeper into the fabric of time than any single seer would have been able to do alone.

Like standing beneath a waterfall, her mind experienced a thousand fates a second. As she scoured the continuum, the Conclave protected her from the torrent, allowing Lyra to focus on Zack's essence. Like a fingerprint, the pattern of his short life was unique and as she concentrated the other lines faded away until there was only one.

Shining brightly against the backdrop of darkened threads, his lifeline arced out into the distance leaving the realms of their continuum far behind. Lyra resisted the urge to follow it, this wasn't about his fate, she reminded herself, grasping the thin stream of gold like a kite string and forcing it down into the locus. She felt its energy being absorbed by the sphere.

When she opened her eyes they were applauding.

In her hands the sphere shone with a beautiful pale light, as if she'd harnessed the dawn.

'Well done!' exclaimed the Grand Seer, patting her on the shoulder. 'Now at least we have something to work with.'

8

SABIEN

The circus was deserted when Sabien returned. The rings and cages were sitting empty, as were the ranks of benches that sloped up into the darkened roof above.

He could still smell the beasts though, their musky scent lay on the sawdust mixed with that of the stale sweat of the performers and the salty-sweet tang of discarded popcorn.

Smells right, he thought, taking off one of his gloves.

He always preferred to walk a crime scene alone. Letting his senses absorb the details subconsciously, waiting for his talent to find the clues that everyone else missed. It was a secret skill, one that could end his career if his boss ever found out.

The term they would use for him was 'Druid'. It was meant as an insult, but it meant nothing, his abilities had solved more cases than the rest of the department combined and he knew they called him 'Sherlock' behind his back.

He ran a hand along the edge of the paint-chipped wooden ring, feeling the lives of the performers dancing

39

beneath his fingers. The *Cirque D'Histoire* was steeped in history, some of which appeared to go back as far as the Pliocene. He was less concerned about the welfare of the extinct animals they imported from the past, or the nefarious trade in illegal artefacts made from their bones in the market outside.

He was searching for something else.

A doppelgänger.

Kaori laughed at him when he'd taken her seriously. She was a scientist who needed to dissect something before she'd believe it really existed. Even though she was a Xenobiologyst, who came into daily contact with some of the most unimaginable monsters in creation, she seemed to draw the line at mythical creatures.

Sabien, however, was raised on angels and demons.

His Irish mother was a devout Catholic, one who'd indoctrinated him from an early age with stories of the heavenly host, the army of God and their battles with the fallen. He was even named after the supreme holy warrior, the Archangel Michael.

Sabien could still hear his mother repeating the litany, kneeling before the statue of the Virgin Mary every Sunday. 'Holy Mary, Mother of God; Saint Michael; all holy angels...'

She was long dead now, and he'd seen more than one devil since, and most of them were very mortal.

He walked slowly around the ring, letting the moments of the previous day play out under his fingertips. The ability to read organic material was a rare talent within the Order, but for some reason druids were treated as freaks, even more so than seers, and not something with which any right-minded member of the Order should be associating.

It was certainly not something to which an inspector of the Protectorate would ever openly admit if he wanted to keep his job.

He could read the timelines encoded in wood and stone, ones that most others would be too scared to touch because of their fractal structure and incredibly long timelines. Weaving with them was dangerous and could easily leave someone left in a distant part of the earth's past from which there was no coming back.

'Can I help you?' asked a deep, French-accented voice.

'Inspector Sabien,' replied Sabien. 'And you are?'

'Benoir Cousineau,' answered the man, stepping out of one of the smaller cages. He wore leather gauntlets that were covered in blood. 'I look after the animals.'

'I thought they'd all been returned to their original time.'

Benoir washed the gloves in a metal bucket and pulled them off. 'The homotherium is too late in her pregnancy to move, it would endanger her litter.'

Sabien looked past the keeper to the large cat that prowled around the inside of the cage, her muzzle still crimson.

'What do you feed them?' asked Sabien.

Benoir shrugged. 'Carrion mostly, the odd inquisitive policeman, whatever we can find.'

Sabien smiled, so many of his conversations with witnesses were spent trying to get them to realise they weren't under suspicion, at least this man had a sense of humour.

'Where were you when the child was abducted?'

Benoir walked into the centre of the main ring and

raised his arms. 'Right here. I was ringmaster and the second act had just come to a close.' He pointed to various points on the outer rim. 'The confectioners were at their stations and the audience were queuing for their treats.'

The inspector stepped out of the ring and went up to the row where Josh and Caitlin had been sitting. They were at the front, which for safety was raised to the height of Benoir's head and had a wire mesh fence running in front of it.

'Has anyone ever been attacked by your beasts?' asked Sabien, touching the metal fence.

Benoir shook his head. 'A few of the staff have come away with the odd scar, but never a member of the audience.'

'And how do you vet your staff?'

'That's a question for Cuvier. I'm not involved in recruitment.'

Sabien rubbed the arm of the chair with his thumb, feeling the grain of the burnished wood, allowing the time-line to unravel. He heard the clamour of the crowd, felt the tent come alive with the anticipation of the audience. He let time flow over him like waves on a beach. Moments came and went until he saw the woman coming towards him.

There was no doubt it was Caitlin Makepiece. Kelly was right when he said that Westinghouse was telling the truth.

She took the child out of his arms and smiled.

The baby seemed disturbed by something as he was transferred. Westinghouse had assumed it was because he needed changing, but Sabien slowed the moment until it was almost still. He got out of his chair and went closer to the mother and child.

And there it was, a crying baby and a mother who wasn't paying it any attention. The maternal instinct was missing, her eyes were fixed on Westinghouse, not on her distressed baby. Whoever this doppelgänger was, it certainly had no feelings for the child.

'What are you doing?' asked Benoir, appearing beside him.

Sabien snapped out of the moment. 'How?'

Benoir's mouth twitched into a half-smile. 'You're not the only one who can weave with organic materials.'

'You're a druid?'

Benoir shrugged. 'I prefer zoologist, but yes, how else do you think I get those animals here?'

An awkward moment passed between them. Sabien had never met another like him, and he was guessing that neither had the Frenchman. Kaori reckoned that statistically there were less than five in the entire Order and none of them were about to start their own club.

'What did you see?' asked Benoir.

'It wasn't her. There was no love between the woman and the child. No maternal instinct. It was her doppelgänger, but why did it take the child?'

Benoir sat down in one of the chairs. 'I need to tell you something, now that we share a secret, I believe I can trust you.'

9

MARCUS

[Chapter House]

Methuselah's parabolic chamber was a small, round room, built from thousands of tiny lensing mirrors. It was a disconcerting sensation to look at an infinite number of versions of yourself; especially when Rufius hadn't changed his clothes in over forty-eight hours.

The chamber was a kind of temporal telescope, one that allowed the user to explore the timeline of anyone who had recently intersected with their own — effectively turning themselves into a vestige.

It was a powerful, if not dangerous tool. The ultimate surveillance apparatus, able to observe any part of a target's life without their knowledge, as long as you could bear the nauseating vertigo that came with standing inside a constantly shifting hall of mirrors.

Methuselah already tried and failed to use it to locate Zachary. Either the child's timeline was too short for the lensing to work or he was no longer in their continuum.

He preferred to believe the former was true.

Rufius stood in the centre of the chamber and slowly opened his eyes, fighting off the urge to throw up as he summoned the memories of Marcus.

The ranger was a notorious wanderer. It had taken Rufius three days to track him down the last time. Since Marcus didn't carry an almanac or a tachyon, Rufius resorted to old-fashioned detective work and a few nefarious contacts who preferred not to be named. It cost him dearly, his private collection of rare single malts had taken a real battering.

The mirrors darkened as Rufius remembered the last moments of the battle at Uruk. Marcus was virtually unrecognisable in his chaos state. The monster that he watched tearing through the Aeon soldiers was an abomination, but a very effective one.

Rufius slowed the images of the fight, studying the killing machine that Marcus became, marvelling at how his entire body transformed into a weapon. Only his eyes retained any sign of humanity, yet they still carried a glint of insanity.

He wondered what could be going through the man's mind while he was in this berserker state. Whether it would be possible to reason with him. Rufius took comfort from the fact that the monster seemed to be aware of whose side he was on, but he wasn't sure how much of Marcus was in control.

Allowing the timeline to move forward a few weeks, Rufius witnessed his departure. The time Marcus spent with Caitlin and the baby at the Chapter House was a complete contrast to the slaughter of the Aeons; this was the Jekyll to his Hyde.

After saying his farewells, Marcus reported to Grandmaster Derado at the Draconian headquarters and received new orders. Rufius watched the two men discuss his next mission. Derado's eyes were like a wolf, never leaving Marcus for a second. The ranger seemed completely unaware of his master's discomfort as they studied the maps of the forgotten corners of history.

His business with Derado concluded, Marcus walked down the spiral staircase of the lighthouse and into the quartermaster's stores.

Rufius hardly recognised the man that reappeared an hour later. He was wearing the travelling fatigues of a Nautonnier, and his head was shaved — nothing like the scruffy shaman that Rufius had picked up in Machu Picchu.

'Where are you off to?' Rufius murmured to himself, pressing further into the man's chronology.

The answer came soon enough.

[Temple of Osiris, Abydos, Egypt. Date: Second Dynasty]

'What are you doing here watchman?' growled Marcus through clenched teeth.

The temple wall behind him was shimmering, a Draconian force field held back the largest breach the Order had ever faced. Hundreds of Dreadnoughts had died during the battle of Abydos, defending the continuum from the nightmare horde of storm-kin that had broken through from the Maelstrom.

It was during this attack that Caitlin's parents disappeared and Marcus had the accident that would change him forever.

'I was going to ask you the same question,' replied Rufius.

'I come here every so often,' Marcus said, holding his hand up to the mirrored surface. 'Part of me craves it.'

The field distorted, bulging as though something on the other side of the breach was trying to reach them.

'They call to me, in my dreams,' he whispered, baring long fangs.

'Something's happened to Zachary, he's been taken.'

Marcus's eyes burned with a manic intensity when he turned to face him. 'Who has taken him?'

Rufius instinctively stepped back, reaching for the hilt of his sword. 'We don't know.'

'Where?'

'That's why I've come for you.'

Dark rage passed like a shadow across Marcus's face and fell away. 'I'm not sure I can help you.'

'Caitlin believes you're the only one who can.'

Marcus shook his head. 'If I don't cross over soon it will become harder to control. The beast within me must be sated.'

'You're going in there?' Rufius nodded to the breach.

'I have no choice.'

Rufius scratched at his beard, an idea forming in his mind.

'Are you still human when you cross?'

Marcus shrugged. 'For the most part, but then sometimes not.'

'Do you think you could find your brother in there?'

The ranger looked confused. 'Easily, his metal ship leaves a large temporal wake. The storm-kin follow it like gulls behind a fishing boat, but why would you need to find Thomas?'

Rufius clapped the man on the shoulder. 'We need to find the *Nautilus* and get her back here, Kelly thinks it's important.'

He seemed surprised. 'You're coming too?'

'Absolutely.'

10

KAORI INTERFACE

[Regent's Park Zoo, London. Date: Present Day]

Kaori Shika sipped her coffee, relishing the warm vapours, letting it revive her tired mind.

She'd been working on the Aeon specimen ever since Sabien left yesterday and her eyes were growing heavy. The only surviving parasite was embedded in the body of Doctor Henry Knox, who'd been kept in stasis since he was apprehended for the Ripper murders in 1888, and she needed to get it out.

Whatever it was that managed to disable their security systems and release their entire collection, had meant it as a diversion. Their real objective were the Aeons extracted from Josh and Champollion. Just by chance, Knox's unit was in maintenance when the breach occurred.

The Victorian doctor's limp body was now floating in a containment field while robotic arms slowly inserted thin wires into his back and neck. Kaori had drunk far too much caffeine to hold a scalpel steady, let alone a fourteen-micrometer probe.

A holographic display, overlaid onto his torso, visualised the procedure as the hair-like needles slid towards the parasite wrapped around the doctor's brain stem.

The break-in had unsettled Kaori and her team, who spent most of their days trying to stop things getting out. Their defences were impenetrable, or so they thought. For the first time in its long history, the Xenobiology Department had failed in their duties, and as Director, she took sole responsibility for it. She needed to know what was so important about these creatures that someone would go to the trouble of breaking in — these parasites were clearly more than just hitchhikers looking for a free ride through history.

Whatever it was, she was determined to find out. The way Caitlin had used the Quindent to remove the Aeon from Josh gave Kaori an idea: an electrical current passed between the probes she was inserting into his body would be enough to stun it. Enough for the parasite to release its grip on the doctor's medulla and for her to perform an extraction.

Or rather the robotic surgical system would.

'Probe deployment complete,' reported an electronic voice, as the arms retracted.

She put down her drink and tapped on the display in front of her.

'Execute Shika-four-five phase-one.'

The code from her extraction programme scrolled up the screen. Fifty virtually simultaneous instructions went into effect in a blur of robotic movement too fast for the eye to see.

Kaori sat back in her chair, listening to the hum of the generators. Seconds later she smelled the metallic taint of ozone as the electric shocks discharged. A minute later, the articulated forceps of the autonomous surgical unit placed the limp carcass of an Aeon into a jar of vitreous preservative fluid.

'Shika-four-five-phase-one complete,' intoned the robot.

Kaori checked the vital signs of the patient. His heart was still in sinus rhythm and there seemed to be a normal amount of brain activity. The only challenge now was going to be how much he remembered.

She wondered what it would be like to wake up to discover you were Jack the Ripper.

'Move to phase two,' she ordered, getting up from her chair and walking over to the scanner.

The arm of the unit turned through one hundred and eighty degrees, depositing the jar inside a white cylindrical MRI.

Enlarged images of the parasite appeared in slices as the sensors slowly mapped its internal structure, something that hadn't been possible while it was still inside Knox.

The internal structure of the creature was more complicated than Kaori anticipated. It was a complex neural machine, that was nearly entirely brain. There were no other significant organs, so whatever it used for energy must have come from the host.

She shivered at the sight of the long proboscis lined with rows of teeth. This was the tool it used to enter the body. A boring machine that could tunnel through human flesh in seconds.

'DNA sequencing commencing,' reported the system as data streamed across the scanner's console.

Base pairs began to form around a helical structure. *Not alien then,* she noted with a tinge of annoyance. She'd been hoping for a new form of genetic material at the very least.

'Biometric interface detected.'

'Sorry?'

'Biometric interface —'

'Yes, I heard that. Where? Show me.'

The display changed as a grainy section of the MRI scan was enlarged and then enhanced.

As the resolution improved it was clear to see a port beneath the segmented section of what could be described as its head.

She walked over to the 3D printer.

'Model the required connector and print.'

The machine whirred into life, its tiny extruder depositing microscopic layers of metal onto the gel base as it recreated the strangest needle assembly Kaori had ever seen.

'This is it?'

'Affirmative.'

She lifted the connector out of the substrate and replaced one of the existing probes on the robotic armature.

'Initiate a secure sandbox and proceed with biological interface.'

The arm rotated through ninety degrees and slowly inserted the connector into the base of the Aeon's skull.

11

CURIOSITY

[Maelstrom]

The Maelstrom reminded Rufius of a kaleidoscope. Watching the buildings shift randomly around him like giant chess pieces, gothic cathedrals slid between streets of Victorian town houses, Roman villas erupted out of ruined Norman castles, and Manhattan skyscrapers folded in on themselves as if made out of paper. It was like they were standing in the middle of an architectural graveyard.

Marcus had brought him to this cluster, where random scraps of history coalesced into a small island of reality for a few minutes before floating off into the infinite void. It was the first solid ground Rufius had stood on since they'd stepped through the breach, which felt like years ago, but could have been minutes, it was hard to gauge the passing of time inside a realm that had none.

Turning into the beast the moment they crossed into the chaos realm, Rufius noted how different Marcus was to the last time. Being inside the Maelstrom made his cryptid skin glow, covering his body in a static blue haze. His transformation seemed more complete somehow; there was no real sign of his humanity, even his eyes darkened.

Yet Marcus managed to keep control of the inner chaos, leaving Rufius on this semi-stable cluster while he went to ask the storm-kin if they knew anything about the location of the *Nautilus*.

Rufius was quite relieved when Marcus suggested that he go alone.

The Maelstrom was filled with nightmarish creatures. The Djinn, or Storm-kin, were grotesque abominations that evolved beyond the strictures of time. Immortal gargoyles driven insane by their never-ending existence, deprived of any form of normality, they preyed on life itself.

Looking down at the circle Marcus left in the dirt around him, Rufius was reminded of something Kelly would draw to ward off evil spirits. The ranger told him it would keep him safe, that no Djinn would cross it. The runic symbols on the four compass points around its edge looked like the bones that the witch Maman Brigitte had used for fate-casting; they were the names of elder gods, she'd told him once and when he walked towards them, they would begin to glow.

Listening to the sounds of clawed creatures skittering in the shadows of the ever-changing architecture, Rufius wondered if Marcus hadn't just tagged him as someone else's lunch.

Rufius estimated it must have been over an hour since Marcus left. Although there was no way to be sure, his tachyon was dead and the various suns that appeared in the rapidly-changing sky were less than reliable; days seem to come and go in minutes, leaving dark, star-less voids in their wake.

He resigned himself to a long wait and taking out his almanac, sat down in the middle of the circle to read.

The pages were unusually still, the notes and chronomaps frozen like a normal printed book. No longer connected to the constant updates from the Copernican actuaries, they were considerably easier to read.

He turned to the report Sim had made on the abduction. It didn't look promising. Rufius put on a pair of reading glasses and held the page close to his face to magnify the tiny notations. Sim's neat handwriting wove around his most recent calculations.

Calculations indicate a seventy-five point three percent probability that no internal actor could have been responsible for the abduction.

'Not one of us,' Rufius mumbled to himself, slightly annoyed at the Copernican inability to state definitively whether something would happen or not.

Without a clearer understanding of the motives, the uncertainty principle is too high. There are too many unknowns to speculate on the perpetrator, Eddington had added in his unmistakable copperplate beneath Sim's conclusion.

'Bloody clackers, think they can find the answers to everything in a slide rule,' huffed Rufius, shutting the book and putting it away.

Looking over the top of his spectacles, he noticed the first of the creatures standing on the outer rim of the circle, its one large, luminous eye staring at him intensely.

Turning slowly as he got to his feet, Rufius saw that he was surrounded by monsters.

'Calm,' he whispered to himself, putting away the

glasses and pulling out his Colt Peacemaker. He had no idea if bullets would have any effect in this timeless world, but just holding the weapon made him feel better.

The one-eyed creature seemed to be floating in space, man-o-war tendrils hung down from the yellow orb. Next to it was something that looked as if it was related to a spider crab. Its shell was blackened, covered in a thick layer of oily tar. The carapace twisted open to reveal rows of sharp teeth. There were others with insect heads attached to bird-like bodies, broken wings folded back and pinned in place with rivets. Humans with limbs replaced with ghostly tentacles and a dozen other nightmarish experiments.

Marcus's circle seemed to be holding them back, but Rufius had no idea for how much longer.

Suddenly the onlookers parted and the ranger, still in beast form, stepped through. He looked as if he'd been in a fight, there were wounds on his arms and blood on his muzzle.

'You all right?' asked Rufius, lowering his gun and pointing at the cuts.

'Blood tithes,' explained Marcus. 'It's a form of currency here, that and the memories that come with it.' He pointed at the weapon and laughed. 'You know that won't work here?'

Rufius shrugged, trying to hide his relief at Marcus's return. 'These are friends of yours I take it?' he said, putting the gun back in its holster.

'More like hired help. They know where the *Nautilus* is, but they wanted to see you before they would show me the location.'

Rufius scowled, puffing out his chest. 'Why?'

'They've never seen a human before, you're a bit of a curiosity.'

'I'm a curiosity?' exclaimed Rufius. 'Have you seen yourselves?'

Marcus growled. 'You need to see them through my eyes. Their appearance is nothing more than a psychic projection, a defence mechanism or in some cases a form of mating ritual. They're actually quite beautiful creatures.'

Rufius held up one of his hands and laughed. 'I'll take your word for it. So, now they've seen me, can we get going?'

The spectators chatted amongst themselves before one of them stepped forward and held out a withered hand towards him.

'I think she likes you,' said Marcus, rubbing the symbols out of the dirt with his foot.

Rufius tried to smile at the tall, thin creature, who looked as if she had been stretched on a rack. 'Are you sure this is such a good idea?'

'Only way we're going to find the ship in this place.'

12

QUEEN

[Anu Ziggurat, Uruk, Sumer. Date: 3100 BC]

The Aeon Queen's body was under strict quarantine. Xeno technicians cordoned off a hundred years in either direction and Sabien's credentials were checked several times before he made it to the site.

He found Kaori in the temple, working with a team of scientists in archaic-looking hazmat suits made of leather, carefully cutting away layers of chrysalis around what was left of the Queen's body by hand.

She would have been an enormous creature, at least eighty-feet long. Sabien stepped carefully through the sticky ichor and what was left of her carcass as he made his way towards Kaori.

'Inspector Sabien, what an unexpected surprise!' she said without the slightest hint of sarcasm. Their relationship was supposed to be a secret, something she kept from her colleagues. It added a sense of drama, a touch of the clandestine, but meant they had to act entirely professional when in the company of others.

'Doctor Shika,' he replied coolly. 'I believe you have some information for me?'

Kaori put down the large-toothed saw she was holding and pulled off her gauntlets. 'Walk with me.'

They moved away from the rest of the team, who exchanged knowing glances with each other; everyone noticed how her eyes lit up whenever he came into the lab.

She pretended to show him one of the soldier drones that was half buried in a corpse on the far side of the temple.

'So, I managed to pull the Aeon out of Doctor Knox without killing either of them,' she said, lowering her voice to a whisper.

'How?'

She arched one of her eyebrows. 'Do you really want to know?'

He shook his head and kicked at the drone's body with his boot.

'Don't do that! Anyway, when I scanned it, I found that the Aeon has this biological interface, kind of like a USB port.'

He stared at her blankly.

She scowled at him. 'How is it I ended up with a technophobe?'

He shrugged. 'I was raised in the nineteen-seventies what do you expect?'

Kaori tried to think of a similar technical analogy that would work. 'Like an RS232 port? Or a game cartridge for an Atari?'

Again a blank stare.

'RJ45? Like on a landline?' She gave up. 'Basically, I found a way to connect to its brain.'

'And?'

Folding her arms over her chest, she scowled at him. 'Do you know how amazingly difficult that is to do?'

'Sorry. Wow! Incredible! And what did you find?'

Kaori sighed. 'I'm not sure I want to tell you now.'

He knelt down as if inspecting the segmented legs of the decaying drone.

'See I'm begging you.'

She smiled, kneeling down beside him. 'Better.'

'What did you find?'

'The data was stored in a really early form of Akkadian, pictograms and cuneiform. It took a while for our translation systems to decipher. The parasite's main purpose seems to have been data collection. They're like knowledge sponges, just soaking up history and moving between hosts, climbing the social ladder until they hit gold.'

'So how did Knox figure in the equation?'

'He was an accident. Happened to be in the wrong place at the wrong time. This particular Aeon had been trapped in the Harpy Tomb in Xanthus until it got excavated by a Victorian explorer named Fellows.'

'I saw what Knox did to those women. That was no accident.'

Kaori shrugged. 'They're a sentient species, trying to survive, just like us.'

He got back up to his feet. 'So, what's this got to do with my case?'

She stood and looked over towards the carcass of the Aeon Queen. 'They don't belong here, someone planted them during the Ubaid period. From what I can gather, it looks like they were monitoring the development of our civilisation. My guess is that the doppelgänger that broke into my lab was retrieving its memories. If they took Caitlin's baby it can only mean one thing.'

'That he was infected?'

She shook her head. 'That he had something they were searching for.'

Sabien rubbed his chin. 'Benoir Cousineau told me that the kid has special abilities, that Lyra thought he was some kind of highly-developed seer.'

Kaori got back to her feet. 'Well, Caitlin spent most of her pregnancy in the Maelstrom, weird shit is the norm out there. I wouldn't be surprised if Zack hasn't come back with a few extra abilities.' She grinned and the outline of her ghast, Ophelia, flickered into ghostly form around her.

Sabien instinctively stepped back as Ophelia's horns grew longer. 'You think they've taken him because he's storm-kin?'

A wicked smile stretched across Kaori's face. 'Nothing wrong with a bit of chaos — some people find it quite attractive.'

He nodded, resisting the urge to kiss her as the shadow of her own djinn faded away.

'That might constitute a motive, still doesn't help with who they are or where they took him.'

'That's the other part I wanted to talk to you about. At exactly the same time as the security breach, when we were all busy trying to recapture the runaways, every single one of our tachyons failed. I didn't think anything of it, since I was too busy rounding up the nightmare horde, but —' She took out a Mark VI tachyon and opened the scorched casing. 'I had my guys look over this, it appears to have been rigged with a remote detonator, and the only person who could trigger it was Grandmaster Konstantine — who has since mysteriously disappeared.'

Sabien smiled. 'Above my pay grade. The boys on the twentieth floor will be dealing with that one.'

She took off one of his gloves and placed the dead tachyon in his palm. 'I'm just saying, you should look into it. That man was involved somehow. It happened just as the others were trying to locate the whereabouts of the Aeon Queen.'

He weighed the watch in his hand, feeling its chronology unfurl around his fingers.

'You know you want to,' she whispered.

'I should arrest you for perverting the course of justice.'

She turned and walked back towards her team. 'Promises, promises.'

He opened the timeline and disappeared.

13

LOCUS

[Chapter House]

Lyra held the locus in both hands, its light flickering like a candle in a storm between her delicate fingers.

'What is it?' asked Caitlin, her eyes widening as she stared into the glow.

'Zachary,' whispered Lyra, her breath misting the glass globe. 'Or a part of him — his essence. We've managed to tether a piece of his timeline in the locus. It's not much, but it does mean he's still alive.'

There were tears in Caitlin's eyes now. 'You're sure?'

Lyra nodded and handed her the sphere. 'Feel it. It's warm. That's a good sign. It means he's okay.'

Caitlin held the fragile object as if it were the most precious thing in the world. Inside the glass sphere, small motes of light rotated in random patterns, like a snow globe.

'Can it tell you where he is?'

Collapsing into one of the larger armchairs, Lyra looked exhausted, dark circles shadowed her eyes. 'No, we've tried, but it was too difficult. His timeline is too short. I only managed to get this because I'd met him. It took a hundred seers to help me harness this, sorry.'

Caitlin tried not to sound too disappointed. 'But he's definitely alive, right?'

Lyra nodded, pulling her knees up under herself and resting her head on the arm of the chair. 'And happy. The colour changes. It's not much, but if you shut your eyes you should be able to sense his emotional state.'

Holding the sphere to her chest, Caitlin closed her eyes and slowly a smile spread across her face.

'I can feel him.'

'The Grand Seer is working on a way to enhance the connection. He thinks with the right amplification we may be able to use it as a rangefinder. To determine how far away he is.'

Lyra stopped talking, realising that Caitlin wasn't really listening.

She was lost in the moment, feeling his breath on her cheek, his heart beating against her chest. She could smell his soft, newborn head as she cradled him in her arms. Her whole body seemed to melt away as the bond between their timelines re-established.

An hour later, Lyra bumped into Josh on her way out of the room. He looked exhausted too, like he hadn't slept for days.

'Is she okay?' he asked, catching the look of concern on Lyra's face.

'She will be. We've managed to create a locus. It's not much, a tiny piece of hope. We may be able to use it to locate Zack if we can get close enough.'

Josh looked past Lyra at Caitlin sitting in front of the fire, staring into the glowing orb.

'He's still alive?'

Lyra nodded. 'He's very special. I don't think they mean him any harm.'

There were tears in Josh's eyes. 'Thank you.'

She hugged him, feeling the tension release in his shoulders. 'We'll find him.'

As her hand stroked his back she instinctively read his timeline. It wasn't something she would usually do to a friend and it was only a brief glimpse, but what Lyra saw made her gasp.

Lyra stepped back, her eyes wide. 'What have you done?' she whispered.

He took a deep breath. 'It's a long story.'

There were hundreds of versions of his life, like an unravelling ball of wool, a multitude of timelines and reboots. Lyra couldn't begin to understand how Josh had done it, but she was sure it wasn't good.

'How many times have you changed the timeline?'

He shrugged, moving to go past her. 'I've lost count.'

Lyra put her arm across the door, barring his way. 'Does she know?'

He shook his head. 'No one does.'

'And all that fuss about building the Infinity Engine?'

'To make sure I didn't screw it up again.'

Lyra looked back at Caitlin. 'You need to tell her. She deserves to know.'

'Not now, not with everything going on with Zack.'

Lyra scowled. 'There will never be a right time. Caitlin loves you, trusts you. You can't carry that burden for much longer. I can see what it's doing to you.'

He nodded, his expression hardening. 'I will. Just let her have this moment.'

She pursed her lips, then finally nodded and dropped her arm. 'Be careful with the locus, they're quite addictive.'

'Thanks.'

Walking away, Lyra turned. 'Just promise me that you won't screw this up.'

14

THE WATCHMAKER

[Antiquarian Watchworks]

The elevator was a cylindrical cage made from ornately-wrought iron. Its bars twisted masterfully into organic shapes of flowers and vines, creating an art-deco masterpiece that had the desired effect on any visitor to the watchmaker — this was a place built by craftsmen.

Sabien entered the cage and the doors slid around to close with a soft click. The sound of the lock made it suddenly feel like a trap, albeit a gilded one. As the winding mechanism slowly lowered him downwards he began to remove his gloves. *Just in case*, he thought to himself, the old habits kicking in before he could stop them.

The cage moved through time as it descended. Sabien watched time pass before his eyes as it travelled towards the watchmaker's office. After a few minutes, the inspector realised they were no longer moving down, but sideways instead, travelling along a temporal corridor that burrowed through the late eighteenth century.

Tachyons were standard field issue amongst all members of the Order since the Mark I was developed by John Harrison in 1759. At its core it was a vestige, a programmable one, but still a simple homing device. Over the years, various grandmasters of the Antiquarian Guild had added their own enhancements to it, some more useful than others. Konstantine followed in the long tradition. The remote detonator was hidden in the upgrade to the radio communications that he sanctioned.

The Protectorate's versions were different from the standard issue. They had made their own modifications, giving it features that would have been seen as dangerous by the other members. Known as 'Black Tachyons' they usually came in pairs, and allowed the wearer to transport another, usually a prisoner, in the same jump. They could also produce a stasis field that would temporarily pause time around them, although that did come with side-effects: temporal amnesia being the most common, which made questioning a subject difficult.

A soft bell chimed to signal that he had reached the destination and the door slid open once more.

Standing in the reception hall was an old man dressed in a houndstooth suit, his beard long and white with tiny bells tied into it.

'Greetings,' said the man, performing a deep bow. 'My name is Chimes.'

'Inspector Sabien,' Sabien responded awkwardly.

'Would you follow me please? The master is expecting you.'

. . .

Sabien followed the strange little man through a series of small studios, each one housing a group of men wearing multi-lensed helmets, poring over the inner workings of a tachyon.

He was surprised to find that they were still built by hand, for some reason he'd assumed that they were manu-factured.

They came to a set of tall wooden doors, inlaid with the symbols of gears and cogs, the insignia of the watchmakers.

Chimes rose on the balls of his feet and tapped lightly on the door, then stepped back and waited for it to be opened. The bells in his beard tinkling as he fidgeted.

Sabien was wondering what the bells were for when the doors suddenly swung open and an old, blind man stood in the doorway to his study.

'Chimes?' the man asked, moving his hand around in the air. 'Where are you? Did you bring him?'

'Here master.' The moment his assistant took a step, the bells gave away his location and the concern in the old man's face melted away. His sightless white eyes lighting on Sabien as if he could still see him.

'Welcome Inspector,' he bowed slightly, as far as his crooked back would let him. 'Please join me.'

Chimes took his master's hand and guided him into the study, which was a tall round room with walls of wooden drawers, each marked with a symbol.

'Every chronometer that's ever been made,' the master watchmaker explained as Chimes deposited him into his seat. 'I test every one of them personally.'

'Even the Mark VI?' Sabien asked.

The old man's expression soured. 'To my eternal shame.'

'It was by design, master,' said Chimes angrily. 'Not your fault!'

The watchmaker nodded somberly. 'Even by design I should have rejected them. It was a terrible idea — the chief artificer should have never agreed to it.'

'The detonator was Konstantine's idea wasn't it?'

The old watchmaker ran his tongue along his dry, papery lips and ran his fingers over the objects on his desk until he found a small metal disc. 'This is the Kalimor, a plate of pure titanium machined to one third of a millimetre in thickness — I can tell by touch if it exceeds that by more than a micrometer. Such is the precision and craft that goes into every one of my watches. Why on earth would I ever want one to be destroyed? They are impossible to lose.' He waved at the cabinets around him, 'We keep a sympathetic copy of every Kalimor that goes into a tachyon for exactly that reason.'

'Konstantine wouldn't listen,' added Chimes, hovering over a teapot.

'You may go,' said the watchmaker.

'But the tea?'

'I'm old but not entirely incapable thank you!' snapped the old man.

Chimes looked like a kicked puppy as he left the room.

'Grandmaster Konstantine has brought shame upon our guild,' he continued once the doors had closed. 'The man was a fool and a charlatan. Only concerned with his own ambition.'

He poured the tea expertly, without spilling a drop and handed a cup to Sabien.

'So, what brings the Protectorate to my door?'

'We're investigating the events surrounding a break-in at the Xenobiology laboratory. We think the tachyon failure may be linked to it.'

The blind man looked confused. 'Interesting. I'm not sure the Grandmaster had any designs on the creatures of the Maelstrom?'

'We believe he may have been colluding with others — part of a wider conspiracy.'

'Rothstein,' the old man muttered like a curse.

'Who's Rothstein.'

The watchmaker drew a long slow breath. 'Have you ever heard of the Medici Collection inspector?'

Sabien shook his head and then remembering, spoke aloud. 'No.'

'Konstantine spent his entire tenure denying the existence of talismans, even though he was secretly collecting them. I may not have my eyes, but I hear things, small pieces of the puzzle that build into a bigger picture.'

The watchmaker told him about Konstantine's obsession, his hidden collection and the agent tasked with finding them.

'Where is Rothstein now?' asked Sabien, writing the name down in his notebook.

'Disappeared along with his master.'

15

MARCUS AND RUFIUS

[Maelstrom]

The *Nautilus* was anchored in a floating graveyard of WW2 battleships. Their old grey hulls scarred and twisted, torn open by torpedoes, drifting silently around the timeship like whales swimming through space.

Rufius wasn't sure of the mechanics behind how Marcus and his menagerie transported him across the void. There was no sense of time passing or distance travelled. Patterns of light and random skeins of time moved in a way that felt as if the void were turning around him, rather than him actually traversing it.

Whatever they did, he found himself standing on the flight deck of the aircraft carrier *USS Enterprise*, while Marcus said farewell to the gruesome posse of biological experiments.

· · ·

The *Nautilus* hung silently in the air above them, a cluster of temporal debris collecting around its hull, trailing off in the general direction of the way they had come.

Thomas Makepiece appeared from the hangar deck of the *Enterprise*, his mouth gaping open in surprise as he spotted Rufius standing between the Hellcats and the Warhawks.

His wife, who was only a few steps behind, crashed into the back of him and they both dropped the crates of parts they were carrying.

Marcus came to stand by Rufius.

He bared his teeth. 'Do you want to tell them? It might sound better coming from a human.'

The long incisors changed his speech pattern, making it hard for him to pronounce certain words, and the gruffness left little room for sympathetic tones.

Rufius nodded and walked towards them. 'Thomas, Juliana, I'm sorry to turn up out of the blue, but we need your help.'

The blood drained out of Caitlin's mother's face as he told them about what had happened to their grandson. She was a strong woman, but Rufius could see that even she was struggling to hold back the tears.

'Where's Cat now?' asked Thomas, when Rufius finished.

'I left her at the Chapter House, with Alixia.'

'Good,' said Thomas, turning to his brother. 'Do you think you can track the one who took him?'

Marcus nodded, folding his arms over his chest. 'Found you in the middle of the infinite void didn't I?'

'You had a little help,' added Rufius.

'Local knowledge, first rule of being a ranger.'

Juliana knelt down and began collecting the supplies she'd dropped. 'Let's stop gassing like old women and get this lot onto the ship. Sooner we get these fitted the better. No time to lose.'

Thomas nodded and gathered up his tray of engine parts. 'The shield bearings need replacing, shouldn't take more than a couple of hours,' he explained.

'Less if you get your arse in gear Thomas Makepiece!' shouted his wife, walking towards the ladder hanging down from their ship. 'And you two, make yourselves useful. There's more parts on the lower hangar deck. Big blue box, can't miss it.'

Everybody did as they were told. Juliana had the kind of voice that old school teachers used to use to silence entire rooms of children.

16

TRUTHS

[Xenobiology Department, London. Date: Present Day]

Sabien watched Kaori pacing impatiently while the others took their seats around the conference table. She was like a child bursting to tell everyone her secret, trying hard to hold her tongue as they took forever to get settled.

Professor Eddington fidgeted uncomfortably, grimacing at the array of touchscreens and holo projectors that lined the walls of the room. Unlike his apprentice, Simeon De Freis, who was fascinated by the three dimensional model of the parasite hovering over the black table like a ghost.

Josh and Caitlin arrived and the temperature in the room seemed to drop a few degrees. Neither of them looked as if they had managed to get any sleep, which was not surprising in the circumstances. Kaori looked pretty strung out too, he assumed she'd pulled an all-nighter after he told her about the kidnapping. There were tremors in her hands from caffeine withdrawal.

This was her show, he was taking a purely spectator role,

sitting at the far end of the table so as to distance himself from Kaori. She shot sideways glances at him, her dark eyes catching him every so often. She had asked him to come and he accepted even though he knew others wouldn't be so keen for him to be there.

The Grand Seer swanned into the room with Lyra Cousineau trailing behind.

'Is that all of us?' asked Kaori, picking up her tablet as if checking a register. 'Where's Westinghouse?'

'Still searching for Marcus I guess,' answered Lyra, taking a seat next to Sim.

Kaori shrugged. 'Fair enough, let's get started.'

She tapped a button on her screen and the lights dimmed.

'I think by now, most of you know this nasty little fellow.' She pointed at the slowly rotating image of the Aeon with a laser pointer.

Josh unconsciously rubbed his neck.

'I've managed to access its memory and it makes for interesting reading.'

Lines of Akkadian script scrolled over the screens on one wall, translated excerpts popping out where Kaori had made notes or highlighted key sections.

'The creature's brain has an organic interface. One that can only be accessed once it's been removed from the host.' She waved her hand and the outer layers of the holographic model disappeared, revealing its brain and central nervous system. 'Most of its neurological infrastructure is dedicated to storing information. This one was discovered by an unfortunate Victorian explorer near Xanthus and from what I've been able to translate so far, it's pretty clear someone placed them in the distant past on purpose.'

'Why?' asked Sim.

Kaori shrugged. 'We're not entirely sure. All we know is that they can store thousands of petabytes of data and they're not native to this planet.'

'So how did they get here?'

'The Anunnaki,' said Caitlin. 'We saw them collecting Aeons in Babylon.'

'Which brings me to my next point,' said Kaori, swiping away the model and replacing it with images of security footage. Grainy frames of the diminutive doctor standing in front of a security door looped through a sequence as they watched her gain clearance and step into the containment facility.

She spoke directly to Caitlin. 'This is the moment when my doppelgänger broke in and stole the Aeon you removed from Josh. It also managed to disable all the safeties on the other containment cells, releasing every single one of our specimens, wreaking havoc within the department. No one even noticed the specimens were missing for two weeks!'

'Your doppelgänger?' queried Professor Eddington, leaning forward to examine the images.

'Yes, I was nowhere near Sec-Con when this was taken and as far as I know I don't have a twin.'

Kaori watched their faces as the penny dropped.

'Rufius was telling the truth,' said Sim.

'As I've already told you,' insisted the Grand Seer, slapping his hand down on the table.

'The creature assumed my identity, right down to the retinal pattern and palm print. There is nothing in our database that has any of those capabilities, nor the ability to infiltrate and disable our security systems.'

'No creature of flesh and bone,' quipped Kelly.

Josh looked confused, but ignored him. 'You think this creature copied Caitlin and took our son?'

Kaori nodded. 'No doubt in my mind, the only question is why. What did Zack have that the Anunnaki could possibly want?'

Caitlin looked into Josh's eyes and he knew what she was going to say.

'It's because he's special,' she said quietly, taking the locus out of her pocket. It glowed faintly in her hand.

Sim gasped. 'What on earth is that?'

'It's a locus,' declared Kelly proudly. 'We've managed to create a temporal connection with Zachary.'

'Can it tell us where he is?' asked Sabien, sitting forward in his chair.

The Grand Seer shook his head, dislodging a number of feathers from his cloak.

'But it does prove he's alive,' Lyra reassured them.

'So, what's so special about your son?' continued Sabien even though Benoir had already told him.

Caitlin stared wide-eyed into the storm of particles spinning inside the sphere. 'He's a powerful seer.'

Eddington scoffed. 'That hardly makes him a target for abduction.'

Josh took the locus from Caitlin and held it up. 'Zack may have acquired some rather special memories. Ones that once belonged to my father.'

Everyone looked confused.

Josh held onto the globe and hoped he was doing the right thing.

'You're not going to like what I'm about to tell you, but if it helps to get Zack back, then I don't care.'

Lyra caught his eye and nodded, as if approving what he was about to do.

Taking a deep breath, Josh's knuckles whitened as he gripped the sphere tightly.

'This isn't the first time I've known you, nor the second. I've been through hundreds of iterations of this timeline trying to find a way to keep you all alive. To keep you safe.'

Sim seemed mildly relieved at the news. 'Well, that explains why my calculations about you never made any sense.'

Josh ignored him and continued, looking directly at Caitlin. 'I've spent so long trying to make everything right: to save my mother; to stop each of you from dying horrible deaths, I'd forgotten what was important — our future.'

He held the sparkling globe towards her face. 'There are millions of ways our lives could have played out, but since you told me about Zack, I can't think of anything I want more than to hold on to this one.'

'How?' demanded Eddington. 'How have you managed to do this?'

Josh held up his other hand, so that they could see his ring. 'I am a Paradox, a child born from a future that never happened. This is Solomon's Ring — it's a talisman. With it I can travel to any part of the past without a vestige.'

'Talismans don't exist,' muttered Eddington.

'According to Grandmaster Konstantine,' corrected Sabien. 'Who had an entire collection of them hidden in a secret vault.'

'How many times?' interrupted Caitlin, her eyes narrowing in disbelief. 'How many times did you restart the timeline?'

Josh sighed. 'More times than I can remember. I've spent so long adjusting the continuum, trying to find the best way forward, I've lost count.'

'Using the Infinity Engine?' she asked through thin white lips as the fire rose in her cheeks.

'That was supposed to help. To make it easier.'

'You created the engine to fix your own timeline?' asked Eddington.

Josh turned towards the professor. 'Actually that wasn't my idea. My father created the original engine, in fact he was the founder of the Order.'

He told them everything and they listened in silence. It felt good to finally share the truth, to relieve himself of the burden that he had carried for so long.

Over the next few hours, Josh told them of the war with the Nihil and the Eschaton Cascade, about Fermi and the paradox of his birth. Tears rolled down his face as he described how his father had gifted him all of his knowledge, before sacrificing himself to protect them.

Caitlin's hard expression slowly softened as he told his story, taking his hand when he described how the Aeon consumed virtually all of his father's memories — except for the last ones that Zack stole from him.

'You've sacrificed so much for us,' said Kaori, getting to her feet. 'Your father sounds like a great man.'

'He was very fond of you too,' replied Josh, sitting back in his seat.

'And you believe he was not from this continuum?' asked Professor Eddington.

'I know he wasn't. I've seen it.'

The professor frowned. 'The multiverse theorem is one

that some of our more eccentric actuaries have been trying to model for years. Statistically it's virtually impossible to quantify.'

Sabien was checking over the notes in his almanac. 'So, you believe that your son was carrying part of your father's memory?'

Josh nodded. 'Yes.'

'And prior to his abduction, the doppelgänger broke into the high security containment and stole the same parasite that took the rest of your father's memories?'

'So she says,' Josh looked at Kaori.

'Do you know what Zack might have taken?' asked Sabien.

Josh shrugged. 'Hard to say from a hundred lifetimes of moments, it could have been anything.'

Kaori snapped her fingers. 'There are patterns to the engrams I downloaded. I might be able to identify which areas of memory are missing.'

'How does that help Zack?' snapped Caitlin, taking the locus back from Josh.

'It gives us a motive,' said Sabien, closing his notebook.

Caitlin scowled. 'Doesn't bring my son back though does it?' She turned to Kaori. 'Do you know where these Aeons came from?'

Doctor Shika shook her head. 'Not yet.'

'I think we're all agreed that they're not from this continuum,' said Sim. 'Our calculations have failed to model any of these outcomes, which can only mean that they fall outside of normal statistical parameters.'

'Meaning what exactly?' asked Caitlin.

'There are more things in heaven and earth, Horatio.

Than are dreamt of in your philosophy,' quoted the Grand Seer, getting to his feet and waving his hands through the holographic images. 'We need to see with new eyes. This is not the work of chance, there is method in their madness.'

No one knew quite how to react to his outburst. There was an awkward silence while everyone processed what exactly he meant.

'So, where do we begin?' said Sim, finally finding his voice. 'How do we find this doppelgänger?'

'Konstantine,' said Sabien. 'I'm convinced he's behind this.'

Josh disagreed. 'He's probably just infected. I think we need to find a way to track them into their timeline.'

'How? They're clearly more advanced than us,' Lyra said, shaking her head. 'I think we need to find out more about the Anunnaki.'

'The best man for that is Uncle Marcus,' said Caitlin, getting to her feet. 'And the Grand Seer is right, I think we're going to need the *Nautilus*. Both of which are probably lost in the Maelstrom right now.'

Lyra frowned and folded her arms. 'Well, I guess we'll have to do it ourselves.'

'I suggest we divide into three teams,' said Eddington calmly, holding up three fingers and counting them off. 'Anunnaki, Konstantine and alternate timelines.'

'We'll take the alternate timelines,' Caitlin said, holding up her hand. Then leaned closer to Josh and whispered. 'I have an idea. We need to go to the library.'

17

THE LIBRARY

[Great Library]

Josh followed Caitlin through the maze of stacks, narrow alleys of towering bookshelves that reached up into a distant ceiling where librarians swung between the tomes on fine steel chains, like circus trapeze acts on the high wire.

Her head was down, shoulders hunched as though she were walking into a headwind, hardly seeming to look where she was going. She'd been raised in the library and knew the layout better than most of the elder librarians. So well in fact, that she didn't need to decrypt the illegible signage that was stencilled in gold at the end of each stack.

Making sharp, seemingly random turns without warning, Josh struggled to keep up with her and was beginning to wonder if she'd notice if he stopped, when she spun around on her heels.

'Hurry up!' she snapped, grabbing hold of his hand. 'I haven't got time to come and find you.'

'Where are we going?' he asked, feeling like a kid being pulled along by his mother.

'Restricted section,' she whispered tersely, taking yet another turn into a corridor of chained leather-bound books. 'We need to find a book called *Codex Arcanum*, written by Johannes Belsarus.'

Josh had heard of him. 'The crazy antiquarian who believed he could travel into the future?'

Caitlin ignored the question. 'So exactly how many times did you restart this timeline?'

Josh wondered how long it would take for her to bring this up. She had an annoying habit of mulling over things. Sometimes it would take weeks for something to resurface, usually just when he thought she'd forgotten about it.

'Like I said, I lost count. More than four hundred times at least. It wasn't like I went back to the beginning of time, most of the changes were in the last thousand years.'

'And do we always end up together?'

'Yes, most of the time,' he winced as he said it. Josh could feel a hole opening up beneath him.

'What happened in the ones where we didn't?'

He paused, trying to decide whether it was worse telling the truth, or just blagging it and hoping they reached their destination before he ran out of road.

'I screwed up, mostly when I tried to take shortcuts. Either you thought I was too cocky, or arrogant. One time you thought I was a stalker.'

'Sounds about right.' She let go of his hand and turned to face him, her eyes were full of fire. 'Would you have restarted this one if I hadn't got pregnant? Wait, have we got pregnant before?'

'No, we haven't,' he protested. 'And maybe — I don't know. We have the Infinity Engine now, it was supposed to make the difference, make it easier for me to see how to save my mum.'

Her hard expression softened, and she took his hand once more, walking at a slower pace.

'She would have been a great grandma.'

'Nanna,' he corrected her. 'She hated grandma. Said it sounded like something from the Waltons.'

Guards were posted on both sides of the front desk of the restricted section. It was a grand, carved wooden architrave that acted as both desk and security gate for the small library that lay beyond. Sitting behind it was an austere woman with steely-blue eyes and silver hair pulled in a tight bun, who studied them over horn-rimmed glasses.

'Head Librarian, what an unexpected pleasure,' she said, her face showing no sign of happiness whatsoever. She had a pinched expression that reminded Josh of a bird of prey.

'Muriel,' replied Caitlin, stepping up to the desk, which came level with her head. 'I would like to enter the restricted section if you please.'

There was obviously some history between the two of them. As Muriel turned the pages of the large register that lay in front of her, Josh could see the sneer gathering at the corners of her mouth.

'You have not made an appointment I take it?'

'No, Muriel,' replied Caitlin trying to remain civil. 'This is something of an emergency.'

'Is there something in particular I can help you with this e-mer-gen-cy?' asked Muriel, over stressing the vowels in the last word. She took a pen from its inkpot and made a note in her book.

Caitlin sighed. 'Do you happen to know where the *Codex Arcanum* is?'

Muriel winced as if she'd just bitten into a lemon. Asking a librarian where something was in the Great Library was tantamount to a curse. The truth was that the years of constant re-indexing had led to chaos, no one really knew where anything was specifically, it was more of a vague notion, like pointing in the general direction of China.

Muriel put down the pen, her hand shaking. 'No one has seen that book in over twenty years.'

'Then I suggest you let me in so I can start looking for it.'

'Very well. But it cannot be removed from the stacks,' the librarian added, nodding to one of the guards.

'I know the rules,' replied Caitlin. 'I think you'll find my grandfather wrote most of them.'

Muriel ignored her and pretended to sort through a pile of papers.

All of the books in the restricted section were stored behind metal grilles. Josh could see that every one of them had a fine brass chain bolted to their leather spines. These were the rarest books in existence, most of which had been recovered from the private collections of deceased wealthy gentleman or libraries that were on the verge of burning down. A few were alleged to be from the Great Library of Alexandria.

The passages were dimly lit. Since naked flames were not allowed and the electric light was at least two hundred years away from being invented, the librarians used fireflies instead. Caught in lamps that hung on stanchions, the small jars flickered with a warm golden light. Caitlin unhooked one and shook it gently, its luminescence increasing until there was enough to light their way.

The place smelled of mouldering paper and old leather, which, Josh realised, was the same way Caitlin's clothes would smell when she came home from work. It wasn't terrible, it was comforting in a strange kind of way, like a pair of his mum's old slippers — not that he would ever tell her that of course.

'We're looking for a large seventeenth-century book with a gold spine. Should be with the other books on the occult.'

Josh studied the rows of gilded spines on the shelves. To him they all looked like seventeenth-century books on the occult.

'Exactly how is Belsarus going to help us with finding Zack?' asked Josh, remembering the forest of continuums that he'd once seen while saving the colonel.

Caitlin was halfway up a small spiral staircase leading to a mezzanine. 'He may never have managed to travel into the future, but before he died, he managed to open a shadow dimension. Apparently, it's where they found Marcus — Belsarus created his own personal zoo of Chimaera in an alternate branch of time.'

'And you think his book can tell you how to cross into it?'

'It's supposed to be a record of his research. Mostly documenting his many failures, but there was a device he invented called a magnetoscope, which was supposed to be able to disrupt the fabric of space-time and create a quantum distortion field.'

Josh frowned, opening a book whose illustrations were mostly about extracting demons from witches. 'Did they know what quantum was in the seventeenth-century?'

She laughed. 'No, of course not, Belsarus called it an Ethereal Portal.'

'And did he ever manage to build this magnetoscope?'

'I assume that's what trapped him in the mirror dimension.'

Josh closed the book and slid it back onto the shelf. 'Doesn't sound very promising.'

'Have you got any better ideas?'

Josh rubbed Solomon's ring with his thumb. It was powerful, it could take him anywhere in their continuum, but he doubted it was strong enough to move them into an entirely different timeline.

They browsed through the books for the next two hours, taking turns at locating various Codices, but never finding the actual one.

Caitlin sat down at the reading table, setting the lantern of fireflies between them.

She signed. 'I'm not sure it's here, and even if it is, it's been misfiled, which effectively means it's lost.'

'And there's no other way to reach Belsarus?'

She shook her head. 'He died in the mirror dimension. Although his brain was preserved, the Draconians managed to salvage it.'

Josh got to his feet. 'Why didn't you say? Let's go.'

'But the man's insane!'

'Can't be any worse than what I carried around in my head for four years.'

18

ARRIVAL

[Aaru]

X-541 placed the naked child carefully into the ceramic basin of the sepulchre and stood back. The glass canopy closed over it, sealing the mewling infant inside a sound-proof chamber.

It was clear that the temporal shift had caused it considerable distress. Transference required a certain amount of resilience, something that the human brain was not designed to withstand. Its sensitive tissue was not accustomed to traversing a quantum corridor.

The synthetic was unsure as to whether it would survive the journey, but it had nonetheless.

'Decontamination sequence commencing,' reported the soft female voice of the unit, repeating the warning in glyphs across the surface of the glass.

The child squirmed while gas filled the interior and ultraviolet light scourged its body of all contaminants. Nothing could be left to chance, no virus or pathogen could be allowed to enter their environment, especially from the cesspit of a world he had just left.

'Analysing,' intoned the voice, as it began the secondary stage.

X-541 studied the biometrics of the fragile human as they scrolled across the glass screen. It was such a tiny, insignificant thing, no longer than his forearm, it was difficult to believe that humanity had managed to survive at all.

While the child was being scanned, X-541 turned towards the main communications port and placed his hand inside. He felt the filaments of the metallic probes slide under the organic layers of skin until they found his primary interface and instantly he was reconnected to the mainframe.

REPORT.

Commanded the system protocol.

X-541 released the data from his secondary memory substrate. Thousands of years of accumulated information streamed through the connection and into the system.

RECEIVED.

He removed his hand from the port, watching the wounds between his fingers reseal.

X-541 PROCEED TO ANUBIS

The messaged scrolled across his vision as his communication node re-registered with the network. Since returning to Aaru, quarantine protocols had locked him out of the central nexus, and even now he only had limited access until his neural cortex was cleared by the gatekeeper, Anubis.

19

RETURN

[Draconian Headquarters]

The *Nautilus* appeared in the dock, its gravity engines whining as the coils powered down.

Ground crews in fireproof uniforms swarmed out of engineering bays around the hangar and began hosing down the hull with jets of water. Steam rose from its long copper surface as they rapidly cooled the ship.

The Watch Commander, Randall McGary, was in the middle of dinner when he was informed of its unexpected arrival. He hastily put on his tunic and made his way down to welcome the Makepieces. The return of the timeship was always something of a special occasion, being the only one of its kind, and more importantly the best source of rare WW2 memorabilia.

Entering the hangar bay, Commander McGary was slightly concerned at the state of the ship. Juliana had clearly driven it hard, the engine housings were still glowing red hot.

He spotted his Chief of Engineering, Reginald Capstone,

on the lower gantry. Reg was scratching his bald head as he watched his team connecting the mooring lines.

'What's up Chief?' McGary asked as he approached.

'Burned out,' Reg replied in a broad Scottish accent whilst staring up at the port engine. 'She's too hot to try and cool, it'll crack the housing. We're going to have to let it cool gradually and then take the whole thing apart.'

'Sorry Reg,' said Juliana, coming around from the tail section. 'Had to push her pretty hard. Do you think you can get her back up and running in twenty-four hours?'

'Not a chance,' said the Chief, shaking his head. 'Do you know how many of those we have in spares?'

'None,' snapped Juliana, 'but I built her from scratch, so I should know how long it would take me, and you have a whole team at your disposal.'

Reg laughed. 'We don't have the advantage of being in the timeless realm Juliana. Us mortals have to get sleep every now and then.'

She scoffed, putting her hands on her hips. 'Forty-eight max. There are spares in the forward cargo hold. Oh, and tell your men to reinforce the plating on the bow and put the cannons back on. I have a feeling we're going into dangerous territory on the next mission.'

'Next mission?' asked the Watch Commander, realising that in his haste he had buttoned his tunic incorrectly. 'We don't have anything scheduled Juliana.'

She stared at him for a second, her jaw grinding as if she were chewing gum. 'Someone's taken my grandson Commander McGary, do you honestly think I'm going to stand around and wait for the bloody Protectorate to find him?'

He snapped to attention. 'No ma'am. We'll have it done in twenty-four.'

The Chief nodded sternly and went to organise his team.

Rufius walked slowly down the gangplank, letting his legs get re-acquainted with gravity. Marcus marched on ahead, his body seeming to have none of the after effects of rejoining the continuum, he'd returned to human form the moment they left the Maelstrom.

Stopping half way down, Rufius took a slow, deep breath. The air tasted so different from the recycled atmosphere on the ship, not to mention the smell of Marcus in his Chimaeric form. He'd forgotten how good it felt to be in linear time once more. The pitching motion of the time-ship was unusual, not unlike being at sea, but there was something odd about its temporal fields that put him off his food. And the dreams were something else entirely.

It took them nearly two days to get back. The hours spent repairing the *Nautilus* were painfully slow, although Rufius knew in reality no time would have passed at all. He felt useless, spending most of his time in his cabin mulling over the kidnapping.

He couldn't help but think about his daughter, though the circumstances were different. He knew exactly what Josh and Caitlin were going through. His wife and child had died whilst trapped in a quarantine zone, surrounded by cholera and typhoid, with no way to reach them. It was a terrible fate, one that he would never be able to put right — the rules of the Order were clear on such things.

At least with Zachary, Rufius might have a chance to save him, especially because now they had Marcus and the *Nautilus*, there weren't many places in the continuum they would be able to hide.

20

BELSARUS

[Cerebrium]

J osh watched bubbles form on the surface of the brain floating in the jar, while Caitlin connected the wires to the copper contacts.

'Are you sure you don't want me to do this?' she asked for the second time, placing the wire mesh on his head.

'No, I'm kind of used to it. Just tell me what I need to ask when I get in there.'

She kissed him gently on the lips. 'Don't blame yourself for this. We'll get him back.'

He tried to smile but failed. Ever since Lyra gave Caitlin the locus she seemed different, less anxious and he wished he could share her sense of optimism.

As far as he was concerned it was all his fault.

WHO? WHAT? WHY?

Came the usual barrage of responses from the slowly waking mind of Belsarus.

JOSHUA JONES

Josh responded through the mental link created by the Intuit.

He closed his eyes, trying to focus on the stream of images appearing in his mind, ignoring the lump of grey matter that was gently fizzing in front of him.

JOSHUA JONES > WHO AM I?

Not a particularly great start, thought Josh. The only other time he'd used the Intuit was before his father had taken residence in his head, learning Ancient Greek from a four-hundred-year-old dead guy called Janto Sargorian.

'He doesn't know who he is,' Josh whispered to Caitlin.

'Johannes Belsarus.'

Josh repeated the name to the mind.

YES. BELSARUS. I KNEW HIM ONCE.

'I think this guy's memories got a little screwed up in that other dimension. He's referring to himself in the third person.'

'Ignore it. As long as he remembers, that's all that matters. Ask him about the magnetoscope. He spent his entire fortune trying to perfect it.'

Josh did as he was asked.

Images of three brass spheres rotating around each other in a bath of mercury appeared in his mind. 'I see them.'

He felt Caitlin take his hand and squeeze it. 'Can you get him to share the plans for it?'

PLANS? DIAGRAMS? Josh asked.

The images of the spheres transformed into schematics of their internal structures. Intricate blueprints streamed into his mind, embedding themselves into his memory.

DANGER!

Came a warning from the mind. It showed Josh a dark,

shadowy realm behind a mirror, hanging on one wall of an old manor house.

'I've got the plans, but he's warning me that it's danger-ous. I can see this dark world on the other side of the mirror.'

'That's the mirror dimension I was talking about. Where he kept Marcus. Ask him about who can build it.'

ENGINEER?

The mind went silent, the mirrored surface shimmering slightly until Josh could see an old man standing on the other side of it.

'I can see him.'

'Who?'

'Belsarus. He's standing on the other side of this mirror, like he's still trapped there. His mouth is moving but I can't hear anything.'

'Don't go through.'

Josh moved closer to the mirror. 'It's only a memory. It can't hurt me.'

'Don't make me disconnect you!' she threatened.

Belsarus raised his hand as if to stop him and began writing in the dust on the surface of his side.

A. L. S. E. T.

'He's writing something on the glass.' Josh spelled out the letters.

'It's backwards. T.E.S.L.A. He's saying we need Tesla.'

21

SABIEN

[Antiquarians HQ]

'Thank you for seeing me at such short notice,' said Sabien.

'Anything I can do to help,' replied Cuvier, getting to his feet and offering his hand. 'Such a terrible thing to happen, the loss of a child, terrible business.'

'Lost, but not dead Grandmaster,' reminded Sabien, ignoring the gesture.

Cuvier retracted his hand, patting his waistcoat and looking slightly embarrassed. 'Yes, quite. So, how can I help you Inspector?'

After the mysterious disappearance of Konstantine, his predecessor, Georges Cuvier was unanimously voted into the position of Grandmaster by the Antiquarian select committee.

Based on the teetering piles of paperwork on the man's desk, it was clear that he was struggling to come to terms with the administrative duties and the dark shadows under his eyes were testament to the long hours he was working, trying to fix the mess that Konstantine had left behind.

The failure of the Tachyon Mark VI paralysed the Order, thousands of people had been left stranded in remote and dangerous parts of history with no way to get home. Rumour was that the Draconians were still searching for over two hundred missing people.

'What do you know about Konstantine?'

Cuvier sighed and sat down behind his desk. 'He was the youngest grandmaster in the history of the guild. We were all impressed by his passion. Antiquarians can be a solitary bunch, and he was nothing if not a charismatic leader. And the work he did on the Minoan texts was outstanding, no one had come close to deciphering it until he recruited Ventris.'

Sabien took out his almanac and pretended to make a note. 'We have reason to believe the Grandmaster may have been involved in the kidnapping of the child.'

Cuvier frowned until his bushy white eyebrows knitted together. 'I knew that the Protectorate were investigating him over the Mark VI debacle, but I wasn't aware that he was responsible for little Zachary's abduction.'

'Are you aware of the Medici Collection?'

The old Frenchman laughed. 'Who isn't? The forbidden talismans of the Anunnaki. Just one of Konstantine's many deceptions.'

'I wish to see it.'

Cuvier grimaced, pushing himself up from his chair. 'Of course, but there's nothing left. The man took it all with him.'

He went to a cabinet of small wooden drawers, peering myopically over his half-moon spectacles at the various symbols etched onto brass plates. 'My men found no trace of his treasure,' he continued, pulling out the contents of various compartments.

After rooting through a dozen, he finally produced a small golden key and handed it over to Sabien.

'No offence, but perhaps there's something that you've missed,' the inspector said, removing one of his gloves. 'The Protectorate has methods that can uncover the most microscopic of details. Thank you for your assistance.'

Taking the key from the Antiquarian, Sabien opened up its timeline and disappeared.

Cuvier slumped back into his chair, took a half-finished bottle of brandy from under a stack of papers, and poured himself a large glass as the sheets toppled onto the floor.

'Bonne chance,' he said, toasting the air where the inspector had just been standing.

Sabien appeared in front of the doors to the Medici Collection. They were just as the old watchmaker described; a complex set of locking mechanisms built into the intricate carvings of the vault.

Except the doors were hanging open.

The official report recorded that the room was sealed after Konstantine's disappearance. It was standard procedure once any high-ranking official was found to be in dereliction of their duties: rights and privileges to all sensitive materials were immediately restricted.

These were his least favourite jobs, tracking down a time traveller came with a whole host of challenges, especially with those who could mask their trail. Unlike linear suspects, where Sabien could simply move back to a last known location and apprehend them, travellers had the ability to lose themselves in the annals of time.

He wasn't allowed, by law, to intercede in the earlier part of the suspect's life. The tenets of the Pre-Crime Act forbade it, mainly because of the disruption it could cause on the rest of the timeline, even if there was clear evidence that the perpetrator was involved in planning the offence at the time.

If Sabien turned up in Konstantine's life and tried to arrest him before he'd actually committed the crime, his defence could argue that this was only one possible future — it was called the 'Uncertainty Principle' and it was very frustrating for a time cop.

Sabien ground his teeth as he stared into the darkness beyond the open door. Knowing that Konstantine had escaped because someone had failed to post a guard was annoying but worse was the thought of having to pick up a cold trail.

He took off his other glove and ran his hands over the door.

The metal locks gave up their life history like a drunk in a bar. In seconds, Sabien knew everyone who'd passed through the portal in the last twenty years.

Thankfully, there hadn't been that many visitors. Mostly old curators with no idea of what they were delivering. As Sabien wound through the timeline he came upon Caitlin and some random young Scriptorian whose timeline felt remarkably similar to Joshua Jones. He made a note of the young man and moved on.

Konstantine's visits were always accompanied by another who failed to register in Sabien's mind. Like a blur on a photograph, an artefact on the lens that couldn't be pulled into focus. The inspector concentrated his senses on the other man, assuming that this was the agent, Rothstein, whom the old watchmaker had mentioned, but the man's identity eluded him.

Confused, he took his hand away and rubbed the palms together. He'd always been able to read a crime scene, it was what he was born to do. The only logical explanation was that Konstantine's accomplice was using some kind of shielding, which meant a technology that wasn't from this timeline.

He stepped inside.

The soles of his boots crunched on the broken glass covering the floor. As his eyes adjusted to the dim light, he could see that every one of the display cases had been smashed.

As Cuvier said, all of the talismans were gone.

Sabien reached out to one of the broken cabinets, his fingers stroking the splintered wooden frame, letting his mind wind back through its chronology as he tried to recapture the original state of the room before Konstantine destroyed everything.

But he couldn't — everything about the place felt wrong.

Countless years spent examining thousands of crime scenes told him there should be evidence. There was something the boffins called the 'law of transference' which stated that: no object could interact with another artefact without leaving something of itself behind. Forensic science was based on exactly this principle.

But this room felt as if it had only just come into existence. There was not a single piece of historical data in it. Even the air tasted too fresh.

Except it wasn't the room, Sabien slowly realised with an inward smile. It was the appearance of one, a room that was created to make everyone believe it was empty, unless you were a druid.

Sabien went back to the doors.

There was no possible way Konstantine would have enough time to collect all of the treasure from this place. Therefore he must have had a contingency plan; a diversion to fool everybody into thinking it was all gone. What better way to fool a tomb robber than to look as if you've already been robbed?

Sabien closed the doors from the inside, sealing himself in. He heard the locking mechanism reset, hundreds of tiny gears meshing together as the deadbolts ground back into place.

He closed his eyes and felt the back of the door. The oak panels warming to his touch, like ice on a lake, he pushed his mind below the surface and into the deep currents beneath.

It was as if the real room was a few millimetres below the shell of the wrecked one. As his senses engaged with the timelines of the hidden space, he heard the sounds of glass cracking and opened his eyes to see the shattered cases restoring themselves, the destruction reversed until each cabinet held a shining talisman once more. Twenty of the most powerful artefacts in the Antiquarian collection sat waiting for their master to return.

'Very clever,' Sabien whispered to himself, realising that he couldn't unlock the door from the inside.

There was at least enough air in the room for thirty minutes. If he didn't find a way out in that time he could suffocate, assuming of course that Konstantine had put a temporal shield around it to stop him jumping out.

Which is exactly what Sabien would have done.

Walking over to one of the cabinets, he opened the case and took out a small golden figurine. 'Now, how the hell do I get out of here?'

22

WORMHOLES

[Chapter House]

Caitlin's parents walked into the study and found their daughter in the middle of a heated debate with Rufius.

'He can't be trusted!' insisted Rufius, his face bright pink beneath his red beard.

'He's travelled into another dimension!' countered Caitlin, pointing at a set of drawings laying on the table. 'And he gave Josh the plans to help us build it!'

Josh was ignoring both of them, bent over a complex blueprint, studiously annotating it with technical details.

Rufius threw his hands in the air. 'The lunatic locked your uncle up like an animal for years. He was deranged when he was alive, God only knows what's happened to him since!'

'He's not a person any more, just a collection of memories, he doesn't have the capacity to lie.'

Rufius raised one eyebrow. 'And you know this for a fact?'

Juliana stepped between them and took her daughter in her arms.

Caitlin seemed to shrink in her mother's embrace, and the pent up emotions that she'd tried so hard to suppress over the last twenty-four hours came flooding back.

Rufius stormed off to get a drink.

'Are you okay?' her mother asked when they finally separated, wiping the tears of her daughter's cheeks. 'Of course you're not, you've lost your baby. Ignore me. I've just spent two long days going crazy.'

'How did you know?' asked Caitlin, her voice hoarse from crying.

'The big bear over there told me,' she said, nodding towards Rufius. 'Walked into the Maelstrom with your uncle. Don't be too hard on him.'

'Hey KitKat,' her father said, trying to smile, but failing. There was more hugging and crying.

'Stop it! The two of you just set each other off!' barked her mother, wiping her eyes. 'This isn't going to get our grandson back is it?'

Alixia and Methuselah came in from the kitchen with trays of food and placed them strategically around Josh, who continued with his work.

'So, what do we know?' asked her mother, between mouthfuls.

Caitlin took out the locus and handed it to her. 'Lyra made this, it's how we know he's still alive.'

Juliana's eyes widened as she examined the small globe. 'Oh my God! It's like I'm holding his hand.'

She gave it to her husband who stared into it like a child at a shop window at Christmas.

'We think he's been taken by the Anunnaki,' said Josh, putting down his pen and rubbing his eyes.

Lyra stepped out of a long mirror at one end of the study and came to sit beside Caitlin's father.

'Where?' asked her mother.

'Another timeline,' growled Rufius before downing a second large glass of wine.

Juliana nodded, helping herself to another portion of the wild boar and putting half of it on to her husband's plate. Thomas hadn't touched his food, he was too distracted listening to Lyra explain how they created the locus.

'Another timeline? How do you figure that?'

'Long story,' said Josh.

'So how do we get him back?'

Josh held up one of the drawings. 'Belsarus gave me the plans for his magnetoscope and the name of the man that can make it — Tesla.'

'Nikola Tesla?' Caitlin's father said, turning back to them. 'The inventor?'

'I guess so.'

'Belsarus was a fool,' said Rufius, sitting back down at the table and pulling the stopper out of a bottle of brandy with his teeth. 'He was convinced he could travel into the future, but ended up squandering his fortune and trapping himself in a mirror dimension to boot.'

'Do you have any better ideas?' demanded Caitlin with a look that should have burned a hole through his forehead.

'The *Nautilus*,' he lifted his glass as if toasting it. 'Finest timeship in the continuum.'

Juliana raised her glass. 'The *only* timeship in the continuum.'

Caitlin turned to her mother. 'Do you think the *Nautilus* could cross into another timeline?'

Her mother frowned. 'I'm not sure. Assuming it's playing by the same fundamental laws of physics, no reason why she couldn't.'

'And if she can't?' asked Rufius.

Juliana thought for a moment, swirling her fork around in her gravy. 'We could end up in a redundant branch or a causality loop.'

Rufius scoffed. 'Assuming there *are* other timelines of course.'

'I've seen them,' snapped Josh.

Juliana ignored them. 'We would need some way of navigating. The Maelstrom is not great on signposting.'

Caitlin took the locus back from her father and turned to Lyra. 'I'm guessing that we could use it to find him?'

Lyra shrugged. 'It's never been tested outside of the continuum. In theory it should be possible, but you would need to listen very carefully.'

Juliana raised one eyebrow at her husband.

'Tesla was an interesting fellow,' said Caitlin's father, changing the subject. 'Favoured alternating current over Edison's DC, had a thing about wireless power too. Very clever for his time.'

'Do you think he can build a magnetoscope?' asked Josh, tapping his pen on the schematics.

Juliana pulled the sheet closer, slipping a pair of spectacles down from her head to perch on the end of her nose. 'I use Tesla coils in the *Nautilus*, and his bladeless turbines. The man was a genius.'

Rufius downed his drink and slammed his glass down on the table. 'But will it work? Even if this Tesla chap could build the damned thing, do we even know that it will allow us to reach Zachary?'

'No one knows.'

'Einstein might,' said Sim, who'd been sitting quietly listening to their conversation. 'Or Rosen.'

'Who?' they asked in unison.

'Nathan Rosen, they worked together on a space-time theory called an Einstein-Rosen bridge — a wormhole.'

When everyone stared at him blankly, Sim lifted up one of Josh's spare sheets of paper. 'Say that space-time could be represented as a two dimensional plane.' Picking up a pencil, he drew two dots, one at each end of the paper then curled the sheet, bringing the ends together and stuck a pencil through the two points. 'They theorised that a wormhole was the fastest way between two points in space.'

'Belsarus was trying to create a wormhole?' asked Juliana, turning the plan upside down.

'You're seriously suggesting we should recruit Einstein?' said Josh, taking back the plans and carefully rolling them up into a tube.

Sim shrugged. 'Why not?'

Caitlin's father coughed. 'I can't wait to hear what Eddington has to say about it.'

Rufius poured himself a third glass. 'I still say the *Nautilus* is our best option, but I have to admit I've always wanted to meet Einstein.'

23

SHADOW PATHS

[Lyra's house]

L yra studied herself in the long mirror, creating tiny ripples on the glass with her fingertips.

The background behind her reflection was of a ruined city, a shadow world slowly decaying in a redundant branch of time. She'd travelled through these discarded realms for years, since she was a child, but something about this particular journey gave her pause.

Benoir appeared behind her, putting his hand around her waist and kissing her neck.

'Are you sure you want to come?' she asked, sliding her hand over his.

'Do I have a choice,' he whispered, nuzzling her ear.

'Of course you do. I don't need a protector, I've used the old paths since I could walk. They take a bit of getting used to.'

'I've travelled through stone, what can be worse than that?'

Lyra thought of the strange things she had seen in the

shadow world, the remnants of people, ghosts some would call them, but there were other things too, hungry things that spent too long in the dark.

'Do you ever have bad dreams?' She turned inside his embrace until she was facing him.

He frowned, the cute wrinkles that she adored appearing in the corners of his eyes. 'Not that I can remember, why?'

'These dead worlds are haunted with things that some would call nightmares, but they're just old memories, like bits of old TV shows on a loop.'

He shrugged, and she could feel the muscles in his arms tightening. 'Like ghosts?'

'And other things.'

'Well, you seem to have survived.'

Lyra bit her lip, the scars on her arms were a testament to all the times she nearly hadn't, but maybe survived was the right word. Compared to the many seers sitting in Bedlam, she was perfectly sane.

She kissed him. 'Just don't say I didn't warn you.'

'The first step into the mirror is like walking through an arctic waterfall,' she explained, pulling on a pair of long leather boots. 'It lasts less than a second but the chill will stay with you for days. I like to think of it as a car wash for your soul.'

He was fiddling with a lantern, filling it with oil and checking the wick.

'How many paths are there?'

She shrugged. 'I've never travelled the same one twice. They have a tendency to move around, it's more a case of remembering where you want to go rather than trying to navigate them.'

'Don't you worry about getting lost?'

Lyra laughed. 'I get lost every time, that's half the fun.'

She could see that he wasn't comfortable with that thought. 'Don't worry, we'll take it slow and pick somewhere easy.'

He gripped her hand tightly as she stepped through the glass. She told him to close his eyes and think of it like the surface of a pond, which he dutifully did, only opening them once they were through.

The shivering was uncontrollable, and Benoir gritted his jaw to stop his teeth from chattering.

She took the lamp from him before he dropped it and hugged him, using her body for warmth.

'So c-c-c-old,' he stuttered as she rubbed his back vigorously.

'It'll pass, but we need to keep moving,' she said, looking at the shadows moving over his shoulder. 'Not a good idea to stand around.'

Walking along the cobbled street, Benoir's breathing eased. He stared up at the ancient gabled houses teetering over them, blocking out the half light of a grey dawn.

'Where was this?'

Lyra was distracted by something behind them. 'What? Oh, Prague I think. Or Bergamo. Or both.' Then lowering her voice. 'Let's turn at the next junction. I think something is following us.'

He looked back, seeing nothing but darkness.

'Like what?'

Eventually they came to a market square and Lyra guided them through the doorway of an old shop.

The ghost of a shopkeeper was busy behind the counter, the grey whiskers of his moustache waggling as he spoke to non-existent customers.

Lyra watched furtively through the mullioned glass while Benoir studied the old man. The loop of time was less than a minute, and he tried to read his lips but the moustache got in the way.

Outside a shadow detached itself from a wall and took the shape of a tall man.

'Benoir,' she whispered. 'Stay very still.'

24

MEDICI

[Medici Collection]

The talismans were dead, their chronologies missing.

Like a criminal wiping away any trace of their fingerprints from a weapon, there wasn't a single moment of history remaining. Sabien couldn't think of anyone who could redact something that entirely. Over the years he'd come across a few talented 'cleaners', devious members of the Order with the ability to eradicate recent events, but none who could have done this kind of work. This was masterful, as though the objects had been reverted to the day they were made, which didn't seem possible looking at their age-worn condition.

Sabien took off his coat. It was starting to get a little warm and that air was beginning to taste stale. He could feel his head begin to ache as the carbon dioxide levels increased.

'Time to be going,' he said to himself, rolling up his shirt sleeves.

Running his fingers along the wood of the cabinets, he

was surprised to find that they too were completely devoid of history — none of the furniture was usable.

Looking around at the collection, Sabien tried to imagine what Konstantine would do if he ever got trapped in here. No one created a bunker like this without building in some kind of safety.

The dials on the tachyons strapped to his forearm were motionless, indicating that time wasn't passing, which meant there were probably stasis field generators embedded in the walls. Cabinets covered every inch of the four walls of the vault from floor to ceiling, but Sabien had a good feeling that there would be granite behind them.

He picked up the serpent staff of some long-forgotten Mayan king and hammered at the back of its cabinet. The mahogany panels took a battering before they finally began to split. It was hard going, and Sabien was panting heavily by the time he saw the first glimmer of stone.

'Finally,' he wheezed, putting his hand through the splintered wood and feeling the cold of the granite under his fingers.

It was dead too.

Sabien tried his other hand, wrenching the planks apart to get his palm onto the stone.

Nothing.

No one could unwrite stone, he thought, *it's impossible.* There wasn't a person alive or dead that could take the millions of years from geological material.

Then the realisation struck him with a chilling certainty.

You're not in Kansas any more Dorothy.

'Not my continuum,' he said, looking around the room with new eyes. 'So nothing has a timeline I can work with.'

They weren't dead at all, just incompatible.

He walked back over to the door, his fingers stroking the

panels with a new found respect. 'So how the devil did you do that then?'

The door failed to answer.

The air was getting thin now, and Sabien felt light-headed. He sat down on the floor and took off his boots and socks, grinding the soles of his feet against the door.

Taking out the St Christopher from around his neck, he kissed it. 'Don't let me down.'

Picking up the blade of an ancient spear he drew its keen edge across his wrist, watching the crimson line rise across his skin. He leaned forward placing his hand so that the blood flowed down his fingers and under the crack between the door and the floor .

'Hail Mary, full of grace,' he recited under his breath, feeling his pulse beating through his arm.

Slowly, the blood trickled through until it breached the border of the stasis field and he felt the time coursing through his veins once more. It was like touching a live wire, and it was enough.

He closed his eyes and stepped back into the safest moment he knew.

Kaori woke to the sound of crashing in the bathroom.

Rising from the bed, she let her ghast surround her, its ethereal armour hardening as she pushed open the door.

Sabien was sprawled on the floor, towels covered in blood as he tried to staunch the bleeding from his wrist.

'What happened to you?' she asked, kneeling down beside him.

Sabien looked up and smiled. 'Forgot my key.'

25

NAZGÛL

[Shadow path]

'Nazgûl,' whispered Lyra, 'Shadow wraiths.'

Benoir crouched beside her, watching as more shapes formed out of the darkness.

'Are they dangerous?'

She nodded. 'They're soul eaters, preying on the lives of those trapped here, what little life that is.'

Lyra bit her bottom lip, her eyes glazing over as she fell into a trance-like state.

He watched as the wraiths drifted over the cobblestones like tatters of old cloaks caught on the wind.

'They are searching for something,' she said in a hoarse whisper. 'There is some kind of sound, like a voice, talking to them.'

'Can you hear what it's saying?'

She shook her head. 'Mostly gibberish. It's repeating over and over, like a madman muttering to himself.'

Benoir realised he'd been holding his breath and let it out slowly.

Lyra's eyes regained their focus and she stood up. 'There's someone else here. I've never encountered another traveller in the shadow paths.'

'Who?' he asked, his eyes flicking back to the window.

She pointed to a cowled figure walking into the square. 'He says his name is Abandon.'

The wraiths circled around Abandon in a kind of macabre dance. He seemed unthreatened by them and raising his hands he removed his hood. Then he stretched out his arms to the creatures, his long fingers moving through their bodies as if they were smoke.

Reluctantly, Benoir followed Lyra out into the street, but it soon became clear that the Nazgûl were only interested in the man.

He was old, his back crooked and bent. His grey robes were tattered at the hem and cuff. White hair fringed a bald head and a long beard threaded with silver rings hung down to his waist.

His eyes shone brightly, they reminded him of stained-glass windows.

As they came closer, Benoir realised the man was singing softly to the shadows, in words he couldn't understand but the tune reminded him of a children's nursery rhyme.

'Master,' Lyra greeted the man deferentially. 'Are you lost?'

The man blinked in amazement, as if seeing them for the first time.

'You are flesh and bone?' he said, with a hint of uncertainty. 'How come you to be walking the shadow paths?'

The song ended, the wraiths drifted away, merging back into the dark places.

'We are searching for a door,' said Lyra cryptically. 'One that leads to another time.'

He frowned, his white eyebrows meeting above his long nose. 'I have seen many such doors on the King's road, they always lead to trouble.'

Benoir was about to ask which king when Lyra cut him off. 'How far have you come?'

The old man sucked in his cheeks, and whistled through his whiskers. 'So far that I forget why I left. Longer than these old bones should have to endure, but yet I still tread the paths, tending to my children.'

'The wraiths?' exclaimed Benoir.

Abandon's eyes saddened. 'They were once lords and princes, now nothing but echoes of forgotten kingdoms. How the mighty have fallen.'

He pulled the hood back over his head. 'Now if you will excuse me, I must be on my way.'

'One last question master,' Lyra pleaded as the man shuffled away, reaching out to touch his shoulder.

The man span around with unnatural speed, a blade suddenly in his hand. 'Have a care girl, I have not wandered all these years without learning to protect myself.'

Lyra saw something else beneath the shadowed cowl, his face no longer that of the benevolent old man, but something else, something dark. The whispering came again, as if he were surrounded by echoes of other lives.

'Be silent,' he said to the air around him.

'Who are you?' Lyra asked.

The shadow seemed to take form and his voice deepened.

'I am Abandon. Shepherd of shadows.'

Lyra bowed slightly, but sensed there was more to him than one name.

'You have had many names I think,' she continued, ignoring the dark tentacles that curled around the edges of his hood.

'More than you can count. What is your question, daughter of the night?'

His old, crooked form was changing, straightening, he grew taller and his rags turned black as midnight.

'Have you ever met the Anunnaki?'

He laughed. 'The shining ones? Call them by their rightful titles.'

'I seek their home world.'

Abandon paused for a moment and then opened his cloak, it was lined with keys.

'There is more than one way to walk that path,' he said, selecting one of the small silver ones. 'But this will take you most of the way.'

26

1905

[Map room]

Josh and Rufius stood patiently in the centre of the room while Professor Eddington and Sim worked the controls of the Infinity Engine.

'There are a number of potential interaction points,' the professor said, manipulating the holographic model until it focused on the inventor's timeline. 'I would suggest we avoid the period prior to his departure from the employ of Thomas Edison, and concentrate on when he became independently wealthy after selling his AC patents to Westinghouse Electric.'

Eddington concentrated the model on 1889. 'We could try approaching him here,' he pointed at a tight knot of activity. 'You could act as overseas investors looking to introduce the polyphase system, or — ' He moved the timeline forward to 1902, 'here, when he lost the confidence of his main financier, J.P. Morgan, for his Wardenclyffe Tower on Long Island.'

Rufius scratched his beard, as he considered the timeline. 'When was he most desperate for funding?'

The professor expanded the timeline to include his later life. 'From this point forward. Tesla spent the next thirty years moving from one hotel to another, running up large bills and never paying them off.'

'We'll take Wardenclyffe,' said Rufius.

'Why not earlier?' asked Josh.

Rufius walked up to the ribbon of light and expanded the events surrounding 1902. 'Long Island is remote enough for us to work without being overseen, and he's just lost J.P. Morgan as a patron. No other investor is going to want to touch him if JP isn't interested. He needs financing and a private project like ours should be appealing enough for his ego and his bank balance.'

Josh considered the idea. It wasn't terrible, but the early twentieth century was nowhere near as technologically advanced as his own era.

'What about Feynman? Shouldn't we bring Tesla up to the nineteen-eighties?'

Eddington shuddered. 'Bad enough that we have to work with electrical current at all. God help us all if we have to work in the age of transistors and nuclear fission.'

Rufius nodded in agreement. 'Wardenclyffe should act as a good base of operations. The nineteen hundreds were still relatively advanced from a technological point of view.'

'Where was Einstein at that time?'

Eddington waved his hand across the flickering lines and they shrank away, re-centering on another major timeline. Josh could tell from the copious amount of annotations and interconnecting branches how influential the physicist had been on the twentieth century.

'1905 was his *annus mirabilis* — his miracle year. He was

working as a patent clerk in Bern, Switzerland, when he published his four groundbreaking papers, including one on the special theory of relativity. He was twenty-six and the University of Zurich will award him a PHD, but it will be three years before he begins teaching theoretical physics at Bern University.' Eddington ran his hands further along the chronology. 'He moved to the United States in 1933, just as Hitler came to power.'

Josh squinted at the timeline. 'So, when did Tesla's Wardenclyffe project run out of money?'

'1905, by 1906 he was mortgaging it to pay off his debts at the Waldorf-Astoria.'

Rufius chuckled. 'That's decided then. We don't need to move either of them out of their own time.'

'And Einstein is still young, in his prime.'

'So what about Rosen?'

Sim appeared from behind one of the control desks. 'He wasn't born until 1909. He didn't meet Einstein until 1934 at Princeton. They worked together for three years.'

Rufius scratched his beard. 'Do we need him right now?'

'His theories have been criticised by other theoretical physicists. Wheeler and Fuller published a paper in 1962 that showed his wormholes would have been unstable.'

'There we go then!' said Rufius, clapping his hands. 'Lets stick with an Einstein-Tesla partnership for now and see where that takes us.'

Eddington agreed, and began to transfer all of the key data to Rufius's almanac.

27

ANUBIS

[Aaru]

Anubis sat motionless on his throne as if carved from marble. The only signs of life were the glowing red eyes shining out of the golden jackal headpiece he wore. They were meant as a warning to those who came before him, that should they be found wanting, their existence would be forfeit.

'Master,' said X-541, bowing before him.

Leaning on his staff, the god rose slowly from his throne, silently summoning his guards. They were synthetics of a similar design to X-541, except their physiology was configured for combat, whereas his was stealth and camouflage.

'Your report is incomplete, Shabti,' said the gatekeeper, his voice augmented by the helmet. Shabti was a derisory term the gods used for synthetics, the servants of the deceased, reminding them they were mere vessels for the souls of others.

The heavily-muscled guards took hold of X-541's arms and forced him to his knees.

Anubis towered over him, standing over nine feet in his ceremonial armour. He was the physical embodiment of the law: judge, jury and executioner, with the power to annihilate X-541 with a single word. In that moment, the synthetic experienced what he could only assume was an entirely human emotion: fear. It was an unusual sensation, suddenly contemplating the end of one's existence, his self-preservation subroutines already processing potential avoidance scenarios.

Keeping his head bowed, he spoke in the language of the gods, a tongue he hadn't used for over three thousand years. 'The symbiote was unable to complete its mission, lord. I have recovered the final engrams in the child.'

'A child,' repeated Anubis. 'You disregarded the first law?'

'It hosts the missing pattern of Thoth, my lord.'

The gatekeeper slammed the base of his staff down on the marble floor and X-541 felt the guards tense, their hands gripping his shoulders tightly.

'You have brought an abomination into the city! You know the punishment for disobeying our laws.'

X-541 lifted his head to Anubis, whose judgement was clear: he would be cast into Duat, the underworld, where his atoms would be recycled.

'The child possesses an exceptional gift,' he pleaded. 'It is a singular being, if you review its biometrics I think you will agree.'

The gatekeeper's head tilted slightly, a sure sign that he was accessing the data.

X-541 recited the prayer of acceptance. 'Great Anubis, weigh my heart as I stand before you and deem me worthy of entrance.'

Slowly, the eyes of the gatekeeper dimmed, the red glow changing to a pale green.

'You are correct. There is reason for further investigation.' He gestured to the guards to release their prisoner. 'You are free to enter the Kingdom of Aaru.'

X-541 got to his feet. The doors behind Anubis opened silently and the god stepped aside to allow him to pass.

28

NAUTILUS

[Nautilus]

'You're going where exactly?' asked Josh, standing in the galley of the timeship.

Caitlin was busy stowing her gear into lockers above their heads.

'They've upgraded the engines, she thinks we can make it through the Maelstrom using the locus.'

Josh looked unconvinced. Caitlin knew this wasn't going to be an easy conversation, which was why she hadn't told him about it. Annoyingly he'd found out anyway.

'You mean the crystal ball that Lyra says might be able to give a general sense of where Zack is?'

Caitlin slammed the hatch closed and scowled at him. 'It's far more accurate than that. Anyway the Maelstrom will reduce the background noise, make it easier to find him.'

'What happened to Belsarus and the magnetoscope?'

She shrugged. 'You can still work on that while I'm away. It's just now we have the *Nautilus*. I think this might be quicker.'

Josh folded his arms and stuck out his jaw, like he always did when he was trying to make a point. 'You can't go.'

'Why?' she asked, crossing her arms over her chest.

'Because you've no idea what's out there. Don't you remember what happened in Babylon? After you left it got a lot worse. They annihilated everyone including me.'

She had to admit he did have a point. Whoever the Anunnaki were, they had advanced technologies and weapons that made their own look like children's toys. But she wasn't prepared to sit around and wait for someone to tell her that her son was dead. Every fibre of her body wanted to go to Zachary, and Lyra's gift had given her the means to find him.

'The *Nautilus* can stay outside of their continuum, at least we will know where he is.'

Josh laughed. 'You're telling me that you won't try and rescue him? That this is just some kind of reconnaissance mission?'

She tried to hide it, but there was no point. 'If I can, I'm going to try and bring him back.'

'How do you know their continuum is even compatible?'

Caitlin shrugged. 'They walked on our world. Stands to reason we should be able to exist in theirs.'

'They can also change their appearance at will. Maybe they've learned to adapt.'

Her father walked backwards through the galley dragging a box filled with ammunition for the forward cannons. He smiled at the two of them and continued without a word.

'You're preparing for a fight?' whispered Josh, after he'd left.

'I'm going to rescue our son. I'll do whatever it takes.'

Josh sat down on one of the couches and put his head in his hands.

'I know you think this is all my fault. I wish I could go back and change it.'

She sat down beside him and put her arm around him. 'I don't. But I have to do this, do you understand? With or without you, this is just something I have to do. Maybe it's the maternal instinct or some other hormonal shit, but if I don't try, I think I'm going to go crazy.'

'I'm coming with you.'

'No, it's better if you stay and work on the Tesseract. We stand more chance if we work on different approaches. At least one of us might reach him. The longer it takes to find him the more likely he could be dead.'

He turned towards her, tears running down his cheeks. 'Don't talk like that.'

She laughed, wiping them away. 'I'm the practical one, remember? Anyway, you're assuming I'm going to fail.'

Josh brushed the hair away from her face and kissed her. 'No,' he said. 'I'm assuming that I am.'

They held each other until her mother arrived and made some comment about needing to be getting on.

Josh watched the *Nautilus* rise gracefully into the air and move out of the dock.

He waved, hoping that she was watching from a window somewhere, but knowing she was already plotting a course into the next dimension.

29

WARDENCLYFFE

[Wardenclyffe, Long Island. 1906]

The strange metal structure rose two hundred feet into the night sky over the sleepy village of Shoreham. Its intricate iron work reminded Josh of the Eiffel Tower and the single story building in front of it was lit by the warm glow of electric light, something that the locals would still come from miles around to marvel at.

It was something that Josh had long taken for granted.

Rufius was already walking up the hill towards the entrance and Josh had to quicken his step to keep up.

It was hard to move fast in the clothes the colonel had chosen. They were heavy, rich fabrics: three-piece suits and overcoats that felt as if they were made from lead. Rufius insisted that this was the usual attire of a European financier — Tesla would expect nothing less from the old world.

The colonel carried Gladstone bags filled with cash. Even though the Order owned some of the oldest invest-ment banks in existence, ones that dwarfed J.P. Morgan, the colonel insisted that nothing would be quite as persuasive as dollar bills. It took the Antiquarians a few days to collect the appropriate legal tender for the period, but here they stood, Josh with Belsarus's plans rolled up in a map case under his arm and Rufius with half a million dollars in two bags.

'Gentleman,' said Tesla, opening the door to them. He dressed like a dandy, his suit was bright and garish. His black hair was thickly-oiled into a parting that went straight down the centre of his head.

'Mr Tesla,' said the colonel, putting down the bags and taking the cigar out of his mouth. 'Pleased to make your acquaintance.'

Tesla took his hand and shook it vigorously. 'A pleasure Mr Rothstein.'

'This is my assistant, Mr Jones.'

The inventor bowed to Josh and then motioned for them both to come inside.

The colonel had chosen the name of a European banking family for obvious reasons, but it was also because his own name, Westinghouse, happened to be the company to which Tesla licensed his patent for the AC motor.

The air inside the large brick building was filled with the metallic tang of ozone. Walking between Tesla's electrical experiments, Josh could feel the hairs rising on his head. Large spiral wheels of copper cable sat at each end of the room and between them stood a transformer with giant metal rings sitting on piles of Bakelite stacks.

'Would you like a demonstration?' asked Tesla, his moustache accentuating the smile as he raised his hand towards the ceiling. There was something of the showman about him.

'No, another time perhaps, we have a train to catch,' said the colonel, nervously eyeing the equipment. 'Shall we go to your office?'

Tesla nodded and led them away from the hum of the coils.

Removing the plans from the map case, Josh unrolled them across the table while Rufius explained.

'We need to build something quite extraordinary, something you'll have never seen before.'

Tesla took out a pair of pince-nez glasses and balanced them on his long nose as he studied the plans.

'This is some kind of graviton?' he asked, pointing at one part of the schematic. 'You're generating gravity waves?'

Rufius smiled and puffed away on his cigar, his voice tinged with just the right amount of Russian to give him the airs of an oligarch. 'See Mr Jones, didn't I tell you that Tesla was the right man for the job?'

Josh nodded deferentially. 'You did Mr Rothstein.'

He could see the colonel seemed to enjoy playing the part of a rich patron. It was an easy role, most of Tesla's previous investors had very little technical knowledge and the more money they had, the less they seemed to know.

'Who designed this?' asked Tesla, moving the first plan away to look at the other sheets.

'Johannes Belsarus,' replied Rufius before Josh could speak. 'A Russian professor at the Lebedev Physical Institute.' It was a good enough lie, Tesla was Serbian by birth so was likely to have heard of the Institute, but having moved to the USA twenty years ago would know little of who was working there.

Tesla's eyes narrowed, and Josh could tell he was only half listening to them.

'What does it do?'

'That's confidential,' said Rufius, producing a contract and a pen. 'If you'll sign this agreement, we can tell you.'

The document was a typical non-disclosure agreement for that time. Tesla had signed many similar ones. He hardly looked at it before signing his name with a flourish.

'I will need an advance,' said Tesla, tapping on the blue-prints. 'Some of these parts are going to be hard to manufacture. The specialists will be expensive.'

Rufius lifted one of the Gladstone bags onto the table, unfastened the catch and pulled it open. 'Funding will not be a problem.'

Josh could see Tesla's eyes light up like a drowning man catching sight of a boat. He was nearly bankrupt and they'd just bailed him out.

He took the bags and deposited them in his safe, returning with a silver tray of fine cut glasses and a bottle of Cognac.

Tesla poured each of them an equal measure. 'Mr Roth-stein, Mr Jones, how shall we toast this new partnership of ours?'

'To the time machine!' said Rufius, taking one of the glasses.

'The time machine,' they toasted, knocking back the brandy in one go.

'One thing I should mention,' the colonel said pouring himself another glass. 'There will be another specialist we wish to oversee the project.'

'Of course, may I ask who?'

'A Swiss theoretical physicist by the name of Einstein. You may have heard of him.'

Tesla nearly dropped his glass. 'Albert Einstein?'

Rufius smiled. 'The very man.'

The inventor sat down heavily in his chair. 'I've read his work on the photoelectric effect, the man is a genius.'

'Then you will be perfectly matched!'

'When will he arrive?'

Rufius winked at Josh and took out his tachyon. 'He should be here in a matter of minutes.'

30

H.G. WELLS

[Swiss Patent Office, Bern. Date: 1906]

Professor Eddington walked into the patent office as though he owned the place. Sim had never seen the man so animated, so human.

'Can I help you?' said the clerk in German.

'I wish to speak with Einstein,' Eddington demanded.

The man put down his fountain pen and clasped his hands together. 'Are you from the newspaper?' he asked in a tone that made it abundantly clear he wasn't in the mood for more journalists.

The professor's face was a perfect picture of aristocratic disdain. 'How dare you! I am the Emeritus Professor of Physics at the Charles University of Prague!'

The clerk looked suitably impressed and got sharply to his feet.

'My apologies Herr Professor, we've had many enquiries since Einstein published his paper. It is not so easy to tell who they are, sometimes they falsify their credentials.'

Eddington handed over his card, it was a perfect forgery,

with his name embossed in gold next to the grand seal of the University.

'Please inform Herr Einstein that Professor Ernst Vingheim wishes to see him.'

While they waited in the front office, Sim took a moment to rehearse his lines. He was nervous, and rightly so, they were about to meet the father of modern physics. Although at this point in history, his work was yet to be recognised for the significant advancement it would make to science.

Einstein was twenty-six years old and unaware of how the rest of his life would be shaped by these revelations. The next twenty years would be spent developing his theories at the Prussian Academy of Sciences in Berlin before moving to America in 1933 and continuing his work at Princeton. All that was to come, right now, they needed to persuade the genius to join them on a project that would challenge the very nature of time.

'Herr Professor?' said a quietly spoken man with kind eyes and a dark moustache.

Eddington bowed his head in greeting. 'Herr Einstein, may we have a moment?'

Einstein looked at the clock, it was nearing midday and they knew that he took his lunch at a nearby cafe everyday at 12:15 precisely.

'Perhaps over lunch?' he suggested genially, taking his coat from the peg.

The cafe was on the corner of two busy streets. A number of office clerks were already queuing to be seated when they arrived. It was a beautiful summer's day, and the sun bathed the tables outside the cosy little restaurant with its red check tablecloths. The blue-eyed waitress took a shine to Sim the moment they sat down at a table.

Einstein ordered a schnitzel with rosti and the others followed suit. He carefully unfolded a napkin and placed it in his lap.

'So Professor Vingheim of the Charles University of Prague, what can I do for you?' There was a slight lilt to his question, one that told them he knew they were not who they purported to be.

Eddington dropped the pretence immediately.

'You are correct of course. My name is Eddington and this is Simeon De Freis. We have come to ask for your help with a most interesting problem.'

The professor took out a pen and wrote a series of equations on his napkin and handed it over to Einstein.

The physicist's eyebrows knitted together as he studied the formulae. He spent nearly ten minutes murmuring to himself before the realisation suddenly dawned on him.

'These are gravitational field equations!'

'It's called an Einstein-Rosen bridge,' Eddington explained, taking back the napkin and spreading it on his lap. 'You will publish a paper on it in 1935, whilst working with Nathan Rosen at Princeton, New Jersey.'

'They become known as wormholes,' added Sim, 'and we need your help in creating one.'

The waitress arrived with their lunches and three tall glasses of beer.

Einstein took the beer eagerly and drank deeply, wiping the remaining froth from his moustache with his napkin.

He frowned, his eyes full of questions. 'How can you know this?'

'We have travelled from the future to find you,'

Eddington said calmly. Sim was slightly taken aback at how easily the Professor broke his golden rule.

Einstein laughed. 'In what? One of Wells's time machines?'

Eddington ignored him and continued. 'We are from an Order who are able to manipulate time. Simeon and I belong to the Guild of Copernicans, our role is to calculate the probabilities of certain outcomes, ones that will affect the future of humanity.'

Einstein raised his eyebrows and blew out his cheeks. 'And how exactly would you do that?'

'We've built a model of the last twelve thousand years. It allows us to predict subtle adjustments to the continuum, which you will come to call space-time.'

He scoffed. 'You're either incredible fantasists or totally insane!'

Eddington turned to Sim. 'Master Simeon if you would care to demonstrate for us.'

Sim nodded, took out his tachyon and disappeared into the past.

This time, when the waitress brought their food, the discussion took the same course as before until Einstein asked the question of: 'How can you know this', and Sim reached over and took the notepad from her apron and showed him the quote that was written on it.

"We are always getting away from the present moment. Our mental existences, which are immaterial and have no dimensions, are passing along the Time-Dimension with a uniform velocity from the cradle to the grave."

It was from 'The Time Machine' by Herbert George Wells and Einstein's eyes widened as he read it.

'We have no need of a time machine,' said Eddington, picking up his knife and cutting into the schnitzel. 'So, now we have your full attention. I suggest we eat, our method of travel tends to work better on a full stomach.'

Shaken, Einstein gave the waitress back her notepad. 'But what about my work?'

'Have you forgotten the first principle of time travel? We can return you here before the clock strikes one,' said Eddington, nodding towards the large clock-tower on the town hall across the square.

'Indeed,' said Einstein, tucking his napkin into his shirt.

31

DOORS

[Medici Collection]

Kaori scanned the door with a hand-held device, while her technicians set up a tripod and mounted what looked like some kind of weapon upon it.

'There's definitely a temporal distortion field behind here,' she said, adjusting one of the dials on her scanner. 'I'm reading high levels of tachyon particles and the quantum distortion is off the scale!'

Sabien loved the way she got so passionate about her work. He had no idea what half of it meant, but she made it sound sexy.

'So, it's from another timeline?' he asked.

Kaori shrugged and clipped the device back on her belt. 'Well, it's certainly not part of our world, the signature's all wrong for this continuum.'

She pushed the doors apart, revealing the empty room once more.

'You say it only happens when the doors are closed?'

Sabien nodded, putting one foot against the door,

wedging it open. 'Yes, but there's no way out once you're in there, it's as if our abilities disappear.'

'Like kryptonite,' she agreed.

'What's that?'

Kaori laughed, walking into the room. 'Come on, you've never read Superman? Kryptonite was this mineral that made him weak, so he lost his powers. There were different colours: red, green, blue — I think there was even a gold. Lex Luthor had a ring made out of it to protect himself from the Man of Steel.'

Sabien looked at her blankly. 'My mother never let me read comics, she said they were the devil's own work.'

Kaori frowned. 'Nice. I'm surprised you survived your childhood as sane as you did.'

The technicians activated the device and a thin line of red light shot out of the muzzle. Kaori stepped out of its path and let the laser scan the back wall of the room.

'What are they doing?' asked Sabien, still hovering on the threshold.

'Laser scanning, mapping the physical dimensions of the room, looking for any signs of a field generator and other shit.'

Sabien laughed. 'That's a technical term is it? Other shit.'

Kaori shrugged, walking back out of the room. 'Sometimes you just got to call it what it is.'

He followed her into the corridor and away from the team.

'So what exactly was in there?' she asked.

'Talismans, at least twenty of them, but they had no power, as if they'd been disconnected from time.'

'Konstantine's private collection,' Kaori said to herself.

'Why on earth was he hoarding the very artefacts he denied ever existed.'

'In a vault sitting in a different timeline,' reminded Sabien, as if she was missing the point.

'Are your people any closer to finding him?'

Sabien shook his head. 'I'd hardly call them my people. The X departments are a law unto themselves, us grunts on the tenth floor get their scraps.'

'Like child abduction?'

'Yeah.'

'So what happens when you report that you've found an inter-dimensional portal?'

'I was hoping we could keep that to ourselves for now.'

'Sure,' she said, taking hold of his bandaged hand. 'How's the wrist?'

'I've had worse.'

She smiled, looking back to see if they were out of sight from her team and kissed him. 'Do me a favour next time and try not to bleed to death on my bathroom floor.'

'Yes, doctor.'

Walking along the corridor of the Great Pyramid, Sabien touched the St. Christopher around his neck and said a silent prayer of thanks to whoever was watching over him.

32

MAESTRO

[Wardenclyffe, Long Island. Date: 1906]

They appeared at the entrance to Tesla's workshop, Eddington catching hold of Einstein's arm as he stumbled forward.

'Mein Gott,' the physicist cursed under his breath. Steadying himself, he took out his pocket watch.

Sim could tell from the distant stare in the physicist's eyes that he was trying to calculate exactly what had just taken place.

'We've travelled six thousand kilometres in less than a minute?'

'Actually we didn't move as such,' explained Sim, 'we simply went back to a different point in the earth's rotation.'

Einstein's moustache twitched as he contemplated the idea. 'If the earth is rotating at approximately a thousand miles per hour, then we've travelled six hours into the future?'

Eddington opened the door to the workshop and

gestured for them to go inside. Sim continued. 'To us, past and future are moot terms. There is a point we cannot travel beyond, we call it the frontier, which is currently moving through the twenty-first century. All time up to that point is effectively in the past.'

Tesla was standing behind a long workbench in the middle of the warehouse, he was deep in thought, poring over a set of plans.

Einstein took a moment to study one of the large metal objects, his hair rising as he reached out to touch it.

'I wouldn't do that if I were you,' warned Eddington with a grimace. 'There's a lethal amount of electrical current running through most of the equipment in this room.'

Rufius appeared out of a side office carrying what appeared to be a large ceramic mushroom. Putting his load down on the bench, he tapped Tesla on the shoulder, nodding toward their visitors.

'Is this truly him?' Tesla asked, walking towards them with his hands raised in welcome.

Eddington nodded. 'Albert Einstein, may I introduce Nikola Tesla.'

Tesla took Einstein's hand and shook it vigorously. 'Maestro, it is a great honour to finally meet you!'

Einstein looked a little taken aback at the enthusiasm. 'Pleased to meet you too,' he replied in broken English clipped by a heavy German accent.

'I have so much to discuss. So many questions!' said Tesla, clapping his hands like a child and beckoning them to follow him.

Reverting to German, the physicist turned back to

Eddington and said quietly: 'You realise that this man is probably insane?'

'I think that may be exactly what we need right now,' replied the professor, taking Einstein gently by the arm. 'Shall we?'

33

NAUTILUS

[Nautilus]

According to the ship's internal clocks they had been travelling at full speed for nearly three days straight.

No one slept, the tension growing steadily worse as everyone wondered how much longer they could go on like this.

Caitlin's mother was pushing the *Nautilus* way beyond its normal tolerances, and the strain it was putting on the ship was beginning to show. A constant low groan ran through the bulkheads now, as the engines struggled to maintain their speed, reminding Caitlin of a dying whale.

'She won't take much more of this,' said her father, voicing the concern everyone else was thinking.

Her mother consulted the navigation system, which consisted of a round oscilloscope screen with a luminescent line sweeping around at thirty-second intervals.

The nearest timeline was still hovering at the edges of the map, like a distant mountain never seeming to get any closer.

'We have no way of gauging distance,' her mother complained, tapping the flickering display until it stabilised. 'One moment is close, the next is off the screen.'

The radar was salvaged from an old minesweeper and had hardly ever been used. Her parents usually travelled through the void using the chaos to their advantage, since they weren't generally heading for a particular destination. They'd spent the last twenty years trying to map what few stable sectors there were: Tycho Station and the Warships Graveyard being two places that generally seemed to stay put.

But to reach an entirely separate continuum was another matter, one that Caitlin was beginning to believe they hadn't really thought through properly.

She sat on the sofa by the observation window and took out the locus, letting its warmth envelop her once more. He was still there, somewhere out in an alternate universe, she could feel his breath on her cheek, his heart beating against her skin, but the sphere gave her no sense as to where exactly that might be.

'Anything?' asked her mother, spotting the glowing sphere.

Caitlin shook her head. 'No.'

'We're going to have to slow down,' insisted her father. 'You need to get some rest.'

Caitlin's mother sighed, throttling back on the power, and engaging the autopilot. 'You're right, I need to sleep and the ship needs a break.' She rubbed her back and got up out of the pilot seat. 'There's nothing else to do but wait.'

Caitlin stared out of the oculus, the large circular window mounted at the front of the bridge, watching the glowing lines of their continuum disappearing into the distance. 'How long do you think?'

Her mother shrugged, taking a steaming cup of tea from her husband and walking over to the window. 'Could be ten minutes, could be ten years. There's no way to know.'

'How about a game of scrabble?' suggested Caitlin's father, going over to the games cupboard.

'Not now Thomas,' protested her mother. 'I need to rest, not worry about what seven-letter word I can make out of six vowels and a Q.'

'Fair enough, thought it might help you to relax.'

'I think a bottle of Macallan and a hot meal would be more like it.'

'Right you are Captain.' He saluted and went off to the galley.

Her mother settled down into one of the leather Chesterfields and put her feet up on the low table.

'Can I hold him?' she asked, putting her hand out.

Reluctantly, Caitlin handed over the locus and watched the lines in her mother's tired face slowly soften as if she were settling into a warm bath.

'It feels stronger,' she murmured, staring into the spiral of lights.

'I thought so too,' agreed Caitlin.

'We should have brought Lyra with us. Maybe she would be able to focus in on his signal.'

'I don't think she would be able to reach him better than me.'

Her mother nodded. 'True enough.'

Her father returned with a bottle of whisky and three glasses. 'Dinner will be ready in an hour.'

They each took a glass and he poured generous measures.

Marcus appeared from the lower deck, rubbing his freshly-shaved head with a towel. The runes tattooed on his skull were still glowing faintly.

'What are we celebrating?'

It was strange seeing him back in his human body. The moment they crossed into the Maelstrom he transformed into his chimaeric form. He was spending longer outside of the ship each day, gathering information and hunting for leads, but there was little to go on and each time he returned he seemed to have collected new wounds.

'The fact that we're not getting anywhere,' said Caitlin's mother sarcastically. 'Did you manage to find anything?'

He took a glass from Thomas and sat down cross-legged on the rug. 'Not much. Most of the storm-kin aren't concerned with the continuums and those that are —' He scratched nonchalantly on a fresh scar on his arm. 'Well, they tend to think of us as prey.'

'I am beginning to think this was a bad idea,' said Caitlin's mother getting to her feet. 'But I'm tired and I need to rest, so let's discuss the options after dinner.'

She handed the locus back to Caitlin and wandered off towards the galley.

'May I?' asked Marcus, holding out his hands like a street beggar.

Caitlin paused for a moment, unsure as to whether to hand it over.

'Promise you won't break it?'

He drew a cross over his heart, the skin turning red where his long, claw-like nails scratched.

She passed it to him and Marcus stared into the dancing lights inside the globe, turning it over as if looking for a way to open it.

'How did they do it?'

Caitlin shrugged. 'No idea, but it took the entire guild to create it.'

'It feels, alive.'

'It's connected to Zack's timeline, while he lives we can reach a part of him.'

Marcus's eyes darkened, the whites disappearing. 'Have you tried to weave with it?'

Caitlin shook her head, reaching out to take it back. 'No. Lyra said that wouldn't be possible.'

He snatched it away from her, making a growling sound deep inside his throat. 'Maybe not inside the continuum. Different rules apply out here.'

Lines of power unwound from the sphere.

'Don't! You promised!' pleaded Caitlin.

His voice grew loud. 'I have touched the infinite chaos of eternity, do you think me so incapable of weaving with this!'

Her mother appeared from the back of the ship, wearing a pair of tartan pyjamas and a garish pair of socks. 'Do you mind? Some of us are trying to rest here!'

'He's trying to reach Zachary!'

'Marcus?'

'I can see him.' Her uncle was rapidly transforming into his chimaera.

'What?'

'We need to turn back.'

'What?' repeated her mother. 'Why?'

'He's too far away. We would age and die a hundred times over before we crossed the distance to his continuum.'

'Where is he?'

'In the hands of the gods.'

. . .

Marcus left the ship before dinner, which was a sombre affair, not made any easier by his absence.

'What do you think he meant?' asked her father, clearing away the plates.

'He's been chasing the elder gods ever since he recovered,' said her mother. 'Everything tends to look like the work of the ancient ones to him.'

Caitlin was staring into the locus, her attempts to weave with it had all failed.

'I don't know how he did it,' she muttered to herself.

Suddenly, there was a loud boom and the ship pitched violently as if it had been hit by a wave. Her father was thrown across the galley, the plates he was carrying smashing across the floor.

A screeching noise echoed along the gangways as the engines tried to compensate for the external forces.

Caitlin and her mother clung to the table as the Nautilus was thrown around like a child's toy.

'Time quake?' asked her father, struggling to get back on his feet.

34

KEYS

Lyra sat in bed staring at the key in her palm. In this world it was a plain-looking artefact with no particular distinguishing marks, but in the shadow realm it had an ornate fob with scroll work and markings that glowed like a magical artefact.

'Morning,' said Benoir walking in with a breakfast tray and a stack of books.

'Did you find it?' she asked, putting down the key and taking a slice of toast from the tray.

He nodded and handed her one of the books. It was old and cloth bound with gold lettering on its worn green cover. The title read *The Wanderer by E.M. Williams*.

'The librarian said Williams spent most of her life documenting stories about Abandon,' said Benoir, sitting down on the side of the bed.

'It's a common theme in many cultures, especially the Nordics, Odin was supposed to appear like an old one-eyed wizard,' Lyra said through a mouthful of toast.

He poured the tea and picked up one of the other books. 'Is there any mention of keys?'

Lyra scanned the indices. 'No, but she mentions doors,' she said, turning to the relevant page she read aloud.

'In all of my research there have been two constant themes: one is that the Wanderer seems to take the form of either an old man with a long white beard or a tall dark hooded figure, and the second is that he could step between worlds using secret doors.'

Benior picked up the key by the chain she had threaded onto it. 'How do we know it will take us to the right place? He might be sending you on a wild goose chase.'

Lyra looked up from her book and frowned. 'I don't. It doesn't have any history.'

'Do we even know what lock it fits?'

Lyra shrugged. 'You're being too logical. I don't think it works like that.'

He put it down on the tray and handed her a cup of tea. 'So, what do we do?'

She sighed. 'I finish my breakfast in peace.'

Benoir left her alone, making some excuse about having to speak to Cuvier. Lyra settled down into the bed with her second cup of tea and the book.

Edith Williams had documented hundreds of sightings of the Wanderer, but never seen him herself. She was an eccentric woman by all accounts, the kind who lived alone with too many cats. She spent her life mapping the shadow paths, a thankless task by all accounts. She diligently devoted each chapter to a different route, beginning with an illustrated chart of her journey.

They were beautifully drawn, with Williams's notes

scribbled in the margins. Some of the landmarks Lyra recognised: The towers of Barad-dûr and Orthanc, the bridge of Khazad-dûm, Mirkwood and the city of Edoras. These were Lyra's names for them, as a child with no map and an overactive imagination, she borrowed names for the nameless places from her favourite book, The Lord of the Rings. Many of them suited their location perfectly and she often wondered whether Tolkien had used the shadow paths himself.

The morning passed quickly as Lyra devoured the various adventures. She was surprised to learn that Edith never used mirrors, preferring to enter the paths through more established gateways such as cemeteries and Lyra's least favourite, ponds.

Lyra discovered the shadow paths by accident. She'd fallen into a deep pool when she was five years old, her sodden dress taking her straight to the bottom. It was dark and cold, and when she finally made it back to the surface she found herself in the shadow realm. Cold and naked, she wandered the paths for days before finding a door, stepping out of a mirror in the study of the Grand Seer, much to his surprise.

The realm became her playground, the infinite paths a never-ending source of inspiration and adventure.

She loved the chaos of it, the random nature of the ancient paths, never thinking once that there may be a pattern to it. Never caring.

Edith had tried to tame them, plotting her charts through the labyrinth, and failed. Her conclusion at the end of the book summarised it perfectly.

'The paths are fractures in time, like weeds growing between cracks in an ancient pavement. They exist in the spaces between the worlds, an accidental oversight in the grand design. There is no underlying pattern, no logical reason for their existence, but still they remain, possibly, the last great mystery in this universe. The Wanderer even more so.'

Lyra closed the book and picked up the key.

'Seems like there's only one way to find out what you unlock,' she said, dangling it between her fingers.

Getting out of bed. She closed the bedroom door and went to the long mirror.

35

GODS

[Aaru]

Anubis looked down at the sleeping infant. It was wrapped in a simple white blanket inside the quarantine chamber which was regulating its temperature and general sustenance.

The gatekeeper removed his jackal helm so as not to frighten the child, temporarily disconnecting from the network and allowing him independent thought once more.

'The Shabti believes it carries the memories of another,' said his daughter, Kebechet, reading X-541's report on a glass tablet.

'The memories of Thoth.'

'The timeless one?' asked Kebechet, putting down the report and walking over to join her father. 'How could such a tiny skull hold the mind of a god?'

'Not in its entirety. The symbiote was able to collect much of his pattern but not all. The Shabti believes this child has somehow managed to secure one important piece of it.'

Kebechet ran her hand over the glass canopy, tracing the glyphs displayed on its surface with her fingers. 'It appears to have an abnormally high psychic quotient.'

'Yes, and a temporal displacement capability.'

'It can move through time?'

'Indeed.' Her father ran his hand over the glass and the symbols changed. 'The Shabti discovered an entire sub-species capable of temporal fluidity. He infiltrated their organisation and subjugated one of their leaders. He believes they were created by Thoth after he abandoned us and escaped into their timeline.'

Kebechet touched three fingers of her right hand to her heart and then her forehead. 'Blessed be the Foresaken.'

Her father repeated the gesture, adding: 'Only through our works shall the pattern be reset.'

The blessing complete, Kebechet went over to the fresco that decorated one wall of the chamber. Like every child, she was raised on the story of their salvation. How the Serpent Queen, Tiamat, rose with her army of demons from the underworld and destroyed their civilisation. How four of the seven gods had fled their world, leaving their faithful subjects to fend for themselves.

'How did Thoth escape Father?'

'That is what we seek to understand, daughter. Those memories are missing from the symbiote recordings. The Shabti insists they are present in the subconscious mind of the child.'

It was written that, after the Cataclysm, their ancestors built a new civilisation in the ashes of the old. Survivors of the great houses, the children of Anu, found the scattered remnants of the old knowledge and developed new sciences, new ways to protect themselves should Tiamat come again. They created armies of synthetics to guard the walls while they slept, learning how to traverse the twelve gates of the underworld and what lay beyond.

But the Forsaken, as they named themselves, never forgot how their gods abandoned them, especially Thoth, who was the master of magic, wisdom and writing. It was widely believed that he had brought down the wrath of Tiamat upon them, and of all the old gods, his secrets were the most highly sought after. The families of the upper houses would be very interested in this foundling.

'How will we extract the knowledge? A symbiote?' she asked.

Anubis shook his head. 'It is too young. We must wait for it to mature.'

She clapped her hands in delight. 'You're going to keep it!'

He smiled, picking up his jackal helmet. 'Your mother is already preparing your old room.'

36

SIXTY-SIX

[New York. Date: May 26, 1930]

The Ministry of Justice was situated in a time loop of the Chrysler building on Forty-Second and Lexington in the heart of New York City during the nine-teen-thirties.

Sabien's office was still part of the homicide division on the tenth floor, although strictly speaking he was not actually a member of the department any more. Investigating temporal murders was hard work, the average detective lasted five years at most, many bailed before that.

Watching someone die over and over again could wear a person down, especially when you knew who did it, but was not allowed to change the outcome — that was a form of mental torture. You either grew a thick skin or you got out.

Sabien should have been a chief inspector by now, he'd watched enough of his colleagues climb the ranks, making their way up towards the twentieth floor.

But that wasn't for him. He hated the idea of flying a

desk and he had the kind of personality that some would call career-limiting — he didn't play well with others.

When he broke the Ripper case, it had cost him his partner, and going back to save her nearly cost him his career.

So now he worked the jobs no one else wanted; missing persons was where they sent cops to die of boredom. He'd been one step away from taking the long walk, but Kaori had saved him.

The long walk was a one-way trip into the past, becoming a distant memory in some town that needed a lawman. It was supposed to be an honourable way to live out the last years of service, but in reality it was a banishment. Sabien knew he would have to take it one day.

The alternative was joining internal affairs, the black hats on floors twenty-one to fifty who spent their days chasing down members of the Order who were breaking the rules. Mallaron's department, the Crows, were like the secret police. If you were stupid enough to use your abilities to win the state lottery or influence an election, you were going to end up in one of their cells. The sub-basement levels of the ministry went down so far they had their own elevator.

Sabien stepped into the brass cage and slid the doors shut. This wasn't his usual car, this lift only stopped at floors fifty through seventy-seven. Today he was going to one of the 'X' divisions, courtesy of his boss, Chief Inspector Avery.

Keeping his gloves on, he ran his fingers down the gilt-edged buttons, wondering what random timelines would be connected to the people who'd travelled up there.

He pushed floor sixty-six, which for some reason reminded him of his mother playing bingo at St Mary's every Wednesday night. 'Clickety Click,' the callers voice echoed in his head. She'd gone there every week for years, raising money for one good cause after another.

The elevator accelerated away from the ground floor, ascending rapidly towards the sixties. He watched the dial above the door as it lit up their progress on an ornate brass plaque.

Avery was his long-suffering boss. The man gave him the usual warning about sticking his nose where it wasn't welcome, but the Chief Inspector knew that there was no changing Sabien's mind once it was set.

'X-Division won't take kindly to you asking questions,' he said, signing the access order. 'They're investigating how Konstantine, a highly respected member of the High Council, turned out to be a traitor. The last thing they need is you turning up with some crazy theory linking him to a child abduction.'

Sabien hadn't told him about what happened in the Medici Collection. The Chief Inspector was a practical kind of guy, he didn't believe in 'spooky shit' as he called it.

'Floor Sixty-Six,' intoned a female voice through the metallic speaker as the doors opened.

Sabien stepped out into the hallway of what could have been a rundown hotel.

Looking back, he checked the number, the light was still glowing behind the sixty-six. For some reason, he'd always expected the floors above the fiftieth to be more lavishly furnished, that as you climbed, the offices would get plusher, the gold a little less tarnished.

A man walked out of one of the rooms at the end of the

corridor. He was wearing a grey tweed suit and carrying a stack of papers. A pipe hung out of one side of his mouth.

'Can I help you?' he said, through gritted teeth.

Sabien took out the pass from Avery. 'I'm looking for Agent Blackstone. Division X-27?'

'Ah yes, follow me,' the man said, turning and pushing a door open with his foot.

The room was filled with filing cabinets, wooden ones that went from floor to ceiling.

The man deposited the stack of papers on an already busy desk, and took the pipe out of his mouth.

'Good to meet you,' he said in a plummy English accent, holding out his hand. 'Jeremy Blackstone.'

'Sabien. Michael Sabien.'

When Sabien didn't take up the offer of a handshake, Blackstone retracted his hand, looking a little embarrassed.

'You'll have to excuse the mess, we don't get too many visitors up here.'

'There are more of you?' Sabien said, looking past the piles of documents.

'Yes, there's Ballard. He's somewhere back there.'

'Present!' shouted a man wearing a tank-top over a white shirt and corduroy trousers, appearing from behind a bookcase.

'You're X-27?' said Sabien, failing to hide his disappointment.

'We are indeed,' Blackstone said proudly. 'Although officially we don't exist, of course.'

Sabien looked at the chaos of document boxes that surrounded their desks. 'And you're leading the investigation into Grandmaster Konstantine?'

Blackstone turned to Ballard as if he was unsure. 'Are we?'

Ballard nodded. 'Yes, that's us. Konstantine is definitely on our chit.'

'And what exactly are you investigating?'

'Oh, we couldn't divulge that I'm afraid, it's all hush-hush. Top secret. You'd need a level sixty clearance to even ask that kind of question.'

Sabien held up the docket that Avery had given him.

Blackstone took it off him and read it before handing it to his colleague.

'Seems like he has it,' noted Ballard, raising an eyebrow.

'Yes, well, in that case, please take a seat Inspector Sabien. Would you like some tea? It may take us a few minutes to find the relevant documents.'

Sabien declined and stood while the two men rooted through desks and drawers looking for the files.

'How many cases are you working on?' he asked, after a few minutes passed with no sign of them getting any closer to finding what they were looking for.

'A few,' replied Ballard.

'Two hundred and fifty-four at last count,' corrected Blackstone. 'We're a bit under resourced.'

Sabien tried not to laugh. 'And what exactly is it that you do?'

'Ah, found the bugger,' said Ballard, pulling a box out of one stack, causing the rest to topple over.

Opening the box, he shuffled through the papers until he came out with one sheet of paper.

'We're temporal accountants, although I prefer the term forensic. We audit the lives of the suspects and develop a profile on their likely location. It's not as glamorous as some of the other departments but I like to think we make a difference.'

'Well said, Jake,' agreed Blackstone.

Ballard pushed his glasses back up his nose and handed Sabien the sheet.

It was typed out on official headed paper with all the required classifications.

Skimming the first two paragraphs, which were mostly detailing out the background rationale for the investigation, Sabien got to the part he was most interested in.

At the end of a long list of locations and times was a single line:

'Suspect now likely to be residing in the early Middle Ages or late twenty-first century.'

He looked up from the report. 'How did you come to that conclusion?'

They both smiled. 'Simple deduction,' said Blackstone, putting the pipe back in his mouth.

'There were only two eras that were not affected by the tachyon destruction: Early Middle Ages, specifically fifth century, around the collapse of the Roman Empire in the West. Can't be much more accurate without actually going there of course. The second option is more of a product of our experience, many suspects go toward the frontier in the hope that the noise from the present will disrupt any chance of us tracking them.'

'Which it does,' Ballard said, taking back the report from Sabien. 'But don't tell anyone. It's a bit of a secret.'

Sabien nodded as if agreeing with them, while inwardly he was trying to process what was happening. All of his preconceptions about the nefarious activities that went on above the sixtieth floor had been destroyed in the last twenty minutes.

'So what do you intend to do next?'

Blackstone puffed away on his pipe. 'Usually we send it upstairs. Let the Crows deal with it, but since you seem so interested we were wondering if you might want to help out on this one?'

Ballard clapped his hands. 'Yes, that would be capital! We've never actually had our own field operative before.'

37

SAARLAND

[Wardenclyffe, Long Island. 1906]

'No, no, no. That won't work,' protested Einstein in German, while Tesla placed one of his coils carefully inside the machine. 'The gravitational forces will disrupt the magnetic flux.'

'The flux needs to be disrupted,' insisted Tesla. 'Read the second schematic. It's clearly based on creating a distortion between the wave emitter and the euclidean capacitor.'

'That is not theoretically possible!' shouted the physicist, picking up the plan. 'Whoever came up with this has not the first idea about Lorentz transformations or special relativity!'

'Nor did we until you discovered it!'

And so they went on.

Josh and Rufius had been subjected to their bickering for over a week now. Tesla was constantly trying to improve on the Belsarus design and Einstein kept repeating how totally impossible the whole idea was.

At first they made the mistake of getting involved in

their arguments, which only lead to the two scientists rounding on them. It was clear that these brilliant egomaniacs hated one thing more than each other and that was the idiots that were paying them to build the impossible.

So they left them to it, which seemed to be working, no matter how much they argued, the magnetoscope was beginning to take shape.

Rufius busied himself with errands for Tesla, finding the most obscure of materials from the remotest regions on the planet. Josh joined him on some of the runs, mainly when he couldn't stand the bickering any longer, or when he wanted to take his mind off what Caitlin was doing.

Wardenclyffe had its very own foundry and machine shop, which meant that Tesla could make most of the parts they needed on site. He was never happier than when he was casting a new piece of Belsarus's puzzle.

'We're going to need better iron,' he muttered, throwing a broken part onto the workbench. 'I can't use this American crap.'

'You need German iron, much higher carbon content,' suggested Einstein, sitting in one of the lounge chairs smoking a pipe.

'Any particular part of Germany?' asked Rufius, getting to his feet and grabbing his overcoat.

'Völklingen in Saarland.'

'And I need titanium,' added Tesla, ignoring his counterpart, 'for the outer casings.'

Einstein nodded. 'Yes. Titanium will lower the Lenz effect.'

'What's that when it's at home?' asked Rufius.

'Titanium is not strongly magnetic. It will help to reduce

the warping, protect the internal mechanism of the machine. Not that it will ever work of course.'

Rufius ignored them both and turned to Josh with a glint in his eye. 'Fancy a trip to Germany?'

Josh nodded, wherever Saarland was it had to be more interesting than staying here.

He was wrong.

Völklingen was a huge ironworks. The massive foundry dominated the landscape like something from an old episode of Doctor Who. The massive network of industrial pipework, chimney towers and processing plant covered over six hectares, as if someone had taken an enormous oil rig apart. The hills surrounding the foundry were all man-made too. Giant heaps of slag and coal piled up in great mounds with rail tracks winding between them leading directly to the furnaces.

The smoke from the chimneys poured out into the stormy sky, turning the clouds a sickly yellow.

Rufius coughed and took out the order that Tesla had given him.

Walking towards the main entrance Josh asked: 'Do you think they'll finish it?'

'I bloody hope so! I don't think I can take much more of their incessant arguing.'

Inside the works, the temperature was close to boiling. Men sweated in stained boiler suits, wearing dark lensed goggles as they poured molten metal into casts. Like a scene from hell, their faces were lit up by the orange glow of sparks as they worked the cooling metal with steam driven hammers.

'What are they making?' Josh shouted over the clang of machines.

'Howitzers,' Rufius said, watching a steaming cylinder of metal being winched out of a cooling bath. 'They're preparing for war.'

38

WORMHOLE

The device sat in the centre of the workshop, hidden beneath a large velvet drape.

As was usual with Tesla there was a sense of theatre about the evening. He had banished everyone from the workshop for the last two days and when they arrived for the demonstration, the rest of his equipment was cleared away, floors swept and chairs placed in a semi-circle around the machine.

Josh and Rufius were joined by Lyra, Benoir, Sim and Eddington who seemed greatly relieved to find that most of the electrical paraphernalia was gone.

'Ladies and Gentlemen,' announced Tesla, appearing from behind the curtain, closely followed by a scowling Einstein. 'It is our pleasure this evening to present you with the world's first and only time machine!'

One of Tesla's assistants pulled on a cord and the velvet cloth disappeared into the ceiling.

Beneath it stood an armillary, a central silver sphere

enclosed in a series of brass rings that began to rotate slowly on different axes around the surface of the metal globe. Power cables snaked across the floor and into the base causing small arcs of blue electricity to ripple across its surface.

It was an impressive feat of engineering, standing at over ten feet, and nothing like the plans that Belsarus had gifted to Josh, but that device had never worked. He assumed that their improvements had made it more effective.

Everyone clapped.

Einstein shook his head and wandered off to help himself to the buffet at the back of the workshop.

'So,' Tesla continued, his eyes following the ill-tempered physicist. 'Thanks to the pioneering work of the maestro!' He gestured to Einstein who was half way through a vol-au-vent. 'We have made some significant modifications to your original design, which we all know was rather archaic.'

Everyone nodded.

'This beautiful creation has the power to create a gravitational distortion field that can hold back the arrow of time.' He stepped away from the now rapidly spinning globe and nodded to one of his assistants who closed the connection on a large circuit breaker.

The rotating rings became a blur.

Einstein came over to sit beside Eddington.

'When this fails, you will take me back to my own time. Yes?'

Eddington nodded. 'As we agreed.'

'Good.'

The room lights dimmed and the central sphere began to glow. As the intensity grew, the air around the machine began to shimmer, like tarmac on a hot day. The waves of temporal energy that washed over them were so intense that

Lyra and Benoir got to their feet and moved back a few rows.

With a sudden burst of light the internal sphere was replaced by a swirling whirlpool of images that slowly stabilised into a mirror-like surface.

'Mein Gott,' exclaimed Einstein under his breath.

They were looking at the workshop, but it was clearly a different time of day.

With all the finesse of a stage magician, Tesla produced a red ball from out of thin air.

'And now the ultimate test.'

He threw the ball into the portal and watched as it bounced across the floor.

Einstein got up from his chair and went closer to the machine. 'It wasn't supposed to work,' he muttered to himself.

Tesla bowed.

'When has it gone?' asked Lyra, her eyes wide with amazement.

'That is a perfectly good question my dear. If everybody would please step to one side.' Tesla waved his arms as if he were parting the Red Sea. They moved aside, creating a wide corridor in front of the machine.

All except Einstein who stood staring into the swirling tunnel of energy. 'Where is the termination point?' he mumbled to himself.

Suddenly the ball flew back out of the shimmering field, bouncing across the empty space. They could see Tesla on the other side of the portal bowing to his audience.

'You created a wormhole into the future?' asked Einstein.

Eddington got to his feet. 'Not exactly, but it's an impressive feat nonetheless.'

'So, if I were to step through there I would go back to the

past?' asked Lyra, trying to sound impressed. Josh briefed all of them that Tesla had no idea of their abilities. Even Einstein had been sworn to secrecy.

Tesla nodded eagerly. 'Nearly thirty seconds. The energy required to go back or forward is exponential, but this is only a prototype. I'm sure with some refinements we could extend that to over a minute.'

It wasn't exactly what Belsarus had hoped to achieve, thought Josh, but it was a start.

'In the same continuum,' corrected Eddington, coming to stand beside Einstein. 'If you're looking to move between continuums, you're going to need to create a tesseract.'

'What's that?' asked Tesla, obviously disappointed at their lack of enthusiasm.

'A four-dimensional wormhole,' muttered Einstein. 'Impossible.'

'And who knows about those?' asked Lyra, ignoring the grumpy physicist.

Eddington paused for a moment, taking off his glasses and rubbing his long nose. 'Let me see, you'd need a quantum field theorist, which would mean 1930s at least.'

Tesla looked confused.

Sim was already searching through his almanac. 'What about Richard Feynman?'

'Who's he?' asked Josh, taking the book from Sim and studying the notes on Feynman's timeline.

'He won the Nobel prize for Physics in 1965. Worked on the Manhattan Project, pioneer in quantum computing and professor of theoretical physics at CalTech,' explained Sim, pointing at various events on the animating lines scrolling across the page.

'Sounds perfect, let's get him,' said Josh, giving Sim back his almanac.

As Sim took the book, something caught his eye.

'The *Nautilus* is on its way home,' he said, studying the flickering symbols on the page. 'There's been some kind of issue.'

Josh turned to Rufius. 'Can you handle this?'

The man scoffed. 'Of course, now get yourself gone.'

'How much power would you need to create this tesseract?' asked Tesla, turning to Einstein.

The German pondered over it for a moment, mentally calculating complex energy equations. 'Assuming that one could actually create such a thing?'

Tesla nodded eagerly.

'The entire energy of an exploding star.'

39
_____

PROJECT Y

[Manhattan Project, Los Alamos, New Mexico. Date: 1943]

The Los Alamos laboratory was situated on a remote mesa high above the arid desert of New Mexico. Its director, Robert Oppenheimer, had established a base of operations there in 1942 to allow his scientists to work in secret on the first atomic bomb.

Sim admired the white-tipped peaks of the Sangre de Cristo Mountains as Rufius drove the Lincoln Continental towards the main gate. The watchman insisted on driving out to the base rather than finding something to get them directly inside. After the war, the laboratory would be turned into a museum and they could have simply taken a tour and disappeared at some convenient point, but Rufius never did anything simply. Instead they were dressed in military uniforms and driving the biggest car in which Sim had ever sat.

The earlier part of the twentieth century was a particularly dangerous period for members of the Order. War made everyone suspicious, and a pair of strangers with unusual accents turning up at a top-secret research base was probably on the first page of the "how-to-identify-a-spy" manual.

Which was why they were dressed like officers of the American Army.

'You should practice your accent,' said Rufius with a strong mid-western twang.

'Do I have to speak?'

Rufius shrugged. 'Always good to have a back story in case we get split up. You could say you're on secondment from British Intelligence I suppose.'

Sim liked the sound of that, James Bond was one of his favourite characters. He used to badger his mother to take him to 1983 just to watch Sean Connery in his last ever Bond film: "Never Say Never Again".

'Don't go thinking you're some kind of double-o-seven,' added Rufius, as if reading his mind. 'They shoot spies in this period. Once they've interrogated them of course.'

Sim shuddered at the thought of being captured. He still had vivid memories of their last mission together, the Battle of Waterloo was a brutal massacre, not something to which a Copernican actuary was supposed to be exposed.

At the security gate, Rufius brought the Lincoln to a gentle stop and wound down the window.

'Good afternoon Corporal,' he said, handing over his papers to the military police officer.

The stoney-faced guard grunted and took the documents into a small wooden hut where he made a call.

Sim could feel the sweat collecting under his shirt collar. There was no air conditioning and the temperature outside was in the forties.

Rufius turned the engine off and lit a cigar.

'What do we do if he refuses us entry?'

The old man laughed, blowing smoke out of his nose. 'I doubt that's gonna happen, but have your tachyon ready if it makes you feel better.'

Sim pulled back the sleeve of his jacket to check his tachyon. He was wearing it like a wristwatch on a leather strap. The dials were rotating normally, which was reassuring, there was nothing like a temporal anomaly near a nuclear test site to make everybody nervous.

He wasn't quite sure how he'd volunteered to accompany Rufius on this mission. Josh opted to stay behind with Einstein and Tesla, who were now arguing about the best way to increase the range of their wormhole. Eddington had also declined, saying he would be too busy calculating the consequences of taking Feynman back to 1906.

Richard Feynman was a brilliant young physicist who went on to work in quantum electrodynamics after his time on the Manhattan Project. The man was nothing like the two geniuses that Josh was having to babysit right now. He was an interesting character, who, according to their records, had presented his time-symmetric theory to Einstein, Pauli and Von Neumann at his very first seminar.

He'd been recruited along with half of the Princeton Physics Department and was currently working on a theory for calculating the yield of a fission bomb, when he wasn't breaking the combination locks on the desks of his colleagues and leaving notes in them.

Feynman was the missing piece of their puzzle, someone who could assist with the quantum calculations required to construct a tesseract and had access to the kind of power they would need to create it — atomic fission.

The MP returned and handed back their papers. His expression hardly changing from before, he motioned for the barrier to be raised and waved them inside the compound.

Feynman was working under Hans Bethe in the Theoretical Division, part of the Physics Laboratory. As they coasted down Trinity Drive, Sim marvelled at the town that had sprung up around the original ranch school. Women and children, the families of the scientists, were walking along the street like it was just a normal day, unaware that somewhere in one of the large brick buildings, a bomb was being developed that would end the Japanese conflict, killing over one hundred thousand people in Nagasaki and Hiroshima.

Rufius pulled the car over and parked. They got out into the sweltering heat and walked into the main campus.

Their uniforms were like a cloak of invisibility, no one questioned their presence or stopped to ask what they were doing there. Within a few minutes they were inside the cool interior of the Physics Lab, waiting to be taken to Feynman's office.

'Gentlemen, how can I help you?' the young physicist greeted them, standing in front of a blackboard covered in chalk equations. He was wearing a clean white shirt, tie and grey flannel trousers, looking more like a school teacher than the father of quantum physics.

Rufius closed the door and nodded to Sim.

Sim took a board eraser and cleared off one of Feynman's longer calculations.

'Hey buddy! Do you mind?' Feynman protested.

Sim ignored him and drew the first of Feynman's quantum particle interaction diagrams. Rufius had convinced Professor Eddington that the easiest way to persuade the physicist to help them was to use equations he wouldn't formulate for another twenty years, but Sim could tell his mentor was not happy about it.

'Electron-positron annihilation,' murmured the scientist, rubbing his chin.

'We're not from the ministry of war,' said Rufius.

Feynman gasped mockingly. 'You're Russian spies?'

'No, that's Fuchs,' said Sim.

The scientist looked genuinely surprised. 'Really? He lends me his Buick most weekends.'

'Forget Fuchs, we're here to make you an offer that could change the course of history.'

40

___

NAUTILUS RETURNS

The *Nautilus* appeared in the dock, its hull still arcing with the residue of the breach energy it had just absorbed.

By the time the technicians wheeled the gantry into position, Caitlin was already at the hatch door and seconds later she was running down the metal steps towards Josh.

'I was wrong,' she said, burying her face in his chest.

Josh held her until the sobbing stopped. Letting the frustration drain away, he was just pleased to just have her back in his arms.

Her parents carried Marcus down the gangway on a stretcher. The ranger looked as if he'd been through a war. There were fresh scars all over his upper body and he seemed to have lost all of his hair.

'What happened to him?' Josh asked into her hair.

'Something attacked the ship, Marcus was outside when it happened. Mum thinks it's to do with the locus. We nearly didn't make it back.'

Josh gripped her tightly. The memory of her lost in the Maelstrom made his blood run cold. 'So he couldn't find Zack?'

'He did. The locus works differently out there, but he's too far away. Marcus said we'd all die of old age before we reached them.'

'I thought the Maelstrom was timeless.'

She pulled away from him, wiping her eyes with the back of her hand. 'Time passes slowly on the *Nautilus*, but we still age.'

Josh couldn't imagine how far away that meant their son was. 'I've missed you.'

'Missed you too,' said Caitlin, kissing him gently.

'Have you managed to build Belsarus's machine?' asked her mother, as the medics took the stretcher.

Josh's mouth twisted into a half-smile. 'Yes, and no. Tesla and Einstein got it working but it can only travel about thirty seconds into the future.'

Her mother looked unimpressed. 'Not enough power?'

'We've sent Rufius and Sim to recruit an atomic expert.'

Caitlin frowned. 'Atomic energy? You're going to use nuclear power?'

Josh knew what he was about to say would sound crazy, but he went ahead all the same. 'Einstein says it's the only way we're going to be able to create a tesseract.'

They went back to the Chapter House, where Alixia and Methuselah were preparing the usual evening meal. Rufius brought Feynman along to meet Einstein and Tesla in an effort to find some neutral territory to discuss their plans. Eddington and Sim were sitting on each side of them, acting as arbitrators for their enormous egos.

Lyra looked relieved to see Caitlin and came over to hug her. There was no need for words, her step-sister could feel the anguish and pain the moment she touched her.

Josh sat down beside the colonel and helped himself to some of the Carpathian Boar. He couldn't remember the last time he'd eaten a proper meal, the slow-roasted meat melted in his mouth.

'How is she?' asked Rufius, nodding at Caitlin who was now in deep conversation with Lyra's mother, Alixia.

'Not good. Apparently the *Nautilus* doesn't have the range to reach him.'

'Did you tell her about our progress?'

Josh lost his appetite and pushed his plate away. 'She's worried about the nuclear option.'

Rufius nodded his head and poured them both a large glass of wine. 'Eddington's not sure about it either. Feynman may be one of the brightest quantum physicists of his age, but exposing Tesla to the potential of nuclear energy thirty years before it was discovered could have long ranging consequences.'

'Not to mention the fact that you've exposed three of the greatest minds of the twentieth century to the possibility of time travel,' said Marcus, limping up to the chair opposite Rufius and sitting down.

'What happened to you?' asked Josh.

Marcus winced as he shifted in the seat. 'Got too close to a pentachion. Those things like to bite first and ask questions later.'

Josh shivered at the thought of a pentachion. They were one of the many nightmarish creatures he had met in the Maelstrom.

'What does Eddington suggest we do?' asked Josh, watching the professor debating something with Feynman.

It seemed to involve moving various pieces of fruit around and holding up forks at different distances.

Rufius chuckled into his wine. 'He wants them all redacted as soon as this is over, just to keep everything in balance.'

Marcus tore the leg off the boar and waved it in front of him. 'Sounds like a good idea. Don't want the Order becoming a household name.'

'Don't want the Order being known at all,' agreed Rufius.

'That way madness lies ,' quoted the Grand Seer, stepping out of the rain through a door behind Marcus. Josh caught a glimpse of a Tudor street before Kelly slammed it closed with his foot.

'Grand Seer,' said Marcus, tearing at the meat with his long teeth. 'I wanted to ask you about that ball you gave my niece.'

'The locus.' Kelly shook off his cloak of black feathers and hung it on the back of his chair.

'Yes, how does it work exactly?'

Rufius groaned.

The Grand Seer pulled out a quill from his cloak and waved it like a wand in the air, leaving faint trails of smoke in its wake. 'The continuum is teeming with millions of tiny little lives, each one singing their very own song. As seers we have learned to listen to these tunes. We can sense their notes like plucked strings in the centre of a symphony.' He played the air with his fingers. 'While you lesser mortals wander through your lives oblivious to the harmonics of the universe around you, we are blessed with appreciating the movement of the spheres.'

Marcus seemed confused. 'So, your orb recorded his sound? Like Edison's phonograph?'

Kelly smiled. 'The orb is tuned to his pattern. Like one of those sonic telegraphs that Bell came up with in the eighteen-eighties.'

'They're called telephones,' corrected Rufius. 'As you know full well.'

The Grand Seer ignored him. 'Lyra was able to hold the signal while the rest of us worked in concert to etch it into the heart of the sphere. The light you see inside is the refraction on the structure that makes up his frequency, it vibrates with the same harmonic as his life.'

'So it's like a fingerprint?' suggested Josh.

Kelly shrugged. 'A crude interpretation, but yes I suppose you could liken it to the unique pattern of your thumb.'

'When I used it in the Maelstrom, I could see him,' said Marcus.

'You saw him?' exclaimed Rufius.

The ranger shrugged and took another bite of meat.

Josh turned towards him feeling the anger warm his cheeks. 'And you thought you'd wait until now to mention it?'

'Careful boy,' warned Marcus, exposing his fangs once more. 'I'm not partial to threats.'

'Just tell us what you saw!' Rufius got up out of his seat.

The others stopped what they were doing and all eyes turned to the argument. The tension between Marcus and Josh was palpable.

'He saw a god,' interrupted Caitlin. 'A jackal-headed god.'

'Anubis?' suggested Kelly.

'Perhaps, we can't be sure,' she continued. 'We don't know if the Anunnaki could have influenced the Egyptians too.'

She walked around the table to join them, sitting next to Marcus.

The scientists went back to their discussions and the others picked at their food keeping one eye on the conversation.

'I think they're looking after him,' she said, putting one hand on her uncle's shoulder. 'Marcus tried everything he could to reach Zack, but it was too far, the journey would have killed us all.'

Rufius sighed and sat back down. 'So let's all hope we can make this damned tesseract work.'

'Well, we do have three of the brightest minds in the history of science,' Caitlin reminded them.

They all looked down the table towards the physicists as Sim stopped Feynman from throwing an apple at Tesla.

41

ATOMIC

[Wardenclyffe, Long Island. 1906]

Feynman studied the wormhole at the centre of the sphere, his eyes widening as Tesla's ball reappeared thirty seconds later.

'You created an Einstein-Rosen bridge?' he observed, rubbing his hand over the two-day beard.

'Who's Rosen?' asked Einstein.

'You haven't met him yet,' said Professor Eddington, scowling at Feynman, who was quickly becoming a liability.

'Sorry, yeah. I keep forgetting,' apologised Feynman.

Tesla motioned to his assistants to shut down the machine.

'We need to increase the range of the device,' the inventor explained as the spinning rings slowed and the wormhole collapsed.

'How far do you need it to go?'

'We need to create an inter-dimensional gateway,' added Josh, before Einstein could interrupt. He had never felt more out of his depth.

Feynman laughed, then realised that they were being serious. 'A tesseract? Are you seriously trying to break into another universe?'

Einstein and Tesla both shrugged at Feynman who was looking to them for support.

'Do you know what kind of power that would need? Ignoring the fact that we all know that it's not physically possible to actually build one.'

'The kind of energy that's released by an atomic bomb?' said Josh.

Feynman ran his hand through his hair. 'And some.'

Tesla sat down and lit a cigarette. 'The trouble with these theoretical physicists is that they don't like getting their hands dirty. The minute you try and do something practical with their work they get all "Oh no, you can't actually do this, it's only a theory!"'

Einstein swore at the inventor in German and stormed off, but Feynman just stood staring at the slowly gyrating spheres.

'You built a wormhole,' he muttered to himself. 'Not something I thought I would see in my lifetime, and he tells me that my research will end the Second World War. Seems like you guys are the ones who get impossible things done. Not sure why you need me, but I'm in.'

'Thank you,' said Josh.

The next few weeks were a blur. They worked late into the night, only taking breaks to sleep in camp beds that Tesla had put up in the offices.

Einstein was slow to come around to Feynman's theories, he seemed to resist the idea of quantum mechanics and no matter how the American explained it, Einstein would counter his argument.

Tesla, on the other hand was only too happy to keep improving on Belsarus's design.

42

BRIDGES

[Shadow Realm]

The key shimmered in her hand, lines of brilliant energy flowing between her fingers. Lyra knew better than to try and weave with it, this was a wayfinder, a navigation device, all she had to do was to follow its light.

The path before her was formed from a maze of bridges. Each ornately carved from wood, they arched over a dark sea of nothingness linking a series of small stone islands together. Every island had three options, the way you had come and two others.

Some of the bridges were beyond repair, making her choice a little easier, but it was the key that she followed, its glow brightening and dimming based on her direction of travel.

Lyra had never been to this place and she named it Moria, after the dwarfish mines beneath the Misty Mountains in the Hobbit.

She passed numerous doors along the way, each one

carved with a different symbol, but the key never seemed to fit.

After a few hours she wondered if Benoir hadn't been right to question whether the Wanderer was more like Loki, the trickster, than Odin. The key appeared to be leading her further into the maze, with little chance of finding her way out.

Finally she came to a dead-end. Both ways ahead were blocked by broken spans and Lyra sat down on the bare rock and considered her options.

'You're not a key at all, are you?' she said, holding the glowing metal object up to her face.

The lights danced before her eyes, fluctuating patterns of gold and amber rotated around the fob — it seemed to shrink as she brought it closer to her face.

Suddenly she knew what she had to do.

'I am the door.'

Opening her mouth she placed the key on her tongue and swallowed.

'You did what?' exclaimed Benoir in disbelief.

Lyra crossed her arms. 'I followed my instincts, and it turns out it was the right thing to do. I told you it's not always logical.'

He lowered his voice. 'But it could have killed you. You could have choked.'

'I'm not a child. I knew what the risks were.'

'And do you feel any different?'

She paused, her eyes shifting from side to side, as if she were checking she had all her marbles. 'Nope.'

'So what happened when you took it?'

'It's hard to describe the sensation without sounding

crazy,' Lyra began, stroking her temple with her fingers. 'It's like the key unlocked something inside my head. Before, my ability was always confined to touch.' She stroked his cheek. 'Except with you of course.'

'And now?'

'Now I can see further. It's like going from a looking glass to a radio telescope. I don't need the Conclave any more,' she said, throwing her arms wide.

Benoir frowned. 'How far exactly?'

Her eyes widened. 'I know where Zack is.'

43

HOLY MAN

[Wales. Middle Ages]

Storm clouds hung low over the grey mountains. Cold sheets of rain lashed down onto the slate hillsides around him, making the shale path slippery and dangerous. The stronghold lay half a mile ahead. A dark, sombre outpost in the middle of nowhere, the original features of its granite walls had been worn smooth by the weather.

Sabien found shelter beneath an outcrop of rock and wiped the water from the face of his tachyon. He wasn't entirely convinced that he was in the right time or place.

Wales in the early Middle Ages was a series of fiefdoms ruled over by various warrior chiefs, each one professing to be the true king. The power vacuum created by the retreat of the Roman Empire had left Britain in a state of civil war, with many chieftains vying for control.

The dials matched Blackstone's projections.

Pulling the sodden cowl over his head once more, Sabien leaned into the howling wind and made his way up the narrow track towards the fortress of Uther Pendragon.

. . .

This was supposed to be the era of Arthurian legends: of magical swords and wizards. Ballard and Blackstone were confident that Konstantine had gone to ground somewhere in the Welsh kingdom of Gwynedd. There was no real factual evidence from the period, but the bardic sagas that influenced the later chronicles of Geoffrey of Monmouth pointed to something unusual during this period. One figure stood out among the heroic tales, that of Myrddin or Merlin as Geoffrey called him in *Prophetiae Merlini*.

Sabien didn't believe in wizards, nor magic, but a prophet was another matter. It was one of the roles that Draconians were known to adopt when stranded in the less enlightened parts of the past. Being able to read the time-lines of everyday objects meant that they could seemingly pass as an oracle in the eyes of the locals. When applied with the right amount of mysticism, it was easy to convince the illiterate peasants of pre-Christian Britain that you could read their fate.

If Konstantine was pretending to be Merlin, he had ingratiated himself with one of the most powerful chieftains in Wales.

None of this made up for the icy rain that was slowly running down his neck and freezing his bones to the core.

The gates to the castle were a tall pair of sturdy oak doors. Two scruffy-looking guards sheltered out of the rain around a brazier, trying to warm their hands, their shields and spears leaning against the door.

'Who goes there?' one of them asked in an archaic form of Welsh.

Sabien resisted the urge to announce himself as 'Lancelot,' and went with 'Geoffrey of Monmouth' instead.

They wouldn't have heard of Geoffrey, not for another thousand years at least, but it didn't matter, as long as they recognised his simple cassock and crucifix as that of a priest he would be safe. Dressing as a monk was Ballard's idea, explaining that the locals tended not to kill holy men. Pagans were a superstitious bunch and didn't like to anger any of the gods if they could help it.

'Approach priest and state thy business.'

The engrams of archaic Welsh were still bedding into Sabien's language centres and the translation was a little rough.

He did as instructed and moved within the shelter of the entrance, relieved to be out of the freezing rain.

'I've come to speak with Uther, on a matter of the church.' Sabien patted the sack that was slung around his shoulder.

'You've come asking for alms?' sneered the second guard. 'We've had nothing but beggars these last few months.'

Sabien shook his head. 'No, I've come to offer you absolution.'

'Hah! And a few saint's bones to boot.'

The trade in religious relics was one of the ways missionaries managed to sustain themselves in these dark times. There were countless fingers of St. Cuthbert in circulation, and numerous toes of Ignatius the Blessed.

Sabien shook his head. 'I carry nothing but the word of the one true God,' he said piously, amazed at how effortlessly those Sunday school teachings of his childhood came back to him now.

'What does your god offer then?' asked the first guard, picking up his pike.

'Salvation. The forgiveness of sin. The Kingdom of Heaven.'

The guard worked his jaw as if chewing tobacco.

'How much will that cost then?'

Sabien laughed, there was something refreshing about their outlook on life.

'Nothing. You just have to surrender yourselves to God.'

The other guard pulled a long knife from his belt. 'I surrender to no one!' he threatened, levelling the blade at Sabien's chest. 'Now, be off with you before I cut off some relics of me own.'

'Don't Dewi, you know it's bad luck to threaten a holy man. You don't know what his god will do.'

'Can't be worse than that bloody warlock,' Dewi said, lowering the knife.

'Hush Dewi, he'll put the evil eye on you and you'll wake up dead like Gwyn.'

'Warlock?' asked Sabien, relaxing and warming his hands over the brazier. 'Uther consorts with a warlock?'

They both made the sign of the eye. 'Aye priest, a dark sort of man with evil in his heart.'

'Then I have definitely come to the right place.' Sabien held up his cross, thinking how proud his mother would have been if she could have seen him now.

'In the name of the Father, the Son and the Holy Ghost, I bless thee.'

The two men looked blankly at him.

'So how many gods was that then?' Dewi asked, rapping on the oak doors with the end of his pike.

'It's complicated.'

44

TESSERACT

[Wardenclyffe, Long Island. 1906]

L ooking at his watch, Tesla raised his hand and everyone fell silent.

Einstein nodded to one of the technicians, who threw the main switch and the rings began to rotate around the sphere.

Josh checked his tachyon, Feynman and the colonel were late. If they didn't make it back in the next minute the entire experiment would be a waste of time.

What was slightly more concerning about their absence was the fact that it meant there had been an issue with the atomic test.

After two solid months of work, Feynman had finally worked out how to harness the power they needed to initiate a tesseract, based on what Rufius had discovered about the Trinity test in 1945. Oppenheimer's team detonated an implosion-design plutonium device nicknamed 'The Gadget' and Feynman developed a way to channel the energy released from the blast into the wormhole in such a way that it would create a self-sustaining portal, one that on paper at least, should allow them to move between timelines.

He'd taken Rufius to the Jornada del Muerto desert, thirty-five miles southeast of Socorro, New Mexico.

Tesla checked his watch again.

45

0529

[New Mexico. Date: July 16, 1945]

Rufius stood on the back of the truck studying the hundred-foot steel tower through a pair of binoculars. It was close to 0520 Mountain Time and the detonation was late. They'd watched the arming crews leave the site last night around 2200 hours, and according to Feynman it was planned to kick off at 0400.

Waking in the night, Rufius had watched a storm sweep over the desert. It had been quite a show, bolts of lightning splitting the sky, illuminating the landscape for miles in every direction. He'd seen the more nervous guards drive away towards the shelters, which were stationed five miles North, West and South of the tower — Rufius didn't blame them, no one wanted to be near a live nuclear weapon in the middle of a thunderstorm.

Feynman was sitting in the truck, trying to reach someone called Bainbridge on the radio to find out what was going on, but there was too much chatter, the frequency was being interfered with by a freight yard in San Antonio.

Suddenly he managed to get a signal, and the voice of Samuel Allison came through clearly, counting down.

'You may want to get in here!' shouted Feynman, sticking his head out of the window.

'I'm fine right here,' said Rufius, putting down the binoculars and sliding the welder's goggles over his eyes.

At 0529 the bomb exploded, a blinding white flash signalling the initial detonation followed by a hemisphere of flame blistering out into the sky. Turning yellow, then red and finally purple as it gathered into a mushroom shape above the site and punched a hole through the clouds.

The light washed the peaks of the mountain range, turning a hazy dawn into midday for a brief second.

Rufius took off his darkened lenses, letting his eyes adjust to the brilliant colours.

The blast wave hit him a few seconds later, like a storm wind, it pushed him back against the side of the truck.

'Was that enough?' he shouted down to Feynman.

'I reckon twenty-two kilotons at least,' said the physicist. 'Let's get back and find out.'

Rufius jumped down from the back of the truck and got in beside him.

'You all right?' he asked, as Feynman stared at the still growing column of smoke.

'Yeah, just trying to imagine what that's going to do to a city.'

'When this is over, maybe I'll take you there,' said Rufius taking out his tachyon and tapping on the dials. 'That's odd.'

'What?'

'Must be the radiation, my tachyon's not working.'

Feynman put the truck into reverse. 'Let's get out of here before someone comes around asking the wrong kind of questions.'

46

TESSERACT

[Wardenclyffe, Long Island. 1906]

Tesla and Einstein both checked their watches.

The connection between the wormhole and the device that Feynman had hidden inside the core of the bomb was holding, but nothing was happening.

Everyone held their breath.

Suddenly Rufius and Feynman appeared out of thin air. They both looked dishevelled. Feynman took one look at the machine and smiled. 'Sorry we're late guys, had a little trouble with radioactive interference.'

'Bloody bomb screwed up the tachyon, couldn't get a fix,' added Rufius.

'And the experiment,' said Einstein. 'There's been no transfer of power.'

Feynman poured himself a drink and slugged it back, then poured another and gave it to Rufius. 'Give it a second.'

As they watched, the surface of the wormhole bulged and a surge of power rippled through the conduits connected to the sphere. Arcs of lightning shot out in every direction, scattering the crowd of technicians and sending sparks off over their heads.

'Here it comes,' shouted Feynman, raising a glass.

The workshop was thrown into darkness as the power overloaded all of Tesla's equipment.

Only the light from the rapidly spinning sphere was visible, except it was no longer a sphere, instead there was an eight foot cube spinning on all three axes.

'Ladies and Gentlemen,' announced Feynman, 'I give you a tesseract!'

47

MOONLIGHT

[Chapter House]

She was dreaming of Zack. They were on holiday somewhere warm with a clear blue sea lapping over the beach while he sat playing on the sand.

Standing in the shallows, Josh was staring at something further out to sea.

Caitlin raised her hand to shade her eyes, and saw that there was a shadow in the water. A dark menacing shape heading towards them.

She shouted to Josh to come out, but he didn't move.

Zack toddled down into the shallows with his bucket and Caitlin felt her heart beating faster as she got to her feet.

'Get out of the water!' she screamed at Josh, running down the beach. He turned around as if hearing her for the first time.

Then something broke the surface, its head was huge, like a dragon with glowing red eyes.

Caitlin woke up with a start.

. . .

'What's the matter,' slurred Josh, turning over in the bed and putting his arm around her. It had been a long day, they'd all celebrated the success of the tesseract and Josh had hit the booze quite hard. She'd let him off, there hadn't been too much to be happy about recently.

'Nothing,' she lied, feeling her heart hammering in her chest, 'go back to sleep.'

She lay still, focusing on her breathing until her pulse slowed. It was the middle of the night and she was wide awake.

The bedroom was shrouded in darkness, except for a single beam of moonlight that slipped through the curtains to create a small circle of silver on the floor. It was a magical light, that made her think of the locus. She picked up the sphere from the beside table and held it close to her chest.

'Hello Mother,' said a voice.

Caitlin sat upright in the bed.

'Hey,' said Josh. 'Are you okay?'

She looked around the room, searching for the voice, but there was no one. 'Did you hear something?'

'Like what?' he said groggily.

'Never mind.'

She got up and went to the window.

'Zack?' she whispered to the lights inside the glass sphere.

They seemed to move in response to her words and as the moonlight struck the locus, some of the rays were deflected, projecting a pattern on the opposite wall.

The scattered light began to take form, the outline of a small boy appeared from the glittering speckles of light.

'Josh,' Caitlin hissed, trying not to scare away the vision.

Josh snored in response.

She turned back to the projection. 'Is that really you? Zachary?'

The outline moved, its hand reaching up as if trying to catch something.

Don't try and find me. Caitlin realised the words were inside her head.

'Where are you?' she said aloud, wanting to move closer, but holding back for fear of losing the light from the moon.

Nowhere and everywhere.

'I don't understand. How are you doing this?'

The gods are teaching me new things, the founder showed me how to use them to reach you.

'Are you safe?'

I am fine Mother, try not to worry. Do not try to find me. I will find you when the time is right.

The light from the moon faded and the outline dissipated like embers from a fire. Caitlin went over to the wall and ran her hand over the old plaster, feeling the cracks and lumps where he had just been.

'Josh, wake up!' she said, jumping onto the bed.

'What?'

She held up the locus, her eyes wide with excitement. 'I saw him. I spoke to Zack.'

He scowled at her. 'He's only seven weeks old. How did you manage that?'

She shook her head. 'He's older. I don't know exactly, but he told me not to try and find him.'

Josh snorted. 'You were dreaming.'

'No, this was real. He said that he would find us.'

'He's seven weeks old!' he repeated, turning over and pulling the sheets over his head.

She ignored him and nestled down into bed, holding the locus up to the moonlight and watched the patterns twisting inside.

48

PREPARING

[Wardenclyffe, Long Island. 1906]

Eddington returned Einstein to his rightful time, the physicist's memories having first been redacted by one of Kelly's most talented seers. The professor left the slightly bemused physicist at the patent office in Bern after lunch with an offer to join the faculty of Prague University and the man was none the wiser.

Tesla and Feynman were making some final adjustments to the tesseract when Josh and Caitlin arrived, followed by Rufius a few seconds later.

They were all wearing Draconian armour and carrying gunsabres.

'Wow,' said Sim at the sight of a squadron of Dread-noughts appearing behind them. They were armed to the teeth and carrying a set of large black cases. 'I take it you're expecting to meet some resistance then?'

Rufius shouldered the rifle and opened up one of the cases, helping himself to a pair of pistols. 'Plan for the worst.'

'Hi,' said Caitlin, giving Sim a tentative smile. 'Where's Lyra?'

He was wandering over towards the elite unit who were busy unpacking their equipment. 'She'll be here. She said she had something to do first.'

Feynman walked over to them, admiring the armour. 'Wow, you guys look like you're going to kick some ass!'

'We've no idea what we're going to find in there,' said Caitlin.

'No, about that,' Feynman folded his arms. 'I can't give you much of a heads up either I'm afraid. The wormhole is a simple corridor between two points.' He pointed at the spinning cube. 'That baby is a whole other level of weird. Nothing we've thrown in there has come back.'

'Yet,' corrected Tesla, wiping the grease from his hands with a cloth. 'Nothing has come back yet.'

'You gotta love his optimism,' said Feynman, slapping the inventor on the shoulder. 'I just want you to understand the risks. This is a gateway into an infinite number of universes. You're going to need something more substantial than a ball of twine to find your way back.'

Caitlin held up the locus. 'We have this.'

'That might not be enough,' said Kaori, walking through the door wearing a Maelstrom EVA suit.

'Doctor Shika,' said Rufius bowing his head slightly. 'I'm not sure this is a mission for the Xeno department.'

Kaori took out an intricate gyroscopic device and handed it to him. 'We've been analysing the environmental data from the Medici Chamber. The room has some interesting anomalies, one of which is that its atomic structures are resonating at an entirely different frequency. One that this device can detect.'

'Meaning what?' asked Rufius, staring blankly at the gyroscope.

'Meaning you can alter the superposition of a universe you're trying to reach by simply observing it,' explained Feynman, taking the device from the big man and examining it. 'This might just work.'

'It's a lodestone?' said Rufius. 'A compass?'

Josh took it from Feynman. 'Does this mean we're not walking into an infinite maze?'

'I think the odds just got a little better,' agreed Feynman.

Kaori went over to one of the weapons cases and drew out a katana. 'Just in case our bullets don't have any effect in there,' she said, sheathing the blade and clipping it to her belt.

Lyra arrived ten minutes later with Benoir in tow.

She looked wired, her eyes were wild, as if she'd been taking drugs. She let go of Benoir's hand and he walked over to Josh who was helping Rufius check over the equipment.

'I need to tell you something,' she said quietly to Caitlin, lowering her voice in case the others overheard.

Taking her by the hand, Caitlin walked out of the workshop and into the cool night air. The view across Long Island Sound was stunning, for a while they simply stood watching the lights of the Bridgeport ferry steaming across from Port Jefferson.

'I've seen Zack, he was fighting a dragon,' Lyra blurted out.

Caitlin gasped, remembering her dream from the night before.

'So did I. I dreamed about a dragon too!'

Lyra bit her bottom lip. 'Did you eat a key as well?'

Caitlin frowned. 'No? What key?'

'It doesn't matter. Tell me what you saw.' Lyra kicked off her shoes and sat down on the damp grass.

Caitlin hadn't been able to explain her nightmare to Josh, nor what had happened afterwards. It felt too real to be a dream, and by the time he woke up the next morning, she'd decided to keep it to herself.

But Lyra was different, she accepted the unusual without question or judgement — so Caitlin told her everything.

Lyra listened intently as she described the way the moonlight refracted on the wall and the voices in her head.

'He's a very powerful seer,' said Lyra, thoughtfully. 'The locus is not a passive connection. I suppose he could have found a way to reach you.'

'But he was older, I couldn't say how much older but at least eight or nine maybe.'

'He was a man in my dream,' said Lyra, staring up into the starry night sky. 'You have no idea what time is like in there. There's no way to know if we are even travelling at the same speed let alone going in the same direction.'

She wrapped her arms around Caitlin's neck and hugged her as best she could through the armour. 'Be careful of the dragon, sister.'

'I will,' Caitlin replied, kissing her on the top of her head.

. . .

When they walked back into the workshop, Caitlin found her parents talking to Josh.

'Ready?' her father said with a nervous smile.

Caitlin tried to put on a brave face. 'As I'll ever be.'

Her mother took off her Draconian insignia and pinned it to Caitlin's breastplate. 'Our very own nautonnier,' she said, with tears welling in her eyes.

'Stay safe KitKat,' added her father, kissing her on the cheek.

Caitlin looked into the spinning cube and put on her helmet.

'Right!' Rufius turned to the Dreadnought squad. 'Let's get this show on the road.'

Feynman paced around the machine as they formed up in a line. Tesla went from one to the other attaching a thin cable between their suits.

The physicist cleared his throat and ran his hand through his hair. 'The tesseract is a hypercube in a state of quantum superposition. Every possible timeline that could ever be exists in there. Think of it as an infinite number of doors to an infinite number of universes. I've no idea what will happen to you while you're in there, but if Doctor Shika's theory is correct, by searching for the right frequency the continuum you're looking for should find you.'

He turned towards the spinning cube, each face filled with other cubes that recursed into infinite versions of themselves.

'Whatever you do, stick together. You all need to observe the same reality or you'll get split up and finding your way back gets a whole lot harder.'

The first Dreadnought stepped up to the portal.

'Good luck, may your god follow you into all of the dark places.'

49

OBSERVER EFFECT

[Tesseract]

One after another, they walked slowly into the tesseract, the line growing taught between them as each paused before disappearing into the mirror-like surface of its event horizon.

Caitlin went last. The helmet made it difficult to turn her head and the visor was steaming up, but she managed to glimpse Lyra and her mother waving as she went through.

It was a strange sensation to walk into the room you'd just left, except now it seemed to stretch off down long corridors in infinite directions. There was an instant sense of vertigo, as if standing on the stairs of an Escher painting, and she closed her eyes for a second to stop herself from throwing up.

Using the static line, she inched her way to join the others. They were clustered in a tight circle, each of them facing a different direction.

'Which way?' asked Rufius over the crude radio Tesla had adapted to fit inside their helmets.

'What does the frequency oscillator say?' asked Kaori, turning to Josh.

He held up the device which was spinning like a children's windmill in a hurricane. 'No idea.'

Kaori held out a gloved hand. 'May I?'

She adjusted the controls on the handle, and as the gyroscope slowed, the walls shifted around them, seemingly responding to the changes in the oscillator.

'Observer effect,' Kaori noted, handing the device back to Josh. 'We're collapsing the number of options by searching for the frequency.'

'But we're still in this continuum,' said Rufius, pointing at the rooms around them.

Kaori shook her head inside her helmet. 'Not necessarily, this is just a single point in time, what we do next will change everything.'

Caitlin took out the locus and watched its intensity change as she moved her hand in a slow arc. Choosing the point when it was brightest she took one step forward. The rooms began to fade away into darkness, as though someone were switching off the lights one by one.

'Stop!' ordered Kaori, grabbing hold of the line between Josh and Caitlin. 'We need to stick together or we'll lose each other.'

'I think he's this way,' replied Caitlin, holding up the locus which glowed like a small sun in her hand.

'That's kind of what the oscillator is saying too,' agreed Josh.

'Fine,' said Kaori, 'just be aware that as soon as we move away from this point it's going to get harder to come back.'

'We'll stay here,' said one of the Dreadnoughts. 'Act as a backstop while you move out to the ends of your tethers.'

There was a general murmur of agreement and like

mountaineers they slowly edged away from the safety of the warehouse and into the darkness.

When each of them had reached the end of their lines they stopped.

No one could see the person in front, only the safety line stretching out to infinity.

'Are you still there?' asked Josh.

'Right behind you,' said Rufius.

'Here,' responded Kaori as did the Dreadnoughts by rote.

'Cat?' said Josh into the silence.

'I think I can see it,' she replied after a long pause.

'So, do we just head in that direction?' asked Josh to no one in particular.

Rufius laughed nervously. 'Glad we only thought of that after we left the quantum physicist behind.'

'The options are narrowing,' whispered Caitlin.

'Caitlin, perhaps you're the lodestone after all,' said Kaori.

50

COURT OF UTHER PENDRAGON

[Pendragon Castle, Wales. Date: 540]

U ther Pendragon sat slumped in his chair, his balding head resting on the table. The remnants of his last meal were scattered across its surface.

Two wiry hunting dogs slept at his feet, while rats and mice scurried between bowls of half-eaten meat, bread and turnips, making the most of their hosts' drunken slumber.

A musty smell of soiled straw and sour beer lingered about the hall, as if no one had opened a window in a very long time. It reminded Sabien of the way a corpse reeked after spending two weeks in a shallow grave in the forest — something he'd experienced more than once.

There were two other men at the table, both equally drunk and dead to the world. They wore badly fitting leather jerkins over patched tunics and carried Roman swords. Sabien assumed that they were either kinsman or bodyguards. Either way, in their current state they weren't a threat.

'My lord,' said one of the maidservants, gently tapping Uther on the shoulder.

'Away!' bellowed the drunken king, throwing out his arm and striking the woman across the face.

She reeled back from the impact, a red welt rising on her cheek. Her eyes were full of fire and hate, but she said nothing and returned to his side.

'There's a priest to see you.'

'What do I want with a damned priest?' he said, raising his head from the table, strands of greasy hair sticking to one side of his face.

Opening one eye he surveyed Sabien. 'And who the bloody hell are you?'

'Geoffrey of Monmouth, sire. I am a chronicler. I've come to write your story.'

'A chronicler? Do you hear that Dafyd?' He threw a goblet at the dark-haired man to his right. 'There's a priest here, wants to write about our humble lives.'

The cup struck the man on the head and his hand moved instinctively to his sword as he stirred.

Sabien nodded, taking out a leather bound book. 'I'm recording the lives of all the great men, for posterity.'

Uther's anger abated, he appeared to like the idea — as Sabien knew he would. Warlords like him tended to be egomaniacs or narcissists and nothing inflated an ego like having someone write your life story.

Dafyd, who bore a striking resemblance to Uther now his face wasn't buried in a pie, got up and brushed the crumbs off his jerkin. 'How do we know he's a scribe? Might be one of Vortigen's men for all we know!'

He pulled out the sword and waved it menacingly at Sabien.

The blade was old, its edge notched and rusting in

places. From its shape he could tell it had once been a Roman Gladius, the sword of a Roman Legionary.

Sabien ignored the threat and opened the book, showing them the richly illustrated manuscript of the Lindisfarne Gospels.

He'd borrowed it from the British Library. According to the Head Scriptorian who signed it out, it took over ten years to create and was worth millions in the present. Which was why he'd made Sabien promise that he wouldn't let it out of his sight, and certainly not allow anyone touch it with their bare hands.

Uther wiped his greasy fingers on his tunic and took the book from him.

Sabien winced, trying not to think what the Head Scriptorian was going to say when he returned it.

Screwing his eyes up until they were tiny dark holes, Uther pretended to read the text. His eyesight was obviously failing, but spectacles wouldn't have made any difference, no one could read in this part of the world, let alone in Latin, which was why the church relied so heavily on illustration.

'You're going to put me in here?' he said, tapping on one of the blank pages and leaving a dirty smudge of a finger print.

'Aye lord, at least two pages.'

'Two pages!' he exclaimed, throwing the book down on the table and standing up to reveal a heavily stained jerkin where he'd obviously thrown up on himself. 'I could fill the whole book with my conquests.'

Sabien bowed. 'My apologies Majesty. I shall send for more vellum.'

Uther nodded, cleaning out a drinking horn with his finger and pouring himself some mead from a jug. 'See that you do, and don't expect any alms while you're about it. You can sleep with the horses until it's finished. Myrtle, see that the priest has something to eat.'

The maid servant scowled and gestured to Sabien to follow her.

Sabien bowed and followed Myrtle out of the room.

51

TROUBLE

[Tesseract]

A strangled scream burst over the radio.

The line connecting Rufius to the Dreadnought behind him went tight, pulling him backwards.

They all heard the sound of gunfire.

Rufius dug his heels in, gripping the cable with both hands as it writhed around like a shark on the end of a fishing line.

'I need backup!' shouted one of the Dreadnoughts.

'Coming to you now!' replied one of his squad.

'No, stay where you are!' Kaori shouted over the radio between the bursts of gunfire. 'We may need to go back. Rufius can you see him?'

'Not quite. I'm going back,' said Rufius through gritted teeth. He released his grip, and arming his gunsabre, he retraced the path along the line, the infinite corridors changing with every step.

The line went slack, and when he came upon the body it was nothing but a mangled collection of blood and armour.

'He's gone,' he reported into the radio. 'Looks like he was attacked by a rubbish truck.'

'I think we should regroup at the insertion point. Everyone retrace your steps,' ordered Kaori.

The static in their headphones changed pitch, there were other voices talking in a thousand different tongues.

'We need to get out of here,' said one of the remaining Dreadnoughts. 'We're not prepared for this.'

'Wait! We're so close,' Caitlin's voice sounded distant, as if she were talking to someone else.

'What can you see?' asked Kaori, feeling the line between her and Josh tightening.

'A desert with pyramids. Egypt I guess.'

'I'm seeing a radioactive wasteland,' replied Kaori. 'I think we're all experiencing something completely different. Our observations are unique, if we stay in here we're going to end up in entirely separate timelines.'

'Or dead,' added Rufius solemnly. 'We have no idea what creatures live in here.'

The sounds of gunfire broke through again.

'We have to get back before we lose the connection,' shouted Kaori.

'Cut us loose,' demanded Josh.

Kaori took out her sword and sliced the line that connected Josh to herself, leaving him tied to Caitlin.

'What are you doing?' said Rufius. 'Are you mad?'

Sheathing the sword, she appeared next to him. 'We have to let them go. There's no way we can take this many people through to one timeline. In fact, we're probably the reason the hypercube won't collapse.'

'You're leaving them in here?' protested Rufius.

'It's the only way they'll ever see their son,' she bent

down and took hold of the boot of the mangled corpse. 'Now let's get back before we lose anyone else.'

'How will we get back?' asked Josh, reaching Caitlin. She was holding the glowing locus like a torch ahead of her .

'We'll find a way,' Caitlin said reassuringly.

Kaori's voice came faintly through their radio. 'Caitlin let your instinct guide you. Josh use the oscillator when you get close, the measurement should collapse the tesseract and the rest of us should find ourselves back in Tesla's warehouse.'

Caitlin nodded and took Josh by the hand. 'Just you and me now, honey.'

They walked forward into the ever-changing maze, Josh staying close to Caitlin.

With every step the worlds around them changed, the number of iterations reducing. The motion of the rapidly changing environment made Josh feel sick, he tried to focus on the route in front of him, but that was hardly any better. So he closed his eyes, letting Caitlin guide him.

In the darkness he heard her singing softly to herself.

52

IGRAINE

[Pendragon Castle, Wales. Date: 540]

Sabien followed Myrtle down a series of winding stone staircases to the kitchens.

A roaring fire was set in the hearth, and a pair of small pigs were roasting on long black spits in front of it.

Three women were busy chopping vegetables under the watchful eye of the cook, who was a large, red-faced woman with a permanent sneer.

'What've you got there Myrtle?' the cook asked as they entered. 'Another mouth to feed?'

'He's a priest,' replied Myrtle. 'His lordship wishes him fed.'

'Does he now! And what does a priest eat?'

'Humble pie,' said one of the servants, making the others cackle.

'Quiet Megan! I'll have none of your cheek. Bread and cheese is all I can spare 'til dinner. Myrtle fetch some more logs for the fire.'

Sabien bowed politely, took off his wet cloak and sat at

the far end of the long table they were using to prepare the meal.

Myrtle left through another door.

The cook clucked her tongue, taking his sodden cloak and hanging it closer to the fire. 'What's your name priest?'

'Geoffrey,' replied Sabien, tearing open the bread. He was glad they hadn't offered him meat, the idea of being a vegetarian in this era was probably tantamount to worshipping Satan.

'Don't see many of your type around here, you come for the warlock I suppose?'

He feigned ignorance. 'Warlock?'

'Aye,' the cook said, planting her wide bottom onto the bench opposite him. 'The warlock. He arrived a few weeks back and the master's not been the same since. I say he's cast a hex on him.'

Sabien crossed himself and the others followed his example.

'And where is this warlock now?'

'His lordship sent him to parley with Vortigen. He should be back soon. It's only two days ride away. Probably less if you can charm the stones like he says.'

Sabien carved off a piece of the cheese and bit into it. The taste was rich and creamy, unlike anything he'd experienced in the twentieth century. His stomach groaned, reminding him he hadn't eaten for two days and he took another slice.

'Good isn't it?' asked the cook, with a wink. 'No one makes a better cheese round these parts.'

He nodded and took another piece, there was no better compliment to a cook than a clean plate.

Myrtle returned with a basket filled with logs. Sabien

was impressed, the thing must have weighed over thirty kilos and she was carrying it under one arm.

'And have you seen him practising the dark arts? Charming stones?' he asked.

The cook leaned across the table and helped herself to a slice of the cheese, her large breasts nearly falling out of her smock in the process. Sabien could smell the sweat on her mixed with something else, something more exotic — perfume.

'Megan has. Says she saw the man step out of a mirror just the other day, didn't you Megan?'

'As if it were a door,' one of the younger girls replied.

'And you say he has influence over your master?'

'His lordship hangs on his every word.'

Sabien turned to Megan. 'Can you show me this mirror?'

The girl blushed, and the others giggled.

'I'll show you,' said Myrtle, putting the last of the logs on the fire. 'It's in the East tower.'

Leaving the warmth of the kitchen, Sabien followed Myrtle through the servants' quarters and up the back stairs into the tower. The stone steps grew colder as they climbed higher, Sabien could feel it through his boots. The soles of Myrtle's feet were black, she had no shoes and he shivered at the thought of how hard their lives must be here.

The room in the East tower had a view over the valley, its small windows paned with mullioned glass that distorted the world beyond. There was a four-poster bed against one wall with sheets of muslin draped as if to preserve it. A simple table and chair stood near the largest window, with a small pile of books and a bottle filled with a golden fluid. He picked it up and sniffed the stopper, it was the same as the scent the cook was wearing.

'Here's the looking glass,' said Myrtle, lighting a candle and holding it up to the mirror.

It was a fine piece of work, the long frame was gilded and carved with ornate flowers and leaves.

'It was her majesty's, Queen Igraine, before she died.'

Sabien took off one of his gloves and touched the frame, feeling the timeline run under his fingers.

'It's beautiful.'

'She was beautiful,' agreed Myrtle, tears welling in her eyes. 'Everything was better then, when she died, something in him died as well.'

'Grief affects us all in different ways,' said Sabien, repeating the words of the priest on the day he came to tell his mother they'd found his father's body.

He could still remember that day. His mother treating the priest like royalty, laying out the best cups for tea.

'And the warlock —'

'Myrddin,' she interrupted him.

'And when Myrddin appeared, did Megan say what he was wearing?'

Myrtle blushed a little. 'She says he was naked as the day he was born.'

'And did he say anything to her?'

She laughed. 'Asked to meet the master, bold as brass, not caring for the fact he wore nothing but air!'

Sabien touched the glass, it was by far the hardest material to read, the surface was cold, far colder than the rest of the room. There was an echo of a path below it, a shadow path.

Myrtle was beginning to look at him strangely. 'Are you a witch finder?'

Sabien snapped his hand away. 'No, I'm a chronicler. I collect stories.'

She frowned. 'What kind of stories?'

'Tales of Kings and Princes. I'm writing a history.'

'Like the Book of Aneirin?'

'Yes, have you read it?' Sabien looked surprised, the book was a collection of poems by the war poet, the so-called "prince of bards".

Myrtle laughed. 'What time have I for letters? We were taught the tales of Owain when we were children.'

Sabien remembered that most stories in these times were passed down through oral traditions, through generations of storytelling.

Myrtle shivered. 'It's getting dark. I should be getting you to the stables before you catch your death up here. Come,' she beckoned, picking up the candle. 'Let's see if we can find you some fresh straw and a warm blanket.'

53

PYRAMIDS

[Arrakeen]

They walked out into a desert, a sea of sand stretching to the horizon in every direction, the sun blazing down from a clear blue sky.

Caitlin lifted her visor and took a long, deep breath.

'It's okay,' she said, decoupling the neck locks and twisting the helmet to take it off. 'We can breathe their air.'

Josh lifted his visor and cautiously sniffed the air. It was dry and warm, the kind that hadn't tasted rain in a very long time.

'Where are we?' he asked, taking his helmet off and looking around.

She shaded her eyes and pointed towards the pyramids that stood out on the horizon. 'I think we're in Egypt.'

'So we're still on Earth?'

Caitlin nodded. 'Well, there aren't many other habitable planets within four light years of this one, so I'm guessing it's the most likely candidate.'

'I just imagined they'd taken him somewhere else.'

'They did,' she said, holding up the locus to her eye and sighting along it as if it were a lens.

'So he's really here?'

'Yup.' Caitlin turned slowly around in a circle, then reversed until she found the strongest signal. 'Somewhere in that direction,' she said, waving her arm in the general vicinity of the pyramids.

They walked in silence for over an hour, the heat of the sun baking the sand and turning the air around them into a shimmering haze. The pyramids seemed to be moving further away and with nothing but footprints to mark their progress, it began to feel like they hadn't moved at all.

Josh stopped to take a drink from his canteen.

The water was bitter and tasted of metal, but it was cold and washed the dust from his throat.

He offered it to Caitlin, but she refused. 'We have to make it last.'

An hour later they stopped again and this time she accepted the drink.

'What was it like having the founder in your head all that time?' she asked, sitting down on the shaded slope of a dune.

Josh hardly knew where to begin. He thought of all the times he'd sat in the library inside his head, the thousands of moments stored in the books lining the walls.

'For a long time he wasn't there. Then fragments of memory started surfacing unannounced and I wouldn't be able to tell what were his and what were mine. He was like someone who'd been in a coma, no concept of time, everything was out of order. Eventually we managed to create the library, where he could organise it all.'

She laughed. 'You created a library in your head?'

'It helped a lot. Whenever we needed something, he could just find it. Snap his fingers and there it would be.'

'If only my library would work like that.'

'But then the Aeon came, and took it all. All his stories, lost forever.'

Caitlin held up her index finger. 'All bar one.'

Josh could still feel the hole in his mind where the last memory should have been, like a tongue probing for a missing tooth, he niggled at it, trying to remember what it was.

Caitlin continued. 'I keep asking myself, what could be so important that they would steal a child?'

'Me too.'

She looked up at him. 'Isn't there anything that you can remember? Something the Anunnaki would want?'

Josh scratched his head. 'Before Babylon, I thought they were just some ancient race, one the founder could harness using talismans to fight the Nihil. I assumed they were long dead spirits, not some kind of avenging group of gods from another dimension.'

'Zack took something from you that they needed,' she said, getting to her feet and brushing the sand off her hands.

'There were too many memories, the man was over a thousand years old, he'd lived through dozens of lifetimes.'

'You still should have told me,' said Caitlin, slinging the gunsabre over her shoulder and starting up the sand dune. 'I thought we told each other everything.'

'I've tried telling you!' he said, raising his voice as she walked away. 'A hundred times I've told you about what I can do. Every time it leads to us breaking up. You can't deal with what I have done, that I changed the timeline. I don't know what else to say, I'm damned either way.'

She turned towards him and walked back.

'Exactly how long did you give it after we broke up each time?'

He looked confused. 'I don't know, maybe a month or two.'

'And then you hit the reset switch?' She tapped on her arm as if she were pressing a button.

'I tried to make up, but you wouldn't listen.'

She folded her arms over her breastplate. 'You have no idea do you? Some things can take years to put back together. You can't just flick a switch and make everything okay. You have to work at it. Just because it's hard doesn't make it wrong.'

'I thought I could fix it,' he said looking at his feet.

She stepped closer to him and put her hand under his chin, lifting his head to meet her eyes. 'Sometimes you can't fix it, sometimes things need to be broken so they can come back stronger.'

'You're not mad at me?'

She laughed. 'Oh, you have no idea, but right now we have to find our son. We can deal with the whole master-of-time-and-space-shit later.'

Josh sighed deeply, it felt like the first time he'd been able to breathe properly in months.

'Now, quit feeling sorry for yourself and start trying to figure out what it was about that creepy old man in your head that would make our son such an interesting prize.'

When they reached the brow of the dune they both stopped.

In the valley below them lay the ruins of a vast city of steel and gold and half of the buildings were ablaze.

Above the towers of tarnished metal floated the three pyramids, hovering in the air like giant mountains, each one casting a dark shadow over the streets below.

The side of the pyramids were covered in a mirror shield so that they reflected the sky, an energy field rippled the air under their bases.

'They're ships?' said Caitlin, hardly able to keep the astonishment out of her voice.

'Warships,' added Josh, pointing at the small craft that were descending to the surface.

Caitlin shaded her eyes and squinted at the tiny stick figures that were engaged in a street battle. The beams of energy from weapons streaked down from the smaller craft, aimed into the buildings where the opposition were taking shelter, destroying them in plumes of blue fire.

'Are you sure Zack is here?' asked Josh, turning towards her.

She took out the locus and held it up to him. 'Positive. He's in there somewhere.' She pointed towards the city.

Josh swung the gunsabre off his shoulder and used the sight to get a better view.

Caitlin opened a flap on her forearm to check her tachyon. She tutted, tapping it. Then shook her arm.

'What's the matter?' asked Josh.

'Tachyon's not working.'

He looked confused. 'Then how are we supposed to get back?'

She unslung her own rifle and started down the slope towards the battle. 'Let's find Zack first and work that out afterwards.'

54

RETURN

[Wardenclyffe, Long Island. 1906]

Kaori and Rufius reappeared in the warehouse dragging the bodies of two dead Dreadnoughts behind them.

'Where are the others? Caitlin and Josh?' asked Caitlin's mother, unable to hide the concern in her voice

'They've gone ahead,' said Kaori, taking off her helmet. 'We had no choice.'

'What happened?' asked Caitlin's father, looking at the bodies of the dead men.

Taking off his gloves, Rufius grimaced at the red welts across his palms where the line had cut through the padding. 'Something attacked them. They didn't stand a chance.'

'You mean something else is alive in there?'

Kaori sat down, pulled off her gloves and unbuckled her breastplate. 'I've no idea. That kind of crushing damage, they could have been hit by a rock or trampled by a dinosaur.'

'So how do we know if Cat and Josh are okay?'

Feynman looked over to the portal, which was returning to its normal state. 'The tesseract's re-established itself, which means they're no longer in it.'

Caitlin's mother took a roll of bandage out of her bag and began wrapping it around Rufius's hand. 'Do you think they've found him?'

Feynman shrugged. 'No way to know for sure.'

A Dreadnought medical team appeared out of thin air and began examining their men.

'Caitlin said she saw pyramids,' added Rufius. 'So maybe Zack's in Egypt?'

'Our Egypt?' Caitlin's father looked confused.

The physicist folded his arms. 'Could be any one of an infinite number of Egypts. One where the Pharaohs are still ruling to this day. That's the problem with the multiverse, the timelines can branch off at any point. Hell, from what you guys have told me this other continuum may have bifurcated from our own a million years ago.'

'Or was never connected,' said Sim.

The medics started to examine Kaori, but she waved them away. 'Let's work on the theory that there's some kind of connection. We know they've been here before and that they've been monitoring the development of our civilisation. It seems logical to assume there's some ulterior motive for coming here.'

'Josh thinks it has something to do with his father,' Rufius reminded them. 'If he really was from another continuum, maybe he was some kind of fugitive, and the Anunnaki were hunting him down.'

'There's only one person left that could tell us,' said Lyra.

Rufius nodded. 'Konstantine.'

55

BATTLE

[Arrakeen]

The streets of the metal city were deserted.

Golden fighter craft screamed low overhead causing Josh and Caitlin to duck for cover as they crept through the narrow alleys.

Burned out shells of buildings smouldered on every corner, sending clouds of thick smoke into the passages, creating an eerie ghost world of half-seen shapes in the maze of alien architecture.

Everything was covered in a layer of sand stirred up by the engines of the enormous ships hovering above them.

Keeping off the main streets, Josh and Caitlin had managed to avoid the roaming patrols of foot soldiers who were systematically clearing the streets of what was left of the opposing forces.

The invading infantry was an impressive sight, standing over seven-feet tall in armour that was obviously inspired by the Egyptian belief system: the symbol for Ra, the sun-God, was embossed on to their burnished breastplates and their helmets were shaped like jackals, hawks or exotic cats. They carried long metal sceptres with ornate heads that fired bolts of energy, instantly vaporising anything in their path.

Pressed against a wall in the shadow of a pyramid, Caitlin looked up into the base of the floating ship. The underside was made from a dark metal and at each of the four corners were recesses housing the pulsing blue halo of enormous thrusters. An eye-shaped opening sat in the centre through which transport ships and fighter craft were constantly moving in and out of the vessel. From the amount of activity she assumed that this was the command centre.

Passing over them, the downward thrust of the engines blew away the smoke, replacing it with a sandstorm of dust and ashes.

Taking out the locus, Caitlin closed her eyes, feeling for the strongest presence of Zack.

As the thrumming sound of the ship faded away, Josh heard a noise from further down the alley. Crouching instinctively, he raised his gunsabre and, leaving Caitlin to her locus, he moved stealthily along the wall.

At a T-junction where the passage intersected with another, Josh found a terrified family of four hiding behind a pile of rubbish. Their faces were pale, eyes wide and their hands shaking as they raised them in surrender. They were dressed in simple robes and the man had a symbol tattooed on his forehead that Josh thought he'd seen before some-where. The wife had one on the palm of her hand.

Josh lowered his rifle and smiled. The parents seemed to relax a little and released their grip on their children. They whispered something in a language that he couldn't understand, but Josh could tell from their expressions that they were still unsure of who he was.

The sound of marching boots echoed along the passageway.

He knelt down beside them and sighted his weapon at the street beyond the corner of the alleyway, waiting for the soldiers to pass by.

Caitlin came to kneel behind him. 'Who are they?' she whispered, staring at the trembling family.

'No idea,' hissed Josh, 'locals I guess.'

Through the gap in the buildings, he watched a detachment of foot soldiers pass by in strict formation. Through the ranks of infantry came a golden chariot, floating level with their helmets, and standing upon it was a glowing figure in golden armour.

'Anunnaki,' Josh gasped, then twisted back against the wall as one of their squad paused at the entrance to the alley.

He held his breath and put his finger to his lips. The family cowered, burying themselves under the rubbish.

They could hear the soldier moving further into the passage, the pneumatic-hiss of his heavy tread, the mechanical grinding of gears, as he came closer.

One of the children coughed. Her mother quickly covered her mouth with her hand but it was too late and there was a low-pitched whine and a series of clicks, the unmistakable sound of his weapon charging.

Josh motioned to Caitlin to cover him. She was naturally a better shot. Her mouth set into a hard, thin line and she nodded, shouldering her gunsabre.

Taking a deep breath, he rolled out of cover and across to the other side of the passage, a bolt of blue narrowly arcing into the sand as he crossed into its firing line.

Josh could hear the weapon charging up once more, and the sound of servos in his armour grinding as the soldier marched on. Seemingly oblivious to the danger, it approached the corner of the alley.

Acting as the decoy, Josh ensured he got his attention by shooting him twice in the head, even at point-blank range the bullets ricocheted off his helmet and into the stone wall.

In one swift movement the soldier rotated his sceptre and aimed the glowing end at Josh.

Slowing her breathing, Caitlin felt her body relax and she gently squeezed the trigger, aiming for the point where the helmet gaped at the nape of the soldier's neck.

The bullet disappeared cleanly beneath the plates of his armour and the soldier froze, his hand reaching up towards his helmet before dropping the staff, collapsing to his knees and onto his front.

Josh sprang to his feet and looked back down the alley to see if any more of the patrol were following, but the entourage had moved on.

Caitlin kicked the staff away from the body and pulled off the helmet.

The head was clearly modelled on a human, but the bullet had shattered the ceramic skull, exposing a lattice of wiring and the remnants of a cybernetic brain.

'It's a robot?' said Josh, glancing up to see the family hastily making their way down the alley.

With some effort, they managed to turn the body over. 'He's about your size,' observed Caitlin, taking off her gloves.

Josh knelt down beside her. 'What are you planning now?'

Caitlin raised her eyes towards the pyramid. 'Zack's on that ship. You can put his gear on and pretend to take me in as a prisoner.'

'Are they taking prisoners?' he asked, shading his eyes as he looked up.

She was already unbuckling her Dreadnought armour. 'Everybody takes prisoners. No point in slaughtering an entire civilisation, otherwise who do you use for slave labour. It's a standard conquest tactic.'

Josh shrugged and picked up the jackal helmet, and began removing bits of the soldier's skull from inside.

56

CHRONICLER

When Sabien woke the next morning the storm had passed.

Walking out into the courtyard, he could still feel a chill in the air, but the sky was clear, the sun strong and warm on his face — finally spring was coming.

Myrtle came out of the kitchen door and emptied a bucket of slops into the swine pen. She wiped her hand across her brow, carefully avoiding the bruise that was purpling around her swollen eye. Sabien could see she wore it like a badge of honour, showing Uther that she could take the punishment.

Sabien took off his leather belt and pulled the woollen tunic over his head. Stripped to the waist he plunged his head into the water barrel, letting the shock of the icy cold wake him.

Throwing his head back as he came out, his long hair flicked water in all directions, catching Myrtle, who was bringing him a linen cloth.

She laughed.

'You're a strange kind of priest,' she said, handing him the cloth, letting her eyes wander over his torso, unashamedly admiring his body.

'I was a warrior once,' he explained, drying his scarred chest. 'Before I found the Lord.'

Sabien realised he was beginning to enjoy this role play a little too much.

Myrtle's expression was hard to read, she clearly wanted to tell him something, but she held back.

'How long since you lost your queen?'

'Three years.'

'Why didn't you leave?'

She bit her bottom lip. 'I've nowhere else to go.'

He pulled the shirt over his head and picked up the crucifix. 'There's always the sisterhood?'

She laughed again. 'What need have I of an invisible god? What I need is a husband who doesn't go off and get himself killed over nothing.'

'You were married?'

Myrtle nodded. 'Once, a long time ago, but he's dead and that's the end of it.'

She picked up her bucket and walked back towards the kitchen door.

'Breakfast's ready when you are, and the warlock has returned.'

'He's here?'

'Aye, he came back in the middle of the night. He's with his lordship right now.'

Sabien went directly to the main hall.

Uther was sitting in his usual chair at the end of the table, his two sons on each side.

Konstantine was standing beside Uther, dressed in long grey robes, a silver chain around his neck and a dark beard clipped into a point, like an evil wizard from a Disney movie.

'Ah yes, the scribe! Myrddin, this is the chronicler I was telling you about!' exclaimed Uther as Sabien entered.

Konstantine's eyes narrowed suspiciously as he walked around the table to greet Sabien.

'A man of letters,' he said, stroking his beard. 'What a pleasure to meet a fellow scholar.'

The last part was spoken in Latin, as if the warlock was testing him.

'A pleasure indeed,' reciprocated Sabien in the same tongue.

Neither offered the other a hand to shake, which suited Sabien. Not wearing his gloves was difficult enough, but touching Konstantine would potentially have blown his cover.

'Enough gobbledygook, speak normal!' ordered Uther.

Konstantine turned back to his master and bowed his head. 'As you wish, my lord.'

Uther continued. 'So, master chronicler, take out your quill. I mean to tell you a tale that will make your heart shudder.'

Sabien sat down at the other end of the dining table and took out his quills and a smooth piece of clean vellum. Konstantine hovered behind him, watching him sharpening his nib and unstopper the bottles of black and gold inks.

'Such a delicate hand,' he said sarcastically as Sabien wrote the first line: *The Chronicle of Uther Pendragon, first of his name.*

The rest of the morning was spent with Uther regaling them with stories of various battles he had fought against Gorlois at Tintagel, and his final victory where he took the hand of the beautiful Igraine.

Konstantine interrupted on numerous occasions, embellishing Uther's description, playing to his ego.

By the time lunch was served, Sabien had written over five long pages of gothic script and his hand was beginning to ache from the calligraphy.

While the servants carried in the food and drink, Uther went to relieve himself and Konstantine came over to inspect Sabien's work.

'It is interesting that we have never met, two learned men in the wilds of Wales,' he said, leafing through the parchment.

Sabien shrugged. 'I have only recently arrived.'

Konstantine smiled. 'And when have you travelled from?' he asked, grabbing Sabien's forearm. 'Who are you? Protectorate?' He pulled back the sleeve of Sabien's right arm to reveal the Ouroboros tattoo.

Sabien jumped to his feet, twisting his arm out of Konstantine's grip. 'You're under arrest.'

Konstantine stepped back and pulled a knife out of his belt.

The two sons watched with great amusement as the tension grew between the two men.

Keeping one eye on the knife, Sabien held up his hand. 'Don't do anything stupid, you know I'm being tracked, the rest of my team will be here presently.'

Konstantine laughed. 'If your team knew I was here they'd have taken me already. You're working alone. I doubt anyone knows you're here.'

He lunged at Sabien, who only just avoided the blade.

The man was fast, but he was faster. He struck out with his foot, hitting Konstantine in the left knee and saw it buckle.

The warlock, seemed to go down, but it was a feint, he swung his right leg out and caught Sabien off balance, knocking him to the floor.

Before he could get to his feet, Konstantine was on top of him, his knees pinning down his shoulders, raising the blade above his head.

Sabien tried to push him off but he was trapped. As the blade came down he heard the sound of breaking pottery, and felt something splash on his face. The weight on his chest toppled off to one side.

Wiping his eyes clear of wine, Sabien found Myrtle standing over Konstantine with the handle of a broken jug in one hand. She was breathing heavily, but there was a wide smile on her face.

'What's occurring?' roared Uther, coming back through the door.

'So what exactly was your plan?' asked Konstantine from the adjacent cell. 'Take me back to face the music?'

'To have your parasite removed.'

Since neither man would explain what had caused the fight, Uther had both of them thrown in his dungeons to cool off. They were dark, cold cells at the lowest level of the castle where even the rats were too afraid to come.

'My symbiote,' corrected Konstantine, 'is as much a part of me as the body it possesses.'

'You're part of a conspiracy, one that endangered the Order, not to mention the manipulation of nineteenth-century Europe.'

Konstantine laughed. 'You really have no idea who we are do you?'

Sabien ignored him. Running his fingers down the grain of the wood of the door, looking for a way to open it.

'I have to take you back, your accomplice has stolen a child.'

'*The child*,' stressed Konstantine, sitting down on the straw bed, 'is irrelevant, the memories it contains however are another matter, but my accomplice will be long gone by now. Even the most powerful ranger couldn't reach him.'

Sabien stepped through the wood of Konstantine's cell door as if it were water.

'Oh, I think you'll find we can.'

Myrtle brought their food an hour later.

Bryn, the guard, took his time finding the right key. She knew that he was sweet on her, and maybe on a dark night with enough mead inside of her, she might have been interested. But now there was another that took her fancy, one who owed her a favour. There was no mistaking the look in Geoffrey's eyes, the man was no priest, not a celibate one at least.

Bryn finally managed to open the door to the warlock's cell, it was empty.

Confused, he turned and went to the other door, finding its key first time. Geoffrey's cell was empty too, except for a small crucifix left on the straw.

Myrtle picked it up and turned it over in her hand. It was solid silver. She smiled as she slipped it into her skirt and went back to help Bryn raise the alarm.

57

PRISONER

[Arrakeen]

J osh marched through the deserted streets with Caitlin in front of him, the staff pointed at her back.

Half a mile from the alley, they came to a large square where a crowd of prisoners were being held in a temporary pen. Dust was settling around a grey transport ship which retracted its wings as they arrived. The whine of its engines winding down drowned out the cries of their captives as the crew unlocked the large cargo bay doors.

None of the other soldiers paid him much attention, even though he was struggling to see through the eyes of the helmet and kept stumbling on the rubble scattered across the plaza.

Caitlin played the part of a captive perfectly, wearing a plain flax dress and keeping her head down as she joined the other prisoners. They were all civilians, mostly women and children and Josh was sad to see they included the family he'd found in the alley.

He went to stand in line with the other guards.

A golden chariot entered the square in a cloud of dust and pulled up close to the row of soldiers.

The Anunnaki surveyed the scene, before stepping down to inspect his men.

His armour rippled with some kind of energy shielding. As he came closer, Josh could feel the electrical charge raising the hairs on the back of his neck. The metal was coated in a luminescent substance that was reacting to the shield, up close he could see that it was tarnished in places. Patches of colour worn away by age. From his waist hung a sabre, its blade glowing with a pale blue light, the same kind of energy that was produced by their staffs.

Beneath the golden bracers strapped to his forearms, Josh could see that his skin bore lines of hieroglyphic tattoos, proving that at least part of him was human, although the lion-headed helmet obscured any sign of his face.

His inspection complete, he nodded towards the open doors of the transport ship and the guards moved with military efficiency to herd the prisoners on board.

Josh took his cue from the others and followed them inside.

They formed into a line across one end of the compound and moved in slow menacing steps, using their staffs like cattle prods to force the prisoners into the cavernous cargo hold.

Suddenly, a force field snapped into place between them as the last guard stepped onto the ship.

Caitlin was standing close to the family, staring wide-eyed through the shimmering wall at him and he forced himself not to react.

A moment later, the cargo doors sealed shut with an ominous grinding boom and he felt the shudder of the engines as the ship began to lift off from the ground.

Josh's boots automatically magnetised to the floor, keeping him from being thrown around as the ship pitched upwards. The other guards moved into alcoves along each side of the hold and harnesses enveloped them, strapping them into position.

He lifted his feet carefully, making for the nearest empty cell, allowing it to shrink wrap him into the recess the moment he settled into it.

The ship accelerated violently and the prisoners were thrown across the hold like clothes in a washing machine. They tried their best to protect the children and the elderly, but with nothing to hold onto but themselves, people began to get lost under the weight of the sprawling bodies. Josh winced at their screams, made worse with every course correction.

Thankfully, the flight was a short one, and a few minutes of acceleration brought them to the underside of the pyramid. As they levelled out, Josh felt the docking clamps take hold of the craft and the engines cut out.

The safety harnesses released and the guards formed a line once more as the force fields came down. The prisoners picked themselves up from the deck, some having to help those who were barely able to stand. When Josh spotted Caitlin she was carrying one of the younger children.

. . .

The doors opened out onto a large hangar bay filled with similar transport ships, all offloading their cargo.

It was a vast space. The sloping interior walls of the pyramid were constructed from staggered levels of what must have been habitation, each floor lined with tiny windows of light.

Hundreds of other ships were docked in the bay. Small fighters glided in silently above them, while larger warships stood menacingly further back on the deck, their ground crews connecting refuelling lines or reloading weapons.

Josh tried to get close to Caitlin as the prisoners filed down the cargo ramp and into the hangar. He could see that the other groups were being manoeuvred towards a holding compound where thousands of people stood behind steel fences.

'Find Zack,' Caitlin mouthed at him, pointing up towards the hollow peak at the top of the pyramid.

He gave an imperceptible nod and then pushed her forward with the butt of his staff.

'You!' commanded one of the senior guards singling Josh out from the others and handing him a tablet. Josh was surprised that he could understand him. 'Go and advise the warden of the tally.'

Josh nodded and turned towards the figure standing at the gate of the compound. He was a large, fat man wearing a crocodile-headed helmet and holding an intricate looking abacus.

Hiding the tablet, Josh walked straight past the warden and into the heart of the ship.

58

NIRGAL

[Pyramid Ship, Arrakeen]

C aitlin sat amongst the other prisoners, trying not to fall asleep.

The guards hadn't bothered to search her when they came aboard and she still could feel the warmth of the locus, tucked away inside her robes. She toyed with the sphere through the pockets of her cloak, stroking it gently with her fingers, softly singing a lullaby to her baby.

Their captors went about their business, oblivious to the prisoners, who were mostly too traumatised to be any trouble.

Looking at the despair in the faces of the people around her, Caitlin wondered what could have provoked the attack. From what she could see, the Anunnaki forces had crushed the local resistance in a matter of minutes. Their superior firepower and technology appeared to be from a far more advanced civilisation.

The prisoners spoke a strange language, one that combined a complex sign language with speech. Sitting in small groups, they made small hand gestures to each other when the guards weren't looking. It was hard to grasp any meaning, but the family managed to convey that they were scribes or librarians — something to do with writing and books.

She noticed there were very few males left amongst the captured, other than children and old men. Caitlin wondered if they'd all died in the fighting.

Too afraid to take the locus out of her pocket, Caitlin spent the first few hours walking amongst the captives, stopping to admire every baby she came across. It was like a form of torture, each one reminding her of how she missed Zachary. The mothers were kind, perhaps sensing her loss. Some even let her hold their child. Her body ached to be close to him again, and it became increasingly harder to give them back.

She searched the entire compound but he wasn't there.

Josh found himself in a strange kind of decontamination chamber at the end of the hangar bay. A series of sliding airlock doors opened and closed sealing him inside a long tube. Archaic glyphs appeared in front of him in glowing neon, obviously some kind of instructions. Josh ignored them and started walking towards the exit when several rings of light slid along the outside of the tube activating jets of steaming gas as they passed. The gas removed every spec of dirt and blood from his armour which, much to his surprise, began to disassemble itself before being removed by a series of robotic arms.

Leaving him naked by the time he made it to the other end.

Outside the chamber, Josh found an alcove with a white

uniform waiting for him. A sequence of cartouches were stitched onto the breast and a line of coloured jewels studded around the collar. As he put on the uniform, he felt the jewels vibrate against his skin.

Josh touched one of the gems and a map flickered into life on a holographic screen a few inches from his face. The display showed the interior levels of the ship in three dimensions and could be rotated with a flick of his finger.

The symbols on the map were similar to the hieroglyphics on his uniform. The level he was currently on was highlighted and had an image of a sail attached to it, which he took to mean 'Ships'. From the floor plan it was clearly the largest single space in the pyramid.

Scrolling through the levels, Josh noticed a pattern of coloured dots appearing beside them. Some matched the jewels on his uniform. He guessed they were access restrictions, which meant he could only travel half way to the top of the ship.

Caitlin had told him to go up, and Josh assumed that the command centre was going to be at the top, if anyone was going to know where his son was, it would be the captain.

Opening the door to the outer corridor, he faced a steady flow of people, each wearing a similar uniform to his own. Men and women going about their business without rushing, their faces passive and unblinking. It was an orderly procession, marching in time to a silent drum, then remembering the wiring in the dead soldier's skull, Josh realised these were simply machines following orders.

Keeping his face impassive, he noted the location of the nearest elevator and stepped into the crowd, matching their pace exactly.

. . .

Caitlin woke up with a jolt. Somebody was shaking her by the shoulder.

It was the mother of the family, her face lined with worry.

Before Caitlin could ask why, the woman raised her eyes towards the gate. Caitlin followed her gaze and saw the strangers entering. They were dressed differently to the guards, who flanked them on two sides. These were either scientists or medics, scanning the prisoners with handheld devices before handing out food and water.

Everyone was getting slowly to their feet and nervously shuffling towards the gates.

Caitlin kept her head down and moved slowly backwards, letting the others cover her retreat.

There was something about the way the medics were acting that felt wrong, the scanner was clearly a type of diagnostic tool and she wondered if they were searching for signs of infection, or worse, some kind of plague.

The guards began to take some of them away, splitting up families without mercy, marking the ones that passed their test on the back of their hand and feeding them.

Her librarians returned smiling with armfuls of food and showed her the symbol.

It was an Akkadian glyph, one that she'd seen before — it was the symbol for Nirgal, the god of death.

Josh stepped out of the elevator, blinking at the bright sunlight. The concourse was lined with windows along its outer side, an azure strip of blue sky stretching out along the entire side of the ship.

There were fewer crew on this floor, which was as high as his access jewels would allow him to go. He walked away from the lift doors with purpose, as they all did, there was no idling, everyone had somewhere to be.

The problem now was that he was still at least thirty floors from the top.

Glancing out of the windows, he could see the ship had risen above the clouds. He tried not to stare, but the sight of the white expanse stretching out below him was breathtaking. As long as he could remember he'd always dreamed of flying, there was something magical about being lifted out of the world, to get a little closer to the stars. They were too poor when he was a kid, and since he joined the Order he never spent long enough in any era with aeroplanes to try.

Walking further along the corridor, Josh caught the sweet aromas of cooking. His stomach groaned, reminding him that it was hours since he last ate anything. Following the scent he came to a luxurious restaurant, where high ranking officials were being served food while enjoying the view.

Men and women were laying on long couches, helping themselves to dishes of exotic fruits. In the centre of their group sat the Anunnaki, still wearing his lion breastplate, regaling them with stories of his conquests.

They were acting differently to the rest of the crew, laughing and drinking, and Josh realised these were real humans, not robots, who were moving silently between the diners with silver trays.

Slipping into the kitchen, Josh picked up a tray of meats that made his mouth water and followed the other waiters out into the dining area.

The Anunnaki snapped his fingers and Josh brought the tray over to him.

'Like Ra himself, we came down out of the sun, they

didn't stand a chance,' he boasted, scooping up a handful of the meat and cramming it into his mouth like a spoilt child.

The language was vaguely familiar, similar to one the founder gifted to him a long time ago, a derivation of Egyptian Coptic.

Josh bowed and turned to the other guests, who ignored him completely.

'And the prisoners? Will they be usable?' asked one of the women. She was wearing a thin, gauzy dress which left nothing to the imagination, including an impressive cartouche tattoo over her left breast.

The General laughed. 'Who knows what he's looking for any more. Once it was about conquest and empire. Now it's just another world, another cull. It's all just sport to me.'

Josh put down the tray and walked mechanically to the preparation area, trying to hide his emotions.

Caitlin was in danger.

She tried her best to avoid them, but somehow they found her. The Nirgal symbols glowed when their machine was close by, and as they searched the crowd, Caitlin stood out like a rabbit in headlights.

One guard grabbed her roughly by the arm, dragging her to the front of the line.

Another held his scanner towards her and slowly moved it down her body.

There was a subtle change in his expression as he read the data on the display. Whatever he was looking for, Caitlin was obviously carrying it.

He gestured to one of the others and they came over to confirm the readout.

Then everything changed.

Suddenly, she was surrounded by guards and escorted out of the compound, moving so quickly that she would have fallen if they hadn't been holding her arms.

A senior-looking official was waiting at the elevator when they finally let her go.

Taking the monitor from the guard, he inspected the display before nodding to the rest of the squad to release her into his care.

He pushed her into the elevator.

59

ISHTAR

[Xenobiology Department, London. Date: Present Day]

'Where did you find him?' asked Rufius, watching Doctor Shika's team preparing the equipment for the extraction.

'At the court of Uther Pendragon,' said Sabien. 'Pretending to be Merlin.'

Rufius grunted, his eyes widening. 'I always wondered how that myth started.'

Doctor Shika turned from her patient and spoke into the intercom. 'He's ready.'

They walked into the operating theatre. Konstantine was strapped to the table, his beard and long hair had been shaved away, and his head locked into a restrictive metal brace.

'You can't do this to me! I have rights.'

'What about the man you've possessed, doesn't he have rights too?' asked Sabien.

'He was a weak little man, with no ambition. I was the

one that gave him a purpose, a reason to reach for greatness,' he hissed.

'You're a parasite living off the lives of others,' added Rufius.

Konstantine smiled. 'You have no idea what I am, what I have seen. I've witnessed Rome burning, the rise and fall of Pharaohs. You think yours is the only way? We have spent millennia watching the human race walking along the edge of extinction. You're a resilient species, somehow you always manage to survive.'

'No thanks to you.'

'Or you. Your pathetic efforts to save the past are just your own form of control. Who's to say your way is any better than ours?'

'Is that why you're here? To save humanity?'

Konstantine laughed. 'No, although some of my kind were more interested in the lives of their hosts than their mission.'

'And your queen?'

'We were promised this timeline.'

'In return for what?'

An alarm went off on one of the biomonitors. Kaori silenced it and looked at the display. 'His vitals are spiking, it's as if the parasite is losing control.'

Konstantine's body arched in pain. 'Kill me please!' he begged them in a different voice.

'Get it back!' shouted Rufius.

Kaori grabbed a syringe. 'I'll give him a sedative, should knock out his conscious mind,' she said injecting a transparent liquid into his IV.

They waited for the drug to take effect.

When Konstantine's eyes opened again they were dark. 'Seems like he had some spirit after all.'

Rufius continued. 'Who promised you this timeline?'

'You call them the Anunnaki, which isn't such a terrible name. To you they must seem like gods.'

'What do they want?'

'They seek one of their own, the timeless one,' his voice trailed off into a whisper.

Sabien leaned closer. 'Why did they take the baby?'

The monitor pinged again.

'His heart isn't going to take much more of this,' Kaori observed, studying the readouts.

Konstantine's face contorted, the tendons in his neck raising like cables as his body started to convulse once more.

'He's going into cardiac arrest. Stand back.'

She keyed something into the medical control panel as her team stepped away from the table.

'Shocking now.'

'Wait!' said Rufius. 'The charge could kill the parasite.' He went over to the side of the bed and leaned in close to Konstantine's ear.

'If I let her shock you, you die and your host lives.'

'I've lived long enough,' Konstantine replied through clenched teeth.

'Where did you take him?'

He coughed, blood trickling from the side of his mouth. 'You'll never know.'

The heart monitor pinged and its line flattening out as Kaori hit the defibrillator.

Konstantine's body arched again as a succession of shocks racked his body.

Rufius stood back and watched for a pulse, after the shocks the wave returned to zero.

Kaori sighed. 'No output.'

As the final breath left the man's body, his eyes opened once more and they were clear.

'The child is carrying the memory of their destruction.'

'How do we reach him?' asked Sabien turning his ear closer to his mouth.

'The statue of Ishtar,' whispered Konstantine before he died.

60

OLD ZACK

[Pyramid Ship, Arrakeen]

'Leave us,' echoed a voice from somewhere above them. Caitlin's escort bowed reverentially and walked slowly backwards towards the elevator keeping his eyes on the floor.

Searching for the speaker, she tilted her head towards the throne sitting high on a golden pyramid in the peak of the ship.

The roof was made of a transparent material, one that gave a three-hundred and sixty degree view of the night sky. It was full of stars and the figure sitting below it was nothing but a silhouette against it.

'This is not your time. What are you doing here?'

'Who are you?' asked Caitlin, straining her eyes in the semi-darkness.

The man sighed heavily, his tone deepened with regret. 'I've had many names: Nirgal, Shamash, Anu, but you knew me once as Zachary.'

'Zachary?' she repeated under her breath, realising he was speaking in English.

The golden pyramid silently collapsed, each step sliding down into the one below it until the throne rested on the floor. The old man pushed himself slowly to his feet, and leaning heavily on a staff, made his way towards her.

'I have scoured the timelines for you. Thousands upon thousands of worlds looking for your pattern. It has taken most of my life and finally here you are. But this is not your Earth, how did you come to be here?'

As he came into the light, Caitlin caught her breath. The man was wearing an ornate death mask like Tutankhamun, his face covered in burnished gold that moved like skin when he spoke.

He lifted one hand to her cheek and brushed it lightly with a gloved finger. They too were covered in a thin layer of gold.

'How do I know it's really you?' she asked.

The old man let go of his staff, which simply floated in mid air and, placing one hand on either side of his head, lifted the mask away. There was a hissing sound as its seals were broken and he let it drop to the floor.

Caitlin gasped. He was truly ancient, his skin grey and deeply lined. A thin tube was running from behind his neck and into his nose.

He looked like a very old version of Josh.

She felt tears welling up in her eyes.

'I told you I would find you,' he continued. 'Yet you have come to me.'

She shook her head, trying to clear her mind, trying to make sense of what she was seeing. 'You were a child, no more than seven weeks old. How can you have aged so much?'

He tried to smile and failed. His thin lips twisting into a sneer, drawn over bejewelled teeth. 'Time is not constant. The continuums move at different speeds. What seems like weeks to you has been hundreds of years for me.'

There was no denying he could have been her son once, but no parent could ever be younger than their child. Except for her own parents of course, who hardly aged in the ten years they'd spent in the Maelstrom.

His eyes flickered from one side to the other. 'Where is my father?'

She considered lying to him. There was something malevolent in his tone, and the destruction she witnessed on the planet below made her question what he was going to do with the captives.

'He's here. Freeing your prisoners, I expect.'

Zack laughed, it was a hollow sound that made her shiver. 'How noble.'

The old man took hold of the staff once more and pressed one of the symbols carved into its shaft. A gilded block rose out of the floor, each side carved with seven winged effigies. He sat down with a groan and motioned for her to join him.

Caitlin sat down beside him. From the side, she could see his balding skull was covered in fine strands of wire that swept back down beneath his golden collar.

'What happened to you?'

'I'm dying, Mother. The Forsaken have the technology to replace my body, but my mind is degrading. Too many years spent traversing the temporal borders has taken its toll.'

'Searching for us?'

He laughed, thumping his staff into the floor. 'Don't let my generals hear you say that! Maahes would have my head. No, my ships, my armada, have cleansed the timelines of so much impurity, so many redundant branches. Like a gardener pruning a rose so that the plant is stronger, and there are so many plants in my garden.'

'Racial cleansing?'

'I prefer to call it refinement.'

He waved his staff and holographic timelines sprang up around them, each one standing like a tree in an infinite forest.

'You have given me a unique gift, mother. One that allows me to anticipate the defects within their timelines,' he explained, his golden fingers teasing the strands of the nearest continuum apart like roots. 'I see the unstable paths that would lead to their destruction.'

Caitlin stared at the twisting shapes around her. Amazed by the thousands of continuums, each one a vital, living thing, branching and building slowly towards their future.

'Why?' was all she could think of to say.

Zack held up the index finger of his left hand, his head twisting as if he were listening. 'Let's wait for father, he shouldn't be long now.'

Josh found a uniform with more senior permissions in the galley. The jewels sewn into its lapel matching those of the highest level on his map.

No one tried to stop him, the kitchen staff continued with their jobs as if he didn't exist.

As it ascended, the elevator car moved onto the outer side of the pyramid, giving Josh a view of the planet from the edge of space. Beyond the blue curve of the Earth, the sky was filled with stars. There were so many, it reminded him of the time in Crete on their way to Selephin; Caitlin had wondered then if there were other planets, other worlds like theirs. They hadn't known then that there could be other versions of Earth.

He prayed she was safe, part of him wanted to go back and find her, but he knew she would want him to find Zack first, only then would they need to work on an escape plan.

The ship was accelerating away from the planet at great speed, which he guessed was going to make things more complicated; no one had considered the possibility that they would find themselves travelling on a spaceship. Josh wasn't sure if he could move back in time once they left the boundaries of Earth.

The elevator chimed, the display coming to rest on a symbol that gave him pause. It was an Ouroboros: the snake eating its tail.

The doors slid open silently and he walked into a forest of holographic timelines.

'Welcome,' said an old man, from somewhere behind the trees.

'Josh?' came Caitlin's voice, 'It's okay, come in.'

She was sitting on an ornate bench with an old man dressed like a Pharaoh. The man looked unusually familiar.

'Cat?'

'I'm fine,' she said, standing up and walking over to him. 'He says he's Zack,' she whispered.

The man got to his feet, leaning heavily on his staff.

The Pharaoh seemed to be struggling to breathe. 'I wouldn't expect you to believe me.'

Josh studied his face. It was like looking into a mirror, one that showed you a version of your future self. Except for his eyes, those were the same as his mother.

'Who are you?' asked Josh.

The old man tried to laugh, but the sound caught in his throat and turned into a wheezing cough.

'After Enkidu stole me from the circus, I was given to the House of Anubis,' he began, easing himself back down onto the bench.

'Enkidu?'

'A synthetic. An X-541 shapeshifter model. Sent to retrieve the symbiote from your timeline. He told me later that he adopted a number of persona that day: first as Dalton Eckhart, disguised as a harlequin, and secondly as you, mother.'

Caitlin was shaking, Josh could feel the tremors running down her arm.

'Where is he now, this Enkidu?' he asked, wondering how it could know about Dalton.

The old man sighed. 'He perished a long time ago, when I was nine years old, when those fools extracted the last memory of the founder.'

Caitlin caught her breath. 'They took it?'

Before she could answer, he raised his hand to her temple. 'Would you like to see what they did to me Mother?'

Zack's eyes shone and there was a sharp pain behind her eyes and then she felt the memories unravel inside her mind.

She was sitting on a throne in the centre of a grand chamber surrounded by priests, each of the white robed clerics silently kneeling in concentric circles around a central dais.

Caitlin could feel Zack's heart beating against his chest. Her little boy was scared, his hands shaking inside the long sleeves of his golden robes.

She jumped at the sound of a large gong being struck. Somehow she knew it was to summon the gods, who entered from doors equally spaced around the chamber.

Wearing the golden headpieces of the jackal, the hawk, the cat and other Egyptian deities, they processed slowly around the chamber, forming a circle around her and laying their ceremonial staffs at her feet.

She felt Zachary stand as the gods bowed before him.

Another chime of the gong sounded, and everyone looked up to the domed ceiling as a large crystal sphere descended slowly on a silver chain.

Inside the glass swam a spectral creature, its snake-like body seemingly made from an iridescent smoke.

The priests began to chant in a low, solemn mantra as the Chief Prophet entered the chamber and walked between them towards her.

'What's happening?' Josh whispered in her ear.

'I can see some kind of creature,' she replied. 'Like something from the Maelstrom.'

'It is Thoth's essence,' explained Zachary. 'The physical manifestation of the memories recovered from the symbiote.'

Fine tendrils of energy curled out from the crystal sphere and wound sinuously towards her. The chanting changed pitch as the Chief Prophet placed a crown on her head. Words formed in his mind and she felt his lips moving in silent prayer.

When the energy connected with the tines of the crown, the pain lanced through her body, like ice running through her veins, every nerve seemed to catch fire.

Caitlin screamed and Zachary broke the connection. She buried her face in Josh's chest, tears running down her cheeks. 'The pain!' she sobbed. 'He was so young.'

61

OPTIONS

[Wardenclyffe, Long Island. 1906]

'You want to use the Medici Collection?' asked Kaori.

'The Medici Collection,' repeated Rufius, standing directly in front of the tesseract, scratching his beard.

Marcus and Sabien were silent, both watching the slowly rotating cubes.

'Well, it may be our only option, since we can't just stroll back in there,' agreed Kaori. 'It'll be impossible to find them.'

'Needle in a haystack,' agreed Rufius.

'Needle in an infinite number of haystacks. And even if we do find them, they may not be the Josh and Caitlin from our timeline.'

'Not to mention whatever killed the Dreadnoughts,' said Sabien.

They fell silent for a moment, remembering the state of the bodies they dragged out of the portal.

'Do you think you could find them? If we went back in?'
Rufius asked Marcus.

Marcus took a long look at the tesseract and snarled.
'Doesn't smell right to me.'

Feynman took the pipe out of his mouth and got up
from his chair. 'What exactly are you guys trying to do?'

They turned towards him, and he could tell from their
expressions that he'd just asked the wrong question.

'Rescue our friends,' growled Rufius.

Feynman went over to a blackboard and drew a circle in
chalk.

'Assume for a moment that this is our timeline.' He drew
another circle at the other end of the board. 'And that this is
the timeline that your friends have moved into.' He drew
another circle that overlapped the two. 'When the tesseract
collapsed there was a moment when both timelines were
connected. You returned here and they to the alternate.'

'Does that mean you can recreate it?' asked Kaori.

Feynman was deep in thought, absentmindedly tapping
the chalk on the same point in the middle of the third circle
until the chalk snapped.

'Do you still have the frequency data from the Medici
Collection?' he asked, beginning to write a long, complex
equation inside the first circle.

Kaori pulled out her almanac and began to read off a
series of numbers as the physicist scribbled them into the
second circle.

Sabien walked over to the blackboard. 'When I was
trapped in there it was as though something had cancelled
out my abilities. I couldn't weave with anything.'

'Not even the talismans?' asked Rufius.

He shook his head. 'Nothing had a chronology.'

'That's because you were operating at the wrong

frequency,' said Feynman, finishing a third equation and looking around. 'Does anyone know where Tesla is?'

One of his assistants was sent to look for the inventor.

'So, they're going to change our frequency?' asked Sabien, studying the formula while Feynman explained the adjustments to the rest of his team.

'I guess so,' said Rufius, scratching his beard.

Kaori patted Sabien on the shoulder. 'Think of it like a decompression chamber. Divers use them all the time to come up from the deep.'

'And we'll be able to come back again?'

'I bloody hope so,' said Rufius.

Marcus scowled. 'I think I prefer my chances in the Maelstrom any day.'

Tesla returned a few minutes later.

'Okay!' announced Feynman, clapping his hands to get their attention. 'We've got a ton of work to do and you guys are going to get really bored hanging out around here. I suggest you grab something to eat and get some rest.'

62

SECRETS

[Pyramid Ship, Arrakeen]

'The priests told me I would feel differently once the memory was removed. That I would be purified of the nightmares.' Zack's face twisted into a sneer. 'They lied.'

Caitlin picked up his mask from the floor. It felt cold to the touch as she turned it over in her hands.

'What did you do?' she asked.

The old man tapped the side of his head with his golden finger. 'Once I recovered from the cleansing, I found my mental abilities had been enhanced in ways you couldn't imagine. An unforeseen side effect of the process I suppose.' He held up his thumb and forefinger. 'Anubis and his false gods became my puppets. Once I could see their innermost desires, their corrupt little fantasies of power, I learned how to reach inside their tiny minds and adjust them.'

'You made yourself a king?' said Josh.

Zack stood, straightening his back until he was as tall as his father. 'I became an emperor.'

'This isn't who you were supposed to be,' said Caitlin, turning to Josh. 'We have to go back and fix this.'

There was anger in his eyes. 'I am not broken mother.'

She glanced at the wires plugged into the base of his skull. 'They've changed you.'

'I've become something greater,' he snapped. 'Like one of the Seven.'

'The Seven?'

He made a sign with three fingers against his heart. 'The real Anunnaki, the seven children of Anu, they are all long dead. Four of them abandoned their people during the Cataclysm, while three remained to fight the great battle against the army of Tiamat. Our entire civilisation was brought to the brink of extinction, the scarce few who survived called themselves the Foresaken. They sent Enkidu in search of the lost gods and his symbiote found the memories of Thoth within your father.'

'They sent the Aeons to find the founder?'

Zack nodded. 'Thoth was the god of wisdom and magic. He held the key to their secrets.'

'What secrets?'

'The stories tell that during the Cataclysm, while the dragon burned the people, the Seven had a weapon that could have saved their people. The Foresaken archives refer to it as a sword named Urshanabi.'

'The ferryman,' translated Caitlin. 'He carries souls across the river of the dead.'

'Where is the sword?' asked Josh.

'No one knows. The Cataclysm erased a million years of history. All that was left were the stories of the gods. Until they discovered his memories.'

'So why didn't they use them to find it?'

'The data from the symbiote was too corrupted, the

synthetic that hosted his mind was nothing more than a babbling madman. But even if they had restored him, no one can go back and undo what was done — the sword was a symbol of power.'

Zack swiped his hand and all but one of the timelines vanished. The remaining timeline enlarged until it stretched high into the apex of the pyramid.

'This is the pattern of my life.' He pointed to one particular node. 'Here when I was three, my adopted father, Anubis, inducted me into their priest class. I excelled as a novice, my abilities were quickly recognised and they began to prepare me for the role of prophet.'

'Because you could see the future?'

A light seemed to burn in his eyes as he spoke. 'Anubis was an ambitious man. He coveted power, he knew Urshanabi would bring him ultimate sovereignty and he saw me as his best chance of finding it.'

He spread out his fingers and the timeline slid beneath them. 'When I reached twenty, I ascended to the Senate. As part of the induction, I was admitted into the sacred archives, the repository of their oldest relics from before the Cataclysm. But I failed, I couldn't find any trace of it.'

Caitlin looked confused. 'You can't travel into the past?'

He shook his head. 'We can travel across dimensions, but not against the flow of time. When they extracted Thoth's memory, I somehow lost your ability to weave the past.'

A long, low sound echoed from somewhere below them, followed by a series of short repeating bursts.

The old man's eyes cleared. 'We have little time, my fleet

is preparing for the jump to the next timeline. I want you to go back and help me find the sword.'

'How?' asked Josh, 'We haven't been able to weave with anything since we got here.'

He held out a golden hand. 'Do you still have the locus?'

Caitlin nodded her head, taking the glass sphere out of her pocket.

Zachary took it from her. Closing his heavy-lidded eyes he pressed it against his forehead. The ball flared brightly, the moments within it reforming inside the glass.

He handed it back to Caitlin. 'I have downloaded my pattern to it. Go back to my ascendancy, the day I visit the archives.'

'Why can't we just go back to when you were taken?' she asked.

He lifted the mask up to his face, its metal forming over the contours once more. 'Because they would come for me again. The only way to stop them is to find the sword. I'm too old and sick to come with you.' He opened his tunic, showing the machinery embedded in his chest. 'But my younger self will know what to do.'

Caitlin let the timeline unwind from around the sphere, the chronology flowing from it like the petals of a flower opening.

'Do you see it mother?' he whispered.

She smiled, her eyes filling with tears.

'Then go.'

63

FREQUENCY

[Medici Collection]

'We need to return him to his own time,' Eddington whispered to Rufius while they watched Feynman tinkering with the modulation suit. 'The longer he stays here the more engrams I will have to redact. His memory will have a significant hole.'

'Just leave him in a bar in New Mexico, he'll blame the mescal,' replied Rufius taking a quick drink from his hip flask and then raising his voice. 'We've been here for hours. Do you think there's any chance we could get on with it?'

Feynman nodded and pocketed his screwdriver. 'All good here, just making sure we don't send you into oblivion.'

Rufius laughed. 'Don't worry lad. I've already been there.'

Tesla and Feynman helped Rufius into the device, which appeared to be a cross between a deep-sea diving suit and an orrery.

'Feels a little tight around the gusset,' complained Rufius as they tightened the bindings.

'We've made it as compact as we can,' said Feynman. 'Be grateful. Our first attempt was the size of a Lincoln Continental.'

'This suit can literally walk through walls,' boasted Tesla, flicking a series of switches on the belt.

A low hum emitted from the circular rings of metal attached to the back of his suit and blue arcs of flux rippled around his body.

Rufius's hair stood up on end.

'Feels a bit weird,' he said, turning around to Eddington, who was doing his best to hide his amusement. 'What?'

The professor shook his head. 'Nothing.'

'Can we proceed?' said Rufius, walking awkwardly towards the doors.

Kaori's team opened them, and he ambled into the empty room. Taking a deep breath, he turned towards them and waved farewell.

The moment the doors shut, Rufius felt the shift begin. The sound of the machine on his back changed pitch, and stronger waves of static rippled over the suit. Like a series of mild electric shocks, he felt the fields pulse through his body.

The room was no longer empty, and just as Sabien described, all of the talismans were back in their cabinets.

Feeling a little dizzy, he walked clumsily over to the statue of Ishtar, a tiny female figurine sitting on a throne like a queen, and took it out of its case.

The timeline unfurled between his tingling fingers. Events and images of an alternate history unravelling in his mind. The Anunnaki civilisation was far older than their own, more ancient than anything he'd ever experienced, and Konstantine was right to call them gods.

They were the powerful, omnipotent beings whose knowledge raised primitive civilisations out of their primeval wilderness.

Rufius could see exactly where they intervened in the early development of his continuum: changing the lives of the nomad hunter-gatherers and teaching them how to farm, how to build — giving them the knowledge that would lead to eventual enlightenment.

But they were not immune from threats of their own. As they grew more powerful, they too were prey to other forces. Something terrible awoke from the Maelstrom, attracted by their advanced technology, their scientists failing to predict the demonic horde that overwhelmed them.

One of their leaders escaped, taking the remnants of his civilisation with him. These were the talismans. What was stored in this room was all that remained of their highly advanced culture.

A dial on his forearm flashed amber, and a bell chimed to remind him that the oxygen levels were becoming dangerously low — his time was nearly up. He turned to the door, placing the figurine inside a pocket on the front of his suit.

'This had better bloody work,' he whispered to himself as he pushed on the panels of the door.

The daylight was intense. Rufius blinked, shading his eyes as he walked out into the courtyard of the temple.

'Never trust an engineer,' he said to himself as a group of priests gathered around him. He looked back to where the doors should have been, only to find a blank stone wall.

64

AARU

[Aaru]

'Are you okay?' asked Josh, stroking the hair away from her face.

Caitlin looked exhausted and there were bruises on her face where she'd been thrown around in the transporter.

'I've felt worse,' she said, trying to smile and failing.

'Was it really him?'

'I don't know. I think so, but he was a monster.'

Josh sighed, shaking his head. 'It wasn't our Zack, they changed him.'

'He was killing people, ending entire civilisations.'

Josh stared at Solomon's Ring, rubbing the cool band with his thumb. 'It's just one future, he's given us the chance to change it.'

Caitlin took his hand. 'I want my baby. Can't we just go back there?'

'You heard what he said, they wouldn't give up until they found him.'

'But who are they if they're not the real Anunnaki?'

'I guess that's what we're here to find out,' said Josh, looking around the room. The walls were decorated with images of different gods.

'Where are we?' he asked, staring at the frescoes.

'These are all from ancient religions,' explained Caitlin, examining the hieroglyphics painted above their heads. Carved Egyptian deities stood alongside Sumerian and Hindu gods, Akkadian beside unknown Chthonic demons.

'That's Amun-Ra, Horus, Osiris and Thoth.' She turned to the opposite wall. 'Anu, Enlil, Ishtar and Enki.'

Josh's eye was drawn to the tentacle-headed creatures surrounding a dragon-headed serpent. 'These look more like something from the Maelstrom.'

'Seems we share some common heritage with this time-line. They had the same gods as us once.'

'Or they were the gods.'

Laid out in the centre of the room were a pair of woven reed mats. Each had a book and quill placed at one end.

Caitlin knelt down. 'I think this is some kind of class-room,' she said, beginning to read.

'This was *his* classroom, he said they were trying to make him a priest.'

A bell chimed somewhere outside and Josh went to the window. Lowering his voice as he peered through the linen curtain. 'Looks like we're in some kind of palace. There's a courtyard down there, and a bunch of bald guys in robes.'

'The text is written in cuneiform, it reads like a history, but it's nothing like any story I've ever heard. These are written as if the gods were real people, it's like their family tree.'

Josh wasn't really paying attention. 'I think they're monks.'

'Priests,' Caitlin corrected him. 'This even talks about

the Chief Prophet of Amun. He was basically the kingmaker, his power was second only to the Pharaoh in Egypt.'

The bell chimed once more. 'I think they're being called to prayer.'

It was her turn to ignore him. 'We need to get out of these clothes.' She got up from the mat. 'This is a sacred place, a temple. There'll be guards — ones that don't like strangers.'

Josh stepped away from the window and went over to the door. 'It's clear.'

The passageway was tiled with white marble, and golden columns lined either side, each one carved with the likeness of a different deity.

A gentle wind stirred the rose petals that were scattered across the floor. The air smelled fresh and cool, as if they were close to the sea.

They walked in bare feet, hiding in the shadows at any sound.

Caitlin found an alcove with robes neatly folded on wooden shelves. They quickly changed and stowed their old clothes into one of the large ceramic urns the priests used for oil.

Reaching the entrance to the temple, Caitlin pulled her cowl over her head and motioned to Josh to do the same. The guards on both sides paid them no attention as they walked slowly out into the sunshine.

A wide river swept down the green valley before them. Across the water, on its far bank, stood a vast walled city, its towers glinting in the midday sun. At its centre rose a large dome-shaped citadel, its golden spires topped with purple and blue pennants.

Josh followed Caitlin down the steps of the temple towards the bridge that spanned the river. They joined a procession of revellers making their way towards the city, dressed in colourful silks carrying blue irises and lotus flowers. There was a sense of carnival among them, as if it were a special day.

'Is this still Earth?' asked Josh, accepting a necklace of petals from a passer-by.

Caitlin stared up at the blue sky. 'No way to know for sure until the stars come out, but they've only got one sun so we're not on Tatooine.'

The bridge was nearly half a mile long, arching high over the river to allow sailing barges to move freely below. There was no sign of the fighter craft, nor the floating pyramids, it was as if they had stepped back thousands of years into the past.

The crowds swelled as they approached the city gates and it was only then as they slowed that Josh noticed everyone around him was wearing a jewel on their left temple.

Caitlin was moving further ahead, and he quickened his pace to catch her up.

'Did you see the jewels?' he whispered in her ear.

She nodded, keeping her head bowed beneath her cowl. 'They glow when others of the same colour are near. I've been watching them for a while now. I think they might be some kind of communication device.'

The guards at the gates wore similar armour and headgear as before, jackal and falcon, their eyes glowing amber. They stood idle, their staffs powered down, watching the revellers enter the city in their thousands.

Caitlin took his hand and moved into the centre of the line of people filing through the tall golden archway.

Pennants flapped in the wind, strung between the tall buildings over the circular courtyard. The crowds divided, taking different paths into the narrow passages that led into the city. As they parted Josh found himself face to face with a jackal-headed guard.

The man raised his hand as if commanding them to stop, but something glowed in the palm of his hand and a beam of light flashed, blinding them and they both fell to the floor unconscious.

65

ENKIDU

[Aaru]

'You are not of this timeline,' said the man, his jackal headpiece transforming into that of a more benign, androgynous human face.

Caitlin and Josh were tied to chairs in a stark cell with no windows. Josh was only half-conscious so Caitlin answered for them. 'We're searching for our son, he was brought here by one of your kind.'

The man was dressed in the dark kimono of a samurai. His inscrutable expression showed no hint of surprise or emotion, though his eyes glowed with a faint blue light as if he was scanning them.

'My kind?'

'You're some kind of robot,' she replied, trying to loosen the bindings on her wrists and failing.

'We prefer the term synthetic. I am a neo-biological entity, with a neural cortex similar to your own, albeit cybernetic. I was designed for reconnaissance, to blend into my surroundings.'

'How do you know we're not from this timeline?' asked Josh, his tongue still numb from the stunning.

'Your pattern is unfamiliar, it is resonating at an unusual frequency, and,' he paused, producing the locus, 'we have nothing that resembles this. What does it do?'

'Give that back!' screamed Caitlin.

The synthetic studied the glowing patterns within it. 'Interesting use of quantum entanglement. Your civilisation was obviously more advanced than I thought, you certainly hadn't mastered quantum dynamics when I left.'

Caitlin gasped. 'You're Enkidu?'

The synthetic's expression softened and his eyes dimmed. 'I haven't heard that name in some time.'

'Where is our son?' snapped Josh.

'I have watched over your child for almost twenty years, he has become quite precious to me,' said Enkidu, his voice full of emotion.

Caitlin frowned. 'But you're a synthetic? A machine?'

'I am still a sentient being.'

'Where is he?' demanded Josh.

'At the House of Anubis being prepared for his ascendancy to the Senate. It is a proud day for all concerned, your son will become a member of the Upper House. He is destined for great things, Anubis believes he will heal the rift that has grown between the Foresaken.'

'We need to see him.'

The synthetic shook his head. 'That is impossible. He is heavily guarded, no one can see him before his investiture, it is part of the rite of passage.'

Caitlin was close to tears. 'I want to see him!'

Josh rocked on his chair, trying to free his hands. 'Listen, we were sent back from the future to help him find a sword

— Urshanabi. Zack believes this is a critical turning point in his timeline — we've seen what he becomes.'

'A God Emperor,' added Caitlin. 'A destroyer of worlds.'

The synthetic's expression went blank. His eyes rapidly flickering from one side to the other as he processed the information.

'This was not foreseen,' he said after a few minutes. 'It cannot be.'

'Why would we lie?' said Caitlin. 'Why would we come here instead of going back to the day you took him?'

He tapped something on his arm and their bonds loosened. 'Come with me.'

66

EMPIRE

[Aaru]

Enkidu took them to a sub-basement deep below the city.

There were hundreds of synthetics working silently inside the long, tomb-like chamber, each one an exact replica.

'We have been trying to predict what he would become,' explained Enkidu as they entered.

'What Zack would become?'

The synthetic nodded. 'Ever since I brought him here, something has disturbed me about his influence on our world.'

'Because he's a seer?'

'He is so much more than that.'

The synthetic took them to one of the workstations. 'From what we have learned from the symbiotes, we know that your Order was capable of predicting the future to some degree. We developed something similar to your algorithm — the Infinity Engine.'

He tapped on a screen and a holographic projection sprang into life before them. It was a complex network of lines weaving back and forth with no sense of linearity.

'I think yours may be broken,' said Josh, walking into the lattice of light.

'Ah no,' said Enkidu. 'Ours includes the higher dimensions. Let me simplify it for you.'

He keyed a sequence into the screen and the ribbons of energy reduced into a single branching continuum.

'We have worked in secret for the last twenty years. Trying to calculate the possibilities created by his influence on our timeline.'

'But Zack knew what you were doing?' asked Caitlin.

The synthetic shook his head. 'Knowing would change the outcome. Part of our problem was understanding what limiting effect Thoth's memory was having on his development. It was only now we recovered a complete sample of his timeline that we're able to fully understand what he was capable of.'

'What do you mean?'

'Your locus,' replied Enkidu, producing the glowing sphere, 'contains a complete record of his life, his pattern.'

Caitlin took the locus from him, her eyes widening at the new structures within it. 'His entire life?'

The synthetic moved the focus of the model to a point further along its axis. 'How old would you say he was?'

'He looked over a hundred, but he said he was much older.'

'According to this chronology, his life spans nearly three hundred years. He built an empire that conquered over a thousand continuums.'

Singling out one specific section of the timeline, Enkidu

expanded key nodes along its path. Their model was far more detailed than the one Josh was used to, they had taken the original and improved it.

'The empire is a scenario we all hoped would never come to pass. There are factions within the Upper House that advocate a more aggressive approach to the management of the continuums, ones who favour conquest. The legacy of the Cataclysm runs deep in our society, many of the elder houses cling to the threat of another attack like a dog gnawing at a bone. Your son has the potential to give them what they most desire; his abilities would ensure they won every battle. Even without Urshanabi, he would become their ultimate weapon.'

'And what if he found the sword?'

Enkidu typed something into the console and the scenario changed, the lines recombining to produce a singular cord that simply ended as if hitting a wall.

'We cannot predict beyond the point at which he discovers it.'

Caitlin walked around the projection, studying the lines that led up to its abrupt end. 'He told us that Anubis wanted to rule over the Senate, to use the sword to ensure his supremacy. That Zack was expected to find it during his initiation, but he failed.'

'After the Cataclysm, the Foresaken were forced to create their own government. The survivors nominated leaders who would become the founders of the Great Houses. Over millennia they have assumed the rituals and rites of the old gods, their descendants sit in the Upper House of the Senate. The Lower House is made up of the commoners and the more scientifically minded. Between them they rule Aaru. As the adopted son of Anubis, Zachary will ascend to the Upper House, it is a great honour, he will be allowed into the Foresaken archives.'

'Which contain the oldest records you possess?'

The synthetic nodded, shutting down the projection. 'Indeed. There is something else I should probably mention. As part of the ceremony your son is to marry the eldest daughter of Anubis.'

'He's getting married?' shrieked Caitlin.

'To Kebechet, yes.'

She struggled to find the right words, her mouth just opening and closing before finally finding her voice. 'How old is she?'

'Kebechet is thirteen years older than Zack.'

'He's marrying an older woman? What does she look like?'

Enkidu's face changed, his skin darkening as his features transformed into a beautiful woman.

'Wow,' said Josh.

Caitlin punched him in the arm. 'That's not the point. Does he love her? Or is this just some political arrangement?'

'They have known each since he was a baby. She has cared for him for most of his life.'

'So he's marrying his babysitter?'

'Sister,' the synthetic corrected her, his face returning to its normal state.

'Any other surprises I need to know about?' she asked sarcastically.

'Well yes, there has been an unexpected development.'

'What?'

'Ten days ago, one of your kind appeared in the Square of Ishtar. A large man with a red beard.'

'Rufius?'

'I do not know his name, but he was taken before the court of Ra who have sentenced him to death.'

Josh swallowed hard. 'Where is he now?'

'Awaiting execution. In the Temple of the Sun.'

67

COBRA

[Aaru]

There was a brief moment, just before the first novice screamed, when Rufius wondered if he might be able to talk his way out of it. The language that streamed out of the frightened child's mouth was reminiscent of an archaic form of Coptic. His memory of ancient Egyptian was a tad rusty, but he caught snippets of phrases that sounded a lot like 'outsider' or 'demon.'

It was hard to be sure.

The rest of the group picked up on the young man's hysteria and soon the whole group overcame their initial shock and escalated into sheer panic.

'Calm down,' he said, waving his hands to show that he meant no harm. They all stepped back and covered their mouths with their scarves as if he were some kind of plague-ridden leper.

'I mean you no harm,' said Rufius in his best Coptic, taking out the figurine and placing it on the floor as a gift.

They stared at him wide-eyed while he struggled out of the cumbersome suit. The commotion was attracting the attention of others, and soon there was quite a crowd gathered around him.

After a few sweaty minutes of wrangling with straps and buckles, Rufius finally managed to step out of it. The crowd seemed to relax, realising that he was, in fact, human.

A tall man, wearing a golden helmet styled on a jackal's head, walked through the group of white robed onlookers. He carried himself like a warrior, holding a long staff with a strangely glowing end that reminded Rufius of a cattle-prod.

'Now hold on fella,' he said, raising his hands. 'No need to get all excited now is there?'

The first shock put Rufius on his knees.

The next one turned out the lights.

'I know you're awake,' said a man's voice from somewhere behind him.

Rufius had been conscious for nearly five minutes, pretending to sleep while he worked out where he was and who else was in the room. His arms were tightly bound to the chair, as were his legs. There was something around his neck, it was warm and smelled of exotic oils.

He opened his eyes slowly, blinking against the light, and found himself looking at a slightly younger version of Josh.

Except it wasn't quite him, the dark-lined eyes were green, like Caitlin's. The man was dressed like a pharaoh, in a white tunic with a golden collar studded with emeralds and amethysts. His head was shaved and his bare arms were covered in heiroglyphs.

'Hello Rufius,' said the pharaoh, smiling, 'how nice to see you again.'

It took a moment for Rufius to realise that the man was speaking in English.

'Zack is that you?' he croaked, his throat dry.

The walls of the room were decorated with effigies of gods, the flat pictographic style reminding him of KV62, the burial chamber of Tutankhamun. Although as his eyes adjusted, he could see that the deities on these walls were not all Egyptian.

Suddenly, the thing around his neck shifted, and Rufius realised there was a snake wrapped around his shoulders.

'What the devil?'

Zack lifted a finger to silence him and continued in a hushed whisper. 'It's a King Cobra. There's nothing to worry about, his mind is under my control. While you cooperate there's no need to be concerned.'

Rufius calmed his breathing and tried not to focus on the deadly reptile that was coiled around his neck.

'I'm intrigued to know how you got here,' continued Zack, stroking the side of Rufius's head with a ringed finger.

His eyes narrowed slightly as he sent a subtle mental probe into Rufius's mind, the kind that even a master redactor like Kelly would have been hard-pushed to achieve.

Show me.

His voice echoed through Rufius's head.

There was nothing Rufius could do, in seconds Zack had located the memory of the modulation suit and after that the Ishtar figurine in the Medici collection.

How very inventive, but why go to all that trouble? Surely not for a child?

His mind delved deeper into the events leading up to his departure.

'You were trying to locate my parents?' said Zack, retreating out of his mind. 'Are they here too?' A flash of confusion flickered across his face. 'I didn't see that.'

'I bloody hope so,' said Rufius, relieved to have the man out of his head.

The snake tightened is coils around Rufius's neck as Zack's eyes darkened.

'This is the wrong time. They come later.'

Rufius could feel his throat constricting, the head of the cobra was close, its tongue flickering near his ear.

'They just want their baby back, you were stolen away before they even really knew you.'

'And you let them take me,' hissed Zachary, the coils growing tighter still.

Rufius hung his head, tears stinging his eyes. 'And don't you think there's not a day goes by that I wish I hadn't? They trusted me with you and I failed them, but I swear that whoever took you was the spitting image of your mother.'

Zack's lips twisted into a wicked smile and the snake relaxed its grip. 'It wasn't your fault old man. The synthetic who took me was capable of emulating any human form. He would have looked exactly like her.'

'Why did they take you?'

Zack tapped his temple. 'I had something they wanted, and as it turned out, they gave me something greater in return.'

'You're not a prisoner?'

He laughed and stood back, showing off his jewels. 'No, the opposite in fact: they're about to initiate me into the Upper House of the Senate. Which is why I can't have oafs like you turning up and spoiling a perfectly good plan.'

'I came to rescue you.'

'Well, you shouldn't have bothered.'

The snake unwrapped itself and slithered down Rufius's body and onto Zack's forearm where it turned back into a golden amulet.

'Amazing how the mind can play tricks don't you think? Guards!'

68

LU'KURRA

[Aaru]

The temple stood on the far bank of the river. Crossing the Bridge of Enki, the synthetic explained how it had become a divide between the religious and secular districts of the city. Josh noticed how the weathered statues lining either side of the bridge began with academics and ended with a pantheon of gods.

Approaching the other side, Caitlin recognised the two towering stone sculptures standing each side of the temple entrance as Sumerian gods, Ishtar and Utu. Their carved faces looking down benevolently on the visitors as they stepped down from the bridge into the Avenue of Light.

Enkidu paused, bowing his head as a patrol of guards passed by, his features suddenly resembling an old priest.

'Anubis is petitioning the Upper House for your son to be granted a new title,' he continued once they were out of earshot. 'He believes that he is the incarnation of Amun-Ra and that his ascension will bring a new era of spiritual alignment to Aaru. Obviously this is a false memory implanted by Zachary, a survival tactic that your father taught him, perhaps?'

Caitlin remembered the ethereal creature trapped inside the crystal sphere. 'Where's Thoth now?'

The synthetic motioned for them to follow him into an avenue of stone obelisks. He kept his voice low. 'The resurrection did not go as planned. Although the engrams extracted from Zachary completed the pattern, the resurrection of the timeless one failed. The Chief Prophet was executed because of it, as were many of my kind.'

Caitlin scoffed. 'They tried to bring him back to life?'

'His physical body is a construct, a Shabti like mine, but his consciousness is entirely human and it is broken. The integrity of his mental state is beyond restoration.'

Josh frowned. 'Shabti?'

The synthetic raised his hands to the seven statues surrounding them. 'A vessel of the gods.'

Josh laughed. 'So you went to all that trouble to end up with a deranged god?'

Enkidu eyes flashed with pain that was quickly hidden. 'They blamed us. Saying that our technology had corrupted him, we became the object of their hate.'

'Couldn't Zack help him?' asked Caitlin.

'He cannot influence a synthetic mind. Our neural cortex does not bend to his will.'

Reaching the entrance to the Temple of the Sun, they stepped aside for a large group of acolytes who were being led out by their priest. The novices were chattering excitedly like a bunch of school children.

'I'm afraid they have made a spectacle of your friend.'

As its name suggested, the inner courtyard of the temple

was bathed in sunlight, its intricately carved walls rising up to an open sky.

In the centre of the space was a stone pillar, a stele covered in hieroglyphics. Attached to it by heavy iron chains was Rufius, roaring like a wild bear at the spectators who gathered around him.

Wearing nothing but a loin cloth, his bare skin bore the red welts of a whipping. Rufius rattled the chains at the priests, raving at them like a mad man.

'He's quite an obstinate character,' added the synthetic.

'You can say that again,' agreed Josh.

'COME ON THEN! I'LL TAKE THE LOT OF YOU!' bellowed Rufius in English, like a drunk outside a pub, oblivious to the fact that the onlookers had no idea what he was saying.

His eyes were wild and there was spittle in his beard. Someone had painted runes onto his chest. Caitlin translated them. 'Death to the Lu'kurra.'

'It's our word for someone not of this realm — an enemy.'

'Ah, the wanderers return!' greeted Rufius, recognising Josh and Caitlin. 'Would you be so kind as to get me out of these chains?' He held up his hands, his wrists red raw around the manacles.

Josh scanned the crowd, spotting the guards standing at both ends of the atrium. They wore the same armoured headpieces as the soldiers they'd met on Arrakeen.

'It would be better if you shouted at us. So not as to draw attention,' Caitlin suggested.

'CAN YOU GET ME OUT OF THESE BLOODY CHAINS?'

Caitlin pretended to be terrified and hid behind Josh.

'There are too many guards,' she whispered.

'I CAN TAKE THEM.'

'No, we'll need a diversion.'

Josh turned to Enkidu. 'Can you create a distraction?'

The synthetic nodded and subtle transformations began to change the shape of his face. He walked away into the crowd.

'Are you okay?' asked Caitlin, over Josh's shoulder.

'I'VE BEEN WORSE,' shouted Rufius. 'GLAD TO SEE YOU TWO ARE ALL RIGHT!'

Someone screamed behind them and the crowd parted, a priest stumbled through the atrium holding his belly, blood gushing from between his fingers.

The temple guards left their posts, running over to assist the man who collapsed on the floor.

In the chaos, Enkidu appeared out of the crowd. He had assumed the shape of one of the guards, his fingers still transforming back from a long blade.

'Take him,' he whispered, breaking the chains with his bare hands.

Josh took off his cloak and wrapped it around Rufius's shoulders.

'Where are we going to go?' asked Caitlin, following the synthetic into the temple.

'Somewhere they won't expect.'

69

TEMPLE

[Temple of the Sun, Aaru]

'I've got some bad news for you,' said Rufius, sitting down heavily on the stone steps of the inner sanctum. 'Zack's in his twenties and his abilities seem to include mind control.' He waggled his fingers next to his head.

'We know,' muttered Caitlin. 'We've met an older version.'

Enkidu brought Rufius some water from one of the fountains. He drank deeply before looking up to study the synthetic.

'Who are you?' asked Rufius, wiping his beard with the back of his hand.

'They call me Enkidu,' the synthetic said with a bow. 'I am the one who took Zachary.'

'But he's helping us now,' explained Caitlin, as Rufius clenched his fists.

'How on earth did you get here?' asked Josh, changing the subject.

Rufius glared at the synthetic while he explained how

Sabien found Konstantine in the court of Uther Pendragon, about the frequency suit and the statue of Ishtar.

'Tesla and Feynman made serious progress after Einstein went back to Switzerland. The miniaturisation of the tesseract was quite an achievement.' He rubbed the bruises on his arms. 'Although, I'm not sure they can use that route again.'

'Zack didn't know you were coming,' said Caitlin. 'So he can't foresee interventions from outside of this continuum.'

Rufius nodded. 'The boy has got some talent that's for sure, but he was surprised to hear that you might be here, said something about it being too early. I get the feeling without you to keep him on the straight and narrow, he's beginning to stray to the dark side.'

Caitlin sat down beside him and told Rufius about the older Zack, the battle on Arrakeen, about the terrible ordeal he had suffered when they extracted the founder's memory.

'So are you going to help him find this sword?' Rufius asked when she finished.

Josh put his arm around her. 'He thinks it's the only way.'

'Why not just go back and take him the moment he got here?' asked Rufius.

Caitlin turned to the synthetic. 'What happened to Zack after you brought him back?'

'Anubis took him from me. He adopted the child, made him one of his family. In retrospect he was probably falling under your son's influence. He spent the next nine years under the protection of one of the oldest families in our society.'

'And if we took him then, would they send someone else back to find him?'

Enkidu nodded. 'Once they assimilated the data from

the symbiote they would realise that a portion of it was missing and send out another Shabti.'

'Were you looking for him all that time?' asked Josh.

Enkidu nodded his head. 'For thousands of years. The symbiotes have been seeded on hundreds of timelines in search of the missing gods. We have learned much from your culture.'

'You were spying on us?' exclaimed Rufius.

'We were seeking knowledge,' corrected the synthetic. 'Following the trails of our lost gods into the old worlds.'

Rufius held up the manacles. 'Old worlds or slave worlds?'

Enkidu held his palms over the metal bracelets and the metal bolts melted away. 'Worlds that have been touched by the Seven.'

Caitlin sighed. 'This isn't helping,' she said, tearing strips from her skirt and wrapping them around Rufius's wrists. 'We need to find this sword.'

'We need the founder,' said Josh, turning to the synthetic. 'Can you get us in to see him?'

Enkidu looked confused by the request. 'He's not operating rationally. I doubt he will be able to help you.'

'I think I know how to reach him.'

Beneath the inner temple, the priests had recreated Duat, the realm of the dead. It was a labyrinth of passages whose walls were adorned with images of Osiris, Lord of the Underworld and the crocodile-headed Ammit, Eater of Hearts.

'This will take us beneath the river and into the city,' explained the synthetic, his palm glowing like a torch.

'It appears we owe a lot of our ancient history to these people,' observed Rufius, running his hand over the frescos.

'Or they borrowed from us,' said Caitlin, lowering her voice. 'He said they were collecting knowledge.'

'I don't think so,' whispered Josh. 'They're much older, some of the memories the founder shared with me go back tens of thousands of years.'

'Do you really believe the founder is a god?' asked Caitlin.

Josh shrugged. 'I don't know, but whatever he is, they've managed to resurrect him, so that gives us a chance to find out.'

Rufius slowed his pace. 'Do you trust him?' he said, nodding to the glowing figure as it moved further ahead.

'I don't think we have a choice. He seems to be genuinely sorry for what he's done to us.'

Rufius grunted. 'He's a machine. They don't have emotions.'

'Not in our world, maybe,' said Caitlin, 'but it's different here. He watched over Zack for years, even after they destroyed the rest of his kind.'

Rufius didn't look convinced.

They surfaced in an alley in the lower quarter of the city. The streets were narrow and full of people and stalls. For a moment it felt as if they had walked into a bazaar in Cairo or Marrakech, the smell of cooking and exotic spices were so familiar. The small golden craft that flew overhead reminded them otherwise.

'Stay here,' ordered Enkidu, his skin darkening until it was the colour of most of the locals.

He negotiated with a nearby trader for three sets of clothes and brought them back into the alleyway.

'You need to wear these, if we are not to raise suspicion.'

Rufius held up the garish silk robe and grimaced as if being asked to wear one of his mother's old dresses.

'This is the fashion,' explained the synthetic, the colour signifies your status as merchant class and I will be your servant as is the custom on market days.'

'Any chance of a weapon?' asked Rufius, struggling to get the kaftan over his head.

'No one carries weapons inside the walls of the city.'

'Apart from the guards,' corrected Rufius.

'The guards are synthetics. The Foresaken are forbidden to carry weapons.'

'Interesting.'

Out in the sun, they began to appreciate their new clothing. The fabric was cool, reflecting the harsh rays and Rufius quickly lost his scowl.

'Where are we?' asked Caitlin, shading her eyes to study the sky.

'This is the city of Aaru.'

'No, I meant what continent? You lived long enough in our timeline to know the nearest comparable city to this.'

The synthetic tilted his head slightly. 'That would be Quito in Ecuador.'

'We're in South America?' said Rufius, slapping his neck and examining the mosquito on his palm. 'Explains the flies.'

'The Forsaken settled near the equator because the northern hemisphere is still mostly under ice.'

'You're in an ice age? What year is this?'

Enkidu turned into a side street and they followed. 'We are six hundred million years behind your timeline.'

Caitlin glanced at Josh, who simply shrugged.

They walked through the back streets, trying not to act like tourists. It was a beautiful place, with architectural influences from many different worlds. To Josh it seemed like a hundred different cities merged into one.

All streets seemed to be leading towards the Citadel, which was a vast structure, dominating the central square. Its white spires towered over the city, and the golden dome shimmered in the sun. Like St. Peter's in Rome, statues of gods looked down on the people from the colonnades that lined the plaza.

'Welcome to the Court of the Four Winds,' said Enkidu.

There was a sense of carnival about the place, performers danced through the crowds dressed in monstrous costumes. In the centre of the square a Chinese dragon was being paraded in a mock battle with a group of men dressed in costumes of Anunnaki. The long silk body of the dragon was filled with children, all squealing as they ran around the square.

Pedlars and hawkers wandered among the crowds, calling out to passers-by, trying to sell food or trinkets. One stepped up to Caitlin and presented an array of jewelled bracelets on both his wrists.

She smiled politely and walked on, but the man was not so easily rejected and kept pace with her while jabbering on in a language she couldn't understand.

The synthetic stepped between them and politely explained to the merchant that they weren't interested, but the expression on the man's face said that he wasn't about to be dissuaded by a servant.

He drew something out from inside his coat, the blade

glinting in the sun for a second before it carved an arc across the air in front of them.

Enkidu's hand was a blur as it took the knife out of his hand, snapping the wrist in the process. The hawker fell to his knees, holding his broken arm and begging for mercy.

The synthetic handed the blade to Rufius, who gratefully accepted it and hid it inside one of his sleeves.

Moving away from the hawker, Josh spotted guards heading in his direction, but by the time they arrived, the man had disappeared into the crowd.

'So crime still exists in this utopia then?' asked Rufius, who seemed to have cheered up immensely.

'It is an inevitable consequence of inequality,' replied the synthetic. 'Where there is a class system, there will be those that seek to better themselves by any means.'

Rufius seemed impressed. 'A philosopher no less.'

70

THOTH

[Aaru]

The observatory was an old grey building on the east side of the square. It had one large gothic tower topped with a brass dome partially open to the sky.

'They're keeping him in the observatory,' said Enkidu, taking them past the building and into a side alley.

'Why?' said Rufius, looking up at the tower.

'The stars seem to be the only thing that calm him,' explained the synthetic, his skin paling back to its usual colour.

Josh looked out into the square, the guards were questioning witnesses, who were pointing in their general direction. 'So, how do you plan to get us in?'

The synthetic's face melted like hot wax. He became older, his hairline receding and greying to white.

He pointed towards a small door recessed into the wall. 'I cannot, but Guruname, Head of the City Guard will not be challenged.'

. . .

The tower was built in ten stories, each one filled with shelves of books and devices from a hundred different timelines.

Enkidu spoke briefly to one of the prison guards. He took his orders without question, and then accompanied them with a serving girl carrying a tray of food.

Josh could hear Rufius's stomach complaining, it sounded like a bear trapped in a well.

'I thought synthetics didn't eat?' Caitlin asked Enkidu.

'They need sustenance just like any biological organism. Although we don't go to the trouble of preparing such lavish dishes. A blended nutrient-rich soup is enough.'

'Sounds delightful,' quipped Rufius, 'remind me not to come to yours for dinner.'

Reaching the doors of the observatory, the guard bowed briefly, making a sign with his right hand before opening them. Placing her tray on a table, the servant did the same.

Caitlin noticed that neither of them would meet Guruname's gaze as they left. The synthetic had obviously chosen wisely, someone whose orders would not be questioned. She wondered what the man could have done to earn such a reputation.

'They still believe Thoth's a god?' she asked, once they were alone. 'Even though he's mad?'

'There are many who still believe. They were raised on the sagas of the old gods. Stories told since the dark times after the Cataclysm. To have one return, no matter how broken, restores their faith.'

Enkidu picked up the tray and they followed him into the observatory.

. . .

It was a vast room. The metal dome was half open, exposing them to a hundred-and-eighty degree panorama of skyline.

'Wow,' exclaimed Rufius. 'That's one hell of a view.'

The synthetic was sitting in a wooden cradle suspended from the thin end of a giant telescope. His head was hairless, but his face was similar to Enkidu's. He was wearing a long white robe with a silver chain around his neck.

As they approached, he turned away from the eyepiece.

'Is it that time already? Venus hasn't risen.'

'Apologies my lord,' said Enkidu, bowing deeply. 'I bring travellers to you.'

With a disgruntled sigh he lifted himself out of the cradle and walked over to them. His eyes narrowed as he studied each one of them in turn. There was no obvious sign of recognition at first, then slowly something changed, his mouth twisted into a wide smile.

'In thirteen eighty-four, slavery was abolished in the British Empire.'

He screwed up his eyes and shook his head, waving his hand in the air.

'That's not what I meant to say! Listen! Joseph Banks joined Captain Cook on the Endeavour in — damn it!'

He took a deep breath, both hands balling into fists as he tried to concentrate.

'Joshua?' he said slowly, his mouth finding it hard to form the words, as if he was speaking English for the first. 'You were my son, Joshua.'

Josh smiled and nodded his head.

'Cait-lin?' asked the founder, breaking her name into two parts.

'And Rufius. King of Scotland.'

Rufius looked confused, but bowed to the man all the same.

When he came to Enkidu, the founder's expression hardened and he wagged a finger in front of the synthetic's face. 'You are not who you seem.'

The face of Guruname melted away, returning to the synthetic's usual features.

The founder clapped his hands in delight. 'An excellent trick!' Then, turning back to Joshua. 'You will have to excuse me, my thoughts are like leaves in a hurricane. The re-indexing of a life as long as mine takes quite some time.'

'Do you mind?' asked Rufius, pointing at the food. 'It's just I haven't eaten for days.'

'Help yourself your Majesty,' the founder said, bowing low.

They sat around a circular table and spent the next hour trying to make sense of his scatterbrained responses. It was frustrating, there would be lucid moments followed by outbursts of entirely unrelated historical trivia.

Josh was finding it hard to believe that this was his father. He looked nothing like him, but there was something about the way he spoke that felt familiar, even if it wasn't his voice.

'You say your son had one of my memories?'

Caitlin took her head out of her hands. 'He said a dragon burned the people — don't you remember?'

The founder tapped his temple. 'I'm sure the answers are in there, but I've no idea where.'

'I do,' said Josh. 'When you gifted me all of your memories they were in pieces, we worked together to make them into a library — you called it a memory palace.'

The founder stared at him blankly.

'You're going to Intuit with him?' said Caitlin, hardly keeping the disbelief from her voice.

'It's the only way, if we can connect our minds, I think we may be able to use the construct we built. It's our only chance of getting some answers.'

They sat the founder in the chair below the telescope and Josh placed his hands on each side of the man's shaven head.

The skin was warm under his thumbs as Josh pressed gently on the founder's temples. For some reason he hadn't expected that.

'What exactly is an Intuit?' Enkidu asked Rufius who was standing at the edge of the observatory shutters staring out across the city.

Rufius grunted. 'Bloody witchcraft. The ability to transfer thoughts and memories between two people. We mostly use it on the departed.'

'On the dead?' the synthetic sounded genuinely surprised.

'We pickle their minds in preservative, it sounds worse than it is, but it allows us to share knowledge and learnings, very useful for imparting language but also incredibly weird.'

Walking between the empty shelves of the library, Josh wondered if this would even work with a cybernetic brain.

The last time the founder had been in his head, he'd nearly lost his mind. The library helped organise the chaos of the man's incredible history, without it they would have both drowned in a sea of random experiences.

Suddenly, he felt the connection initiate between them and thousands of pages filled the air, twisting like a tornado around him, each one a single moment torn from a book of memories.

'Where are you?' he called out into the storm.

Clutching a small book, his father appeared through the swirling clouds of notes. He was Lord Dee once more, with short grey hair and a beard. Josh wasn't sure if he was recreating the image of the founder from his own memories, or if the old man was remembering, but it was good to see his face.

The tornado calmed as his father approached, the pages falling to the floor like leaves, creating a carpet of paper around them.

'Where are we?' he asked.

'It's a library, we built it together. Don't you remember?'

The founder scowled. 'I'm a collection of memories Joshua, I don't make new ones.'

Josh knelt down and picked up a few of the handwritten pages.

'June thirteen, seventeen-sixty,' he read the title aloud. 'Today we observed a total eclipse of the sun.'

As he continued to read, other pages lifted from the scattered piles across the floor, adding themselves to the one he was holding. Soon, he was holding a thick manuscript around which a binding stitched itself and then a leather cover with the numbers '1760' engraved into its front.

'A good year by all accounts,' said the founder as more books began to collect on the shelves around them.

In a blur, the memories organised themselves, the

library filling with a seemingly endless collection of volumes.

As the last of the pages flew into the final tome, his father held out the small book he had been holding onto so dearly.

'I think this is what you have been looking for. It's not like the others.'

The cover was well-worn and locked with brass latches on top and bottom.

Opening it carefully, Josh read the frontispiece aloud so that Caitlin would hear.

'I am the last of the Seven. The first of our name, creators of worlds.'

Turning through a few pages he stopped and read again.

'We mastered the higher dimensions, allowing us to travel between continuums. We discovered other, nascent, worlds and shared our knowledge. There were many failures before we realised that they were too immature, by then they had come to worship us as gods.

'On the last day, when Tiamat awoke, and our civilisation ended. My escape came at a terrible price —'

Josh felt the memory coming to life. The thick stone walls of a subterranean shelter solidified around him and suddenly there were people rushing past him, hugging their children and what was left of their belongings.

Deep, booming explosions rocked the underground passage, sending clouds of dust and stone down on the heads of the fleeing crowd. Everyone screamed as the lights flickered and went out. In the darkness Josh could feel the panic, smell the fear on them.

Caught up in the flow of bodies that were making their

way deeper underground, Josh had no choice but to follow them. People stumbled and fell in front of him, hands brushed against his legs as he was carried along, unable to stop to help.

Another strike shook the bunker. This time, Josh felt the rush of hot air on his face as a searing fireball lit up the passage behind him.

Roaring over the heads of the refugees, he watched them catch fire, bodies flailing around engulfed in flame as it raced like a wave towards him.

Turning a corner, he found himself in a cavernous space filled with groups of frightened families huddling against the far wall where a large steel door was embedded into the rock.

Someone was waving at him, a woman and her child. Part of the memory recognised them as the founder's wife and daughter. Josh let the moment play out. The heat against his back, the ring on his finger glowed as he embraced them and engaged his personal force field.

When the fireball receded, no one else had survived. The small bubble had protected his family from the searing flames, but the chamber was filled with charred remains and ashes.

Another explosion echoed down the shaft.

Lifting up the child, Josh felt the founder take the hand of his wife and lead them through the carnage to the steel door. It was sealed shut with bodies piled up against it. Telling his daughter to close her eyes, he put her down and activated the door with his ring. The thick metal shutter rolled up slowly, and as soon as the gap was wide enough he pushed them through.

Closing the blast door behind him, he led them down a brightly lit corridor beyond. Through the founder's memory, Josh could understand the markings on the various signs that they passed. This was some kind of experimental research facility. The signs read like a military installation, each one a warning about dangerous materials or biohazards within.

'What is this place?' his wife asked, carrying their daughter.

'Somewhere I never thought I would have to bring you.'

He came to a door marked with the symbol of a snake eating its own tail.

The Ouroboros, thought Josh.

The founder keyed a sequence into the security panel and placed his ring against the symbol. The door slid away silently, revealing a laboratory filled with organic-looking machines.

'We need to leave this timeline,' he told her, ushering them into the room.

The lights in the corridor dimmed, and they felt the tremor as another blast rocked through the complex.

'Now!' he barked, pushing them towards a pod standing in the middle of the equipment.

'Thoth,' came a voice from the doorway. 'What are you doing?'

The silhouette of an Anunnaki, his armour field glowing in the semi-darkness, stood in the doorway.

'Saving my family, Enlil,' the founder replied, flicking a series of switches on the control panel and watching the power levels rising.

'We need to use the sword,' said Enlil.

'It is too late for the weapon, there is no one left to save.'

Enlil dragged himself into the room, his leg was badly damaged and one of his arms lay limp against his side.

'It was designed for this, there will be some who will have found shelter.'

The founder ignored him and continued to prepare the pod.

'Thoth,' pleaded Enlil, raising his arm, the sound of the weapon charging caught the founder's attention. 'Don't make me do this.'

He turned towards his friend. 'There isn't enough power, they've taken out the dam, there's not enough in reserve to sustain more than a single burst. I need to think about saving my family.'

'We are your family!' screamed Enlil, firing his weapon.

The energy bolt lit up the room, striking the conduit above their heads, sending sparks of blue in all directions. His daughter screamed.

The founder raised his hand and a ball of light knocked Enlil off his feet.

Turning back to his wife, he found her trapped under a pile of rubble beside the body of their daughter, the end of a thin metal spar lodged in her chest.

Josh could feel the pain and grief that surged through his father's body as he rushed to them. His wife's face was pale with wide staring eyes. Her breathing shallow and ragged. The founder brushed the hair from her forehead and kissed her gently.

'Can you heal her?' asked his wife, her eyes full of tears.

The founder examined his daughter, the spike had pierced her lung and was close to her aorta.

'It's too close to her heart,' he said,

On the other side of the room Enlil was stirring.

'You have to go,' whispered his wife, her skin white with dust like a china doll.

'I'm not leaving her.'

He looked into his wife's eyes and watched her life fade away.

Enlil's blast clipped his shoulder and spun him around, his armour protecting him from the worst of the damage.

The last part of the memory was of him running towards the machine.

'What happened next?' asked Josh, taking his hands away from the founder's head and noticing that the synthetic's face had transformed into that of his father.

'I crossed into your timeline.'

'Didn't you save her?'

The founder shook his head. 'The Djinn must have destroyed my equipment. When I tried to return the gate was gone.'

Josh told them what he had seen. 'Zack lived with those nightmares for nine years. Carrying the guilt of something he didn't do,' he said, wiping the tears from his cheeks.

Caitlin sighed. 'That would explain what he became.'

'Where is the weapon now?' asked Rufius.

The founder rubbed his hand over his chin as if trying to stroke a beard that wasn't there.

'Buried deep beneath the city, lost under thousands of years of Aaru — assuming the research facility survived the attack.'

Caitlin drew in a deep breath. 'What does this sword actually do?'

The founder looked up, his eyes darkening as they focused on her face. 'The Sword of Time. We named it "Urshanabi". It could slice through the temporal cohesion of an individual's timeline — used on a person, they would simply cease to exist, on a wider scale it could eradicate an entire civilisation.'

Josh looked puzzled. 'What were you going to do with that?'

'It was a by-product of my research. An accidental discovery that should have been destroyed, but the science academy saw it as a way to defend ourselves.'

'You were trying to manipulate time?'

He shook his head. 'We were trying to understand the nature of time.'

'You were building a time machine,' insisted Rufius.

'Enlil said it could have saved your people,' Josh reminded him.

The founder shook his head. 'It would have destroyed them all, the core would have been too unstable without the power to contain it.'

'That's why he sent us here,' said Caitlin, walking towards the edge and looking out over the city. 'Zack never found the weapon. He wants to go back and do what you wouldn't. He's been haunted by those memories for years.'

'How?'

Enkidu pointed towards a set of ceremonial robes hanging by the founder's bed. 'On the day that he becomes a member of the Senate, he will be given access to the sacred archives. Ones that lay hidden in the foundations of the original city, deep below the citadel.'

'There's no way to reach him before that happens?'

The synthetic picked up the founder's headpiece. 'Not for us, but Thoth would be an honoured guest.'

'And he cannot read a neuronic mind. I will be sitting beside Anubis when Zack is sworn in.'

71

NAUTILUS

[Draconian Headquarters, Ascension Island. Date: 1927]

Feynman walked out of the engine room, his smiling face smeared with oil. 'That's one hell of an engine,' he said, wiping his hands.

Tesla followed close behind. 'She's beautiful.'

Juliana Makepiece folded her arms, beaming with pride. 'Took me nearly twenty years to get her running true, and she still has a few eccentricities, but she's a good ship.'

'She's a masterpiece,' enthused Tesla. 'And she can truly travel through time?'

Juliana's pride faltered a little. 'Well, she's not exactly a time machine as such. More of a kind of go-around-the-outside kind of girl.'

Tesla looked confused.

'Probably better if we skipped the details. There are some things that are best left to the imagination. Have you managed to adapt the modulator to work without breaking her?'

'Yeah,' said Feynman, 'and how did you get on with retrofitting the tesseract into the breaching array?'

She tapped the bulkhead with her wrench. 'Piece of cake.'

'Someone mention cake?' said her husband, walking in with a tray of cups and a teapot.

'Your timing is impeccable,' his wife replied, helping herself.

'What is it with you guys and tea?' said Feynman, taking out a hip flask. 'This deserves a proper drink, don't you think?'

'Who said it was tea?' said Thomas, pouring a cup and handing it to the physicist.

Feynman sniffed it and his eyes widened.

He poured out two more and handed them out. 'Fifty-year-old Glen Mhor. Cheers!'

Tesla looked confused. 'In a teacup?'

'Beggars can't be choosers,' explained Juliana, 'on a ship of this size, space is a premium.'

Feynman raised his cup and toasted. 'Well, here's to the *Nautilus*, may she fly on the wings of angels.'

He went to clink his cup with Juliana, but she pulled her hand away.

'Sorry, it's an old naval superstition. They say the sound woke the souls of the dead.'

'Understood.'

'So, shall we take her out for a test drive?' asked Tesla, walking over to the controls. 'I've been dying to see her in action.'

Thomas looked at Juliana. 'Well strictly speaking, we're not supposed to —'

Juliana interrupted. 'It's top-secret technology, Professor

Eddington was very clear that you weren't to see her in operation.'

'Cross my heart and hope to die?' Feynman drew an 'X' over his breast.

She put down her cup and sat in her pilot seat. 'Okay. They're going to wipe your memory anyway, you might as well enjoy it.'

The pitch of the engines changed. Juliana moved a series of levers, and tapped on a pressure gauge until the needle moved back out of the red.

72

SENATE

[Senate, Aaru]

The Senate was housed on the opposite side of the square to the Citadel.

'Only the Foresaken are allowed to attend the ceremony,' Enkidu said, placing jewels on their temples. 'These access stones will allow you to enter as honoured members of the Science Academy. The sentinels will not question your presence.'

He walked towards the doors, the guards bowing slightly to him as he entered.

The entrance hall of the Senate was crowded with the city's aristocracy. The powerful and wealthy citizens of Aaru paraded around the arched colonnades in expensive silk gowns and golden headdresses in the shapes of their respective gods, before making their way into the central chamber.

Passing through a grand arched entrance carved with thirty-foot high effigies of the Seven, they followed synthetic up an ornate staircase to the second floor.

The main chamber was built on three tiers, each set back further than the last, like an inverted pyramid.

On the highest tier, the public gallery was filled with citizens watching in silence as the gods, dressed in elaborate animal-headed costumes, took their seats in the Upper House. The statues of the Seven, sat on thrones of gold, were arranged along one wall of the first floor. The founder was below them in the centre muttering to himself like the mad man everyone believed him to be.

On the ground level, the members of the Lower House filed into the chamber. Enkidu had explained that they were mostly drawn from the rich merchant classes. Caitlin could tell from the intricate jewelled headdresses and fine silk robes that they were hardly commoners.

'Where's Zack?' whispered Caitlin, scanning the crowd like an anxious mother at her first school prize-giving.

'He will be called to the Seven by Anubis,' explained the synthetic, watching the jackal-headed god getting to his feet and raising the staff of office.

'Bring forth those who seek to ascend,' he commanded in an obviously amplified voice.

A blast of horns announced Zachary's arrival and drums beat out time as he was carried through the ranks of the Lower House in a litter on the shoulders of four heavily-muscled slaves, wearing a long flowing cloak and a white toga.

Caitlin caught her breath, he looked so handsome in his ceremonial robes, holding his head high like a caesar entering the Colosseum. Zack was flanked on each side by lines of guards wearing the heads of falcons and lions. Behind his entourage, Kebechet walked alone carrying the train of his cloak.

'A military escort?' whispered Josh.

'They are from the houses of Montu and Maahes, the ones who are sponsoring his ascendancy.'

Caitlin looked confused. 'I thought that he was under Anubis's protection?'

The synthetic nodded to one of the lesser members of the Upper House. 'Maahes has become Zachary's mentor since he left the priesthood. The Lord of Slaughter has been petitioning the senate for an army for years. He's been filling Zack's head with stories of conquest.'

Josh recognised Maahes, the Lion breasted Anunnaki from the battle on Arrakeen.

The litter bearers stopped at the bottom of a staircase leading up to the Upper House and lowered Zack to the floor.

Anubis stepped down to meet him as he ascended. The symbolism wasn't lost on the rest of the congregation, who began to chant as Zack removed his cloak and bowed before the master of ceremonies.

Thoth was led down to stand beside Anubis, holding up a head modelled on a falcon with a ruby disc mounted above it.

'Amun-Ra,' murmured Enkidu. 'They are to anoint him as a sun god.'

A silence fell across the room as the helmet was placed over Zack's head and the entire senate spontaneously applauded.

'So what now?' asked Josh.

'We hope that the founder was able to place the psychic dampener in the helmet,' replied Rufius, turning to Enkidu. 'How long do we have?'

'The ceremony will continue with Zack paying homage

to each of the Seven. Then they will retire to the sacred archives where Zack will be presented with the key to its secrets.'

There was a sharp intake of breath from the audience as Thoth turned to follow Zack and stumbled.

Anubis went to help the old man back to his feet. Zack hardly seemed to notice as he made his way towards the upper floor.

Rufius stepped back from the balcony. 'The founder's playing his part. We have to reach Zack before they give him access to the archives.'

The synthetic led them down a winding set of stairs carved into the stone, the sounds of the crowd echoing through the chamber as they descended.

'The chamber of Enlil is hidden deep below the Citadel.'

'And the archives?'

'They lie within, but only the representatives of the Upper Houses are allowed into them and those that have sworn never to speak of it.'

Rufius scoffed. 'If the sword's going to be anywhere, it will be down there. What happens in the next part of the ceremony?'

'He will be left alone in the chamber. It is supposed to represent the final act of his ascendancy, he will commune with the ancestors and be reborn as a god.'

'Can you get me in there before he reaches it?' asked Rufius.

'Better if I go,' said Caitlin.

'No,' said Josh. 'He's already got inside your head once. I'll do it.'

. . .

Reaching the lower level, they found Enlil's chamber empty.

The room was decorated with the usual bas-reliefs of the various deities. Lit by oil lamps that threw deep shadows over the gods' faces, it wasn't hard to imagine how impressive it would be to the uninitiated. On the far side of the room was a door that appeared to have no lock. Enkidu's finger transformed into a long silver key which he inserted into the eye of one of the gods and the door slid open.

73

CRYOGENIAN

[Nautilus]

'Bringing the tesseract online,' warned Tesla, standing behind his newly installed controls.

Juliana checked a series of dials on her dashboard. 'All systems in the green.'

Feynman stood in front of the oculus window, watching random clusters of moments scudding past the bow as the ship ploughed through the Maelstrom.

'So these are like remnants of time?' he asked Thomas, who was a little merry, having helped himself to a third shot of whisky.

'I like to think of them as tiny bubbles of happiness drifting in a vast ocean of despair.'

The physicist raised his cup. 'I'll drink to that!'

'We could use a little help here!' said Juliana in a tone that Thomas knew should not be ignored.

'Coming!'

She pulled back a series of levers. 'Bring the resonator online and tune it to our own frequency.'

'Aye, aye, Captain!' Her husband saluted before settling down into an old leather armchair surrounded by dials.

Feynman was pouring himself another drink from the teapot when he saw something out of the corner of his eye. 'Hey, I think I just saw a giant squid.'

Juliana's hand froze over one of the levers. 'What did it look like exactly?'

'You know, tentacles, big glowing eye. Come to think of it maybe it was more like an octopus. Sorry octopi.'

She glanced nervously at her husband. 'Honey, how long until we're ready to jump?'

'Give me a break,' he said, waving the instruction manual over his head. 'I've only just got on to page two.'

Juliana flicked on the automatic pilot and lifted herself out of her chair. 'Were the magazines for the forward cannons reloaded before we left?'

Thomas nodded. 'Did them myself, why?'

Something heavy hit the hull, sending a resounding boom echoing through the ship.

'Iceberg?' said Feynman, half-joking.

An ulcerated tentacle attached itself to the outside of the window, leaving a thick smear of putrefying ichor across the segmented panes.

'You don't want to know,' snapped Juliana. 'Nikola, do you think you can fly this thing?'

Tesla nodded and stepped out from behind the tesseract controls.

'Thomas, I'll be in the forward gunnery, please hurry up.'

She ran to a hatch at the end of the bridge and jumped through it feet first.

. . .

Running along the gangway to the cannons, Juliana was thrown against the bulkhead as a second collision knocked the ship off course. This time it was followed by a long screeching sound as though something were dragging its claws along the side of the ship.

'Goddam pentachions,' she said, putting on her headset and strapping herself into the bucket-like seat. Pulling a lever, the chair descended into the gunnery position on the front of the ship.

'How are we doing Thomas?' she whispered into the radio.

'Another two pages and I should be ready,' Thomas's voice crackled through the headphones.

Juliana took hold of the firing controls and placed her feet into the positioning system. Pushing down with her left to rotate around three hundred and sixty degrees, she searched for the bitch that was scratching her beautiful ship.

The turret rotated back around towards the bridge and the creature came into her sights. It must have been five times bigger than the *Nautilus*, one of the largest specimens she'd ever seen.

This was the second time they'd encountered a pentachion in as many days and that bothered her. They were usually to be found in the Mordant Quadrant and never ventured so close to the continuum. Juliana wondered if it was something about the fields the tesseract was throwing off that was attracting them.

In the past they would simply outrun it, but she knew once the creature connected with the hull it wasn't going to let go.

The readings showed both cannons were fully charged and she could feel their energy vibrating through her hands as she fired the first round of plasma torpedos into the body of the enormous bloated cephalopod.

Since they were fighting in a timeless vacuum there was no satisfying recoil when the shots were fired, nor satisfying scream of pain when the electrostatic charges found their mark. The creature's arms simply went rigid as the shocks short-circuited its nervous system, releasing its grip on the hull.

'Thomas,' she whispered. 'Now would be good.'

'Nearly there, just got to recalibrate the thingy.'

Something else caught her eye, and she pushed down on the right pedal, rolling the gun turret over until she was upside down.

Below the ship, keeping pace with it, was something Juliana could only describe as a swarm of pentachions. At that precise moment, she couldn't recall the collective noun for a group of eight-legged giant Kraken, but swarm was what they were doing, and they were getting closer.

The stunned body of the first monster was drifting slowly away from the ship, and she watched as some of its comrades duly gathered it up and began to eat it.

There was something very strange about semi-transparent creatures eating each other, the glowing internal structures doing little to hide the digestion process.

'THOMAS!'

'Yes, dear,' he replied, slurring his words slightly. 'I think I've got it.'

She was about to tell him to wait until she got out of the gunnery section when suddenly the universe appeared around her.

There was a sense of relief, followed by rage, which she vented over the radio to her husband in a series of four-letter expletives.

Calming down, Juliana realised that the planet they were orbiting showed distinct signs of glaciation. 'Thomas, what year do you have on the clock?'

His voice crackled through her headset. 'Erm. I'd say we're pretty far back. I'm reading in the minus six-hundred and fifty.'

'Million?'

'Yup.'

Drifting into the daylight side of the planet, Juliana saw vast sheets of white covering most of the northern hemisphere.

'Snowball Earth,' she muttered to herself, turning on the mic once more. 'Tell Feynman we've arrived in the Cryogenian and break out the snow shoes.'

74

SECRETS

[Chamber of Enlil, Aaru]

Josh waited in the darkened room, going back over Caitlin's last instructions.

'Number one: don't let him take the helmet off.' She counted on her fingers. 'Two, under no circumstances tell him about his future self. Three, don't let him read any of the books in there, don't let him even touch them.'

The term 'books' was an overstatement, as was 'sacred archive'. Their holy relics were like something from a fire sale. Burned scraps of paper and battered old objects were arranged carefully on glass shelves like precious jewels. It was a pitifully small collection, but all that remained of their original civilisation.

Josh picked up one of the singed pages, his fingers searching for a chronology but finding none — it was just a piece of paper, nothing more.

. . .

There was a noise outside the room, a scraping of stone as the lock was opened and a line of light divided the room.

Standing outside was the falcon-headed god.

'Hello father,' said Zack, his voice amplified by the technology embedded in the helmet.

'Zachary,' Josh greeted his son.

Zack stepped inside, his glowing eyes illuminating the room. 'Where's Mother?'

'Close by.'

The doors closed, sealing them in.

'The last remnants of the golden age,' said Zack, touching some of the exhibits. 'Strange to think that this is all that remains of their old world.'

'Not everything, there are your grandfather's memories.'

'So there are. Maahes informs me that his mind is finally clearing. I assume that was your doing?' Zack paused, tapping the side of the helmet. 'Interesting. I cannot read you, have you done something clever father? Or is it that ring of yours?'

Josh could feel his heart hammering inside his chest. It was strange to be standing before a son who was now only a few years younger and considerably more powerful.

Before Josh could stop him, Zack removed his helmet. His lips twisting into a familiar wry smile, Caitlin's smile. 'Did you think I couldn't see this far ahead? That I wouldn't know you would come here?' He spoke English with a slight Middle-Eastern accent.

He had Caitlin's eyes and nose too, and what Josh's mother would have called a 'movie star' jaw line. She would have adored her grandson, it was a shame they would never get to meet.

'Why did you send us here?'

'You know the answer to that already.'

'To change your past,' replied Josh.

Looking down inside the helmet, Zack took out Enkidu's device and examined it. 'A dampening field, a little too advanced for you I think? Who's been helping you?'

Josh felt Zack's mental probe slide into his mind, instantly taking control of his motor functions, paralysing his body, leaving him with nothing but the power of speech.

'Enkidu is alive?' exclaimed Zack, finding the memory of his old retainer. 'They told me he was destroyed.'

'He wants to help you,' said Josh through clenched teeth.

Zack's expression soured. 'Give me your ring Father,' he commanded, his voice seeming to break into a hundred parts, and like a marionette on invisible strings, Josh's right arm rose.

The golden band glowed brightly as he took the ring from Josh's finger and placed it on his own.

'I have spent most of my life abiding by the teachings of the Cataclysm and the stories of the Seven. One in particular regarding Thoth's ring, it was supposed to ensure the wearer never aged. A childish myth, but earned him the name of the Timeless One.'

Kissing the ring, he turned back to the display cases and raised his hand. 'None of them knew what they have truly lost. That they once had the ultimate weapon and didn't use it.'

Lines of stress appeared in the glass panes, frost-like patterns spreading across them until they shattered into a million sparkling shards.

'Your grandfather had good reasons not to — it was unstable.'

Turning back towards him, Zack sneered. 'He abandoned his own people. Left them to die.'

'They killed his family!'

The last moments of the founder's memory resurfaced in Josh's mind, and Zack's mental probes latched onto it.

'I remember this differently,' he said, a flicker of confusion passing across his face. He turned the event over, examining it from all sides. 'Are you trying to deceive me?'

The probes went deeper, like tree roots burying into the emotions attached to it, following the grief down until he found the final memory of Josh's mother.

His son winced, sharing the pain Josh left buried within it.

'You let her die?'

Josh could feel hot tears on his cheeks. 'Everybody dies, some things are inevitable.'

'You're wrong Father. You had the power to change it.'

'See for yourself,' said Josh, opening his mind and showing him all of the ways that he tried to save her.

Zack absorbed them eagerly, like a child learning to walk. He studied all the ways Josh weaved with the ring, until he was satisfied he could harness its power. Withdrawing his mind, Josh felt his senses return.

Walking to one of the broken cases, Zack took an artefact from inside. Holding it in his right hand, the ring began to glow brightly. 'Now, I have the power too.'

'You're going to change the past?'

'You're forgetting that I've seen it all. The weapon can defeat Tiamat and restore the Anunnaki to their rightful place. Become the true gods we once were.'

Lines of energy began to unravel from the artefact.

'You can't make it right, you've seen how I failed. You have to make peace with the past and move on,' said Josh.

Zack teased at the ribbons of light with the fingers of his left hand. 'So says the man who would sacrifice everything to have his baby back.'

'I've seen what you become. What the power will do to you.'

Zack laughed. 'So you're a seer now? You've made so many bad decisions Father,' he whispered, placing his hand gently on Josh's cheek. 'Would you like me to fix you Daddy? Shall I take away all of that guilt and pain?'

Josh shook his head.

'As you wish. I doubt that we shall meet again, but I thank you for the lesson, I shall treasure it for eternity.'

Zack's body flickered for a second and then faded out of existence.

75

PROBLEMS

[Draconian Headquarters, Ascension Island. Date: 1927]

'So it attracts pentachions,' said Marcus, inspecting the large rents in the side of the ship. They ran the length of the hull and were nearly three feet wide. 'How long did you have before they appeared this time?'

'I'd say about ten minutes.'

'And how long does it take for the tesseract to establish itself?'

Juliana glared at her husband who was busy organising the repair crew. 'A sober person could probably do it in under ten, but it would be close. It's not the tesseract per se, it's the guidance system, the resonator needs to establish a stable frequency.'

Marcus ran his hand over his scarred head. 'Do you think you could get it down any lower?'

She shrugged. 'Maybe, but they're getting quicker too.'

'Can't you jump inside the continuum?' asked Sabien.

Juliana sucked air in through her teeth. 'Not safe. We've no idea what it could do to the fabric of spacetime.'

'But you sent Rufius through?'

'And the room collapsed! Kaori's team are still digging through the rubble. We can only hope that he got out before the thing imploded.'

Feynman came down the gangplank carrying a pair of snowshoes and wearing a broad grin.

'Wait until I tell the boys back at Los Alamos.'

Sabien tapped his watch. 'I think it's about time we got you back there.' He gave Juliana a knowing look and raised his voice. 'Just need to take you up to the medica to check you're not contaminated with any prehistoric bugs. You too Mr Tesla.'

They followed him dutifully out of the hangar.

Juliana sighed, staring at the gaping rents in the hull. 'I don't think she could take much more of that kind of punishment. Do you have any ideas on how we could keep the penta-chion away?'

Marcus crossed his arms and tilted his head like a dog trying to understand its master. 'We'd need some kind of diversion.'

'What do they like more than a quantum field oscillator?'

He shrugged. 'A breach?'

She considered the idea for a second and then shook her head. 'No, we couldn't do that. Grandmaster Derado would have our arses.'

'Not if we opened it somewhere ancient and unin-habited.'

Her eyes lit up as she caught his meaning. 'Like six hundred and fifty-million years ancient?'

'Where there's nothing but snow, ice and a few amoeba.'

She stroked the hull of her ship. 'It would make for an interesting fossil record that's for sure. Keep the palaeontologists busy for decades. I could pull them through and leave them stranded. The *Nautilus* would seal the breach on the way back out.'

'It would be a dangerous manoeuvre, you'd have the entire convocation on your tail.'

Juliana clicked her fingers. 'Convocation of pentachions. I knew it had a collective noun. I went with swarm, it seemed fitting at the time.'

She nodded towards the crew who were welding brass sheets over the holes. 'Once they're done, I'm going to electrify the hull. Tesla has left me a few of his toys. The static from his coils should give them a nasty shock.'

'So are you going to tell Grandmaster Derado?'

She patted Marcus on the arm. 'I think it will sound better coming from you.'

Two days later, as they were finishing the repairs, Lyra walked into the hangar carrying a small case, as if she were going on holiday.

Juliana was checking the port engine when she appeared.

'Hello love, you off somewhere?'

Lyra put down her case and smiled. 'I'm coming with you.'

Juliana put down her wrench and climbed down the ladder. 'Are you now?'

'I have to be there. I've seen it.'

Caitlin's mother knew of Lyra's skills, and there was no denying that a seer on board would be an advantage, but this was a dangerous mission and there was no room for spectators.

'This isn't a recon mission love, we're going to be facing some dangerous opposition.'

Lyra ran her hand along the new plates on the hull. 'I know. The pentachions are drawn to the songs, the *Nautilus* sings to them.'

'The frequency oscillator?'

Lyra nodded. 'The music of time. It drives them crazy.'

Juliana put the wrench into her tool belt and folded her arms over her chest. 'You'll need to do your bit, we don't carry passengers.'

Lyra picked up her bag. 'I know.'

[Chamber of Enlil, Aaru]

'Y ou gave him your ring?' asked Caitlin, failing to hide the disbelief in her voice.

Josh nodded.

'Because you let him take off his helmet.'

He nodded again.

She sighed and shook her head. 'And now he's gone back to fight the Djinn single-handed. Why do I listen to you?'

Picking up the helmet, Enkidu closed his eyes, his hands glowing through the skin.

'He found the dampening field,' said Josh.

'I am aware,' the synthetic said through tight lips.

'How long before they notice he's gone?' asked Rufius.

'Two or three hours. I have re-configured the biometric sensors to simulate a meditative state.' Enkidu placed the helmet on a shelf like an exhibit. 'They will assume he is communing with the ancestors.'

The founder came out of the archives holding a piece of old parchment, one of the holy relics. 'This was from the

Book of Carthen, there were over a hundred volumes of his histories. Now all we have left is this one page.'

Snatching the page from him, Caitlin's eyes narrowed briefly as she searched for any trace of a chronology and found nothing. 'Is there any way to follow him back there?'

'There is the sword,' the founder suggested, staring at the far wall.

Rufius grunted. 'I thought you said it was unstable.'

The founder ignored him, distracted by the symbols carved onto its surface. 'I know this place.' He raised a finger towards it and traced the signs out in the air.

Caitlin squinted at the hieroglyphs. 'Can we get a bit more light in here?'

Enkidu obliging raised his glowing hand up to the engraving.

Above the writing were seven figures carved into a horizontal block. Their heads surrounded by rays of light, a pair of wings stretching behind them.

'Angels?' suggested Rufius.

'The Seven,' said the founder, turning to Enkidu. 'Can you generate an electrostatic discharge?'

The synthetic nodded. 'Up to twenty-thousand watts.'

Caitlin finished translating the script. 'This says it's the entrance to the halls of the Seven.'

The founder tapped on one of the symbols above an image of a winged god. 'Here.'

Enkidu pressed his hands together and slowly pulled them apart. A small ball of energy formed between the synthetic's palms, growing in intensity as the gap widened.

The ball leapt from his hands and into the symbol, which instantly lit up with blue light. Other glyphs followed suit, until an arch of glowing characters formed in the stone.

The founder took Josh's hand and pressed it against a blank stone.

'You should be carrying enough genetic material to register as a close relative of Thoth.'

The stone felt warm to the touch and Josh could sense something beneath the surface.

There was a grinding noise deep inside the wall and the door slowly raised. Behind it, Josh could see a dimly lit corridor sloping downwards. He recognised the symbols on the walls, they were the same as the ones in the founder's research bunker.

'Quickly!' interrupted Enkidu as the door slid slowly upwards. 'The mechanism is old, and my energy will not power it for long.'

They ducked under the thick slab of steel and into the corridor beyond. The synthetic was the last to cross as the door slammed down into position.

Light from the ceiling panels flickered into life as ancient sensors reacted to their presence. The long passage was deathly quiet, the stale air smelled of decay and dust, as if they'd entered some ancient tomb.

Striding ahead, the founder took the lead and they followed him down through a series of long sloping passages and staircases.

The facility was a vast complex carved out of the bedrock. It reminded Josh of a nuclear bunker from the nineteen-sixties, one that had been redecorated by the Pharaohs.

They passed locked doors and corridors blocked by cave-ins. It was clear that the place had taken a beating during the final days of the conflict.

Finally, they reached a large laboratory. Three skeletons

lay on the floor: one, a child from the size, had a metal spike through its ribcage, one adult was laying next to it under a pile of rubble. On the far side of the chamber lay another, still in its armour which was covered in rust.

Enkidu and Rufius went to examine the fallen warrior while the founder knelt beside the child and whispered a silent prayer over it.

'They were his family,' Josh whispered to Caitlin.

They left the others and walked over to the collection of decaying equipment covered in thick layers of spider webbing.

'This was how my father escaped to our timeline,' explained Josh, brushing aside the web on a large circular portal. 'It's some kind of tesseract I guess.'

The equipment surrounding the portal looked as if it had been grown rather than built, made from a hard material like the carapace of a beetle.

'Part of me wishes he never had,' Caitlin said sourly, wiping the dust from a control panel.

'Zack saw all of this, he needed me to bring the ring to this place at this time.'

'So he can kill himself trying to stop the Djinn?'

Josh smiled. 'He's just like you. Trying to save the world.'

A sob caught in her throat. 'We haven't changed a thing.'

He wrapped his arms around her, hugging her tightly. 'We'll get him back.'

She pushed him away. 'How? Unless we get the memory out of him he's doomed, he's never going to stop trying.'

Josh looked down at his bare hands, a white line around his finger where the ring used to be. 'We've beaten them once, we can do it again.'

Caitlin touched one of the cables leading to the portal, it turned to dust in her hand. 'Assuming Thoth can get us back there.'

'The gods may yet assist us,' said the synthetic, coming to join them. He was wearing the gauntlets of the dead warrior. 'He was Enlil, greatest of the Anunnaki. With this we should be able to defeat Tiamat.'

'Well by all accounts it didn't work the last time, I think we're going to need more than a pair of fancy gloves,' joked Rufius.

Enkidu raised his hand and the jewels embedded within its palms began to glow. Rufius floated ten feet into the air.

'Okay, Okay,' he said, waving his hands around. 'Put me down you fool and find me a pair of those.'

The founder got to his feet and brushed off his knees. 'They are probably the only pair in existence. The armoury was destroyed during the initial attack by Tiamat's forces. I believe she had spies within the city, either that or she could sense the energy signatures of our weapons.'

'And the sword? Did it survive?'

The founder shrugged. 'It was well shielded, let's hope they never discovered it.'

He turned and walked towards a heavy steel door. 'Joshua, we will need your genetic code once more.'

77

CATACLYSM

[Aaru]

The desolation of Aaru was nearly complete.

Zack stood amongst the ruins of the library still holding the book he'd taken from the archive. He hardly recognised the city through the smoke and ash raining down from a sickly-coloured sky. Everything was covered in a dark dust that smelled of charred meat.

He could hear the sounds of battle raging somewhere within the walls — the heroes of the Cataclysm: Anu, Enlil and Enki were fighting to save their people, while others, like Thoth, were making their escape. It was the forsaking, the crucial moment when four of their gods abandoned them.

Stumbling through the shattered ruins of the old building, he climbed out into what was left of the Court of the Four Winds. Across the plaza rose the dome of the Citadel, cracked open like an egg, with a black, winged serpent coiled around its walls tearing at the golden panels — she looked exactly like the pictures on the walls of the temple, the Goddess of Chaos, Tiamat.

As if sensing his presence, Tiamat raised her head to the sky and vomited a boiling cloud of black smoke into the air. The dark gas formed into nightmarish creatures that swirled above the Citadel like a shoal of dark fish. They wove backwards and forwards around its spires until the building was cloaked in a hurricane of darkness.

With no way to enter the research facility from the Citadel, Zack decided it would be wiser to take the secret tunnels from the Temple of the Sun.

Moving away from the approaching storm and towards the river, he was relieved to find that the bridge was damaged but still passable.

Corpses littered the road. The bodies of people trying to escape the city lay twisted and broken like old toys, most of them were missing their eyes.

Zack always assumed the stories of demons they used to tell to the novices were exaggerated to scare the children. The elder priests would take great pleasure in threatening him with graphic tales of monsters, ones that waited in the shadows to claim the unfaithful or false of heart. Now, as he picked his way among the dead, he could see the terror on their faces and knew that it was worse than anything he could have imagined. Wisps of smoke escaped from their mouths, curling into ghostly forms as it escaped and for a moment he wondered if they might be their souls ascending.

Looking back over his shoulder, he watched the last of the Citadel disappear, consumed by the dark mass and broke into a run.

78

URSHANABI

[Research facility, Aaru]

Behind the steel door, they found themselves inside a vast, hollowed-out cavern. A winding ramp curved down towards what appeared to be a small power plant half-buried in the floor.

A large glowing sphere sat in the centre of a network of vine-like structures.

'It seems to be still functional,' said the founder, looking over a series of control panels.

'How?' asked Caitlin.

'I'll run some integrity tests,' said the founder, wiping the dust from a screen. 'Check the power levels.'

The energy from the sphere made Josh's skin tingle as they moved closer. It was a familiar sensation, the kind that would leave fractal patterns on his skin.

'Doesn't look much like a sword,' observed Rufius. 'More like a fairground ride.'

The founder ignored him, focusing his attention on the readouts which were just strange swirling patterns of colour.

Caitlin took out the locus, the particles were nothing more than dying embers. 'There's something wrong with the pattern, it's fading.'

'It's as I hoped,' said the founder, 'the Forsaken repaired the power grid after the attack, they've used my original design.'

'How is it still here? I thought Zack was going to destroy it?'

Josh took a deep breath, letting it out slowly. 'I told him not to do it.'

She rounded on him. 'What did you say?'

'I warned him that it was unstable.'

Enkidu made a gesture with his hand. 'You changed the pattern.'

'So what happened?' asked Rufius.

Josh shrugged. 'Looks like he took my advice.'

Caitlin frowned. 'Or he failed. We need to get back there now!'

They watched in silence while the founder manipulated the timeline within the sphere. Millions of tiny strands unwound like fraying rope at the point where the Cataclysm occurred, with only a few hundred lines continuing beyond into the future.

The founder singled out one golden thread. 'Zack has returned to the moment when Aaru falls.'

Caitlin climbed up onto the platform. 'This is the end of your civilisation?' she said, staring into the lines of light.

'Yes, millions of souls were lost in a matter of hours,' added Enkidu.

Rufius scratched his beard. 'How did he manage to get back there?'

'He learned to use Solomon's ring,' said Josh, coming to stand beside Caitlin. 'Can you put us in there?'

The founder looked up from the controls and nodded. 'I can, but there may be no way to bring you back.'

'We always knew this might be a one-way trip,' added Rufius, putting his hand on Caitlin's shoulder. 'But we've got this far.'

Caitlin smiled and placed her hand over his. 'I have to go. I can't ask you to make the same sacrifice.'

'Not another word,' he said, turning to the founder. 'Maestro, three tickets to the end of the world if you please!'

'Make that four,' said Enkidu, stepping next to Josh.

79

EVEREST

[Cryogenian, Earth]

The *Nautilus* burst into the bright blue sky over the mountains, and Juliana pulled up hard to keep her bow from hitting the craggy peaks of the massif. The brass hull grazed over the snowy summit and she banked right to avoid crashing into a proto-Everest.

In the ship's wake came a swarm of tangled giant squid-like shapes, their bodies solidifying as they entered the temporal realm, and, suddenly trapped within a gravitational field, their heavy bodies fell towards the Earth.

'Shut down the aperture,' commanded Juliana into a speaking tube.

'Closed,' replied the tinny voice of her husband.

She pulled the ship around and guided it gently down a broad flat valley, which was now littered with the bodies of pentachions. Juliana imagined what George Mallory would think of them when he arrived in 1921.

'Prepare the oscillator and open a new aperture,' she ordered, powering up the engines once more.

Lyra nodded and flicked a series of switches, listening to the change in pitch.

The *Nautilus* accelerated along the valley, the jet wash from its exhaust stirring the snow drifts along the floor into clouds of ice that covered the bodies of the rapidly freezing creatures.

As they sped towards the lower slopes of the mountain a new portal opened.

'Steady,' she whispered to herself. 'Thomas, the moment we re-enter the Maelstrom I want you to engage the tesseract.'

'Aye, Aye Captain.'

Juliana checked her readouts, everything was nominal.

'Okay girls and boys, hold onto your hats, we're going in.'

The ship slid silently into the shimmering portal, forty feet from the base of the mountain.

Six hundred and fifty million years later, a British reconnaissance expedition led by George Mallory, would come to stand on the same spot unaware of the nightmarish creatures that lay frozen in the ice beneath their feet. Their eyes would be drawn to the mighty peak of Everest, looking for a route to the summit.

80

ALPHA

[Aaru]

The sky was full of Djinn.

Bloated, gaseous creatures the size of zeppelins floated over the rooftops of the city, their transparent abdomens filled with dark, egg-shaped bombs. Giant winged scorpions swarmed around them, collecting the eggs from festering sores along their sides and dropping them across the city.

A decaying Wyrrm swam lazily overhead, its sinuous body nearly three hundred feet long. As it passed over Josh and Caitlin, a trailing tentacle struck the tower of a nearby building like a wrecking ball. Huge chunks of debris fell into the street around them, knocking them all to the ground.

'Where are we?' groaned Caitlin, shaking the dust out of her hair.

'South of the Citadel,' answered Enkidu, helping her to

stand. 'My sensors tell me the enemy's land forces are approaching the city walls.'

Rufius was nowhere to be seen.

The synthetic found Josh under a pile of rubble and it took the two of them a few tense minutes to clear the debris away before Caitlin was sure he was still breathing.

'Hey, we made it,' she said, brushing the grit out of his eyes.

Josh coughed, drawing a sharp breath and pushing himself up on his elbows. A dark shadow passed over them and they looked up into the belly of a heavily laden blimp.

'We need to get off the streets,' wheezed Josh. 'We're too exposed out here and we don't have any weapons.'

'Not strictly true,' said Rufius, stepping out of a doorway carrying an armful of power staffs. 'These beauties should do some damage.'

They each took a staff and followed Enkidu through a series of narrow streets and down into a sewer tunnel. There were others sheltering further back in the passage, their faces covered in ash and blood, their eyes wide with fear.

'So where's Zachary?' asked Rufius, breathing hard. Josh noticed he was holding his side.

The synthetic paused for a moment, his pupils fading to white. 'There is no network here, not one that I can detect at least. I have no way to determine his location, nor an accurate map of the city.'

Caitlin took out the locus and handed it to the synthetic. 'Try this.'

He held the globe in his glowing hand and the pattern began to stir within it. 'Below the temple. I think he's trying to use the tunnels to reach the facility.'

Coughing, Rufius grimaced, spitting blood onto the floor.

'Are you hurt?' asked Caitlin.

She pulled up his tunic. The skin was purpling around his ribs.

'Took a bit of a beating from those Temple Guards, then half a building fell on me. Might have cracked a rib or two.'

Enkidu handed the locus back to Caitlin and placed his hand against Rufius's side.

'Three, in fact, I can reduce the swelling and heal the fractures if you wish.'

Rufius grunted his approval and the synthetic's fingers seemed to melt into his skin.

Josh stood at the mouth of the tunnel, watching the sky darkening as the Nihil swarmed over the Citadel.

'You've fought them before haven't you?' asked Caitlin, coming to stand beside him.

He nodded, his throat tightening as the memory of her broken body came flooding back. 'We did, but it took everything we had to stop them.'

'How did you beat them?'

'They don't deal well with linear time. Especially when you drop a few hundred thousand years on them in one go.'

Her eyes widened. 'You took all of them down?'

Josh shook his head. 'They're a hive mind, if you can find the alpha you can neutralise their entire army.'

She slipped her arm around his waist.

Josh took a deep breath, pulling her closer to him. 'You realise if we try and change this we may never meet?'

'If we stop the Djinn, the founder never leaves, never crosses over to our timeline.'

'I never exist.'

'The Order never exists.'

'We could literally cancel out everything in one go.'

Caitlin smiled and kissed him. 'Causality's a bitch.'

Rufius coughed to get their attention. 'When you two love birds are quite finished. I believe we have a Cataclysm to prevent.'

Josh turned and smiled, the colonel looked his old self once more, ready to take on an army of nightmares.

'So, how do we help Zack?'

Enkidu came out of the shadows, wearing the gauntlets of Enlil. 'The stories told of a great battle where the last of the Anunnaki faced Tiamat.'

'The Dragon that burned everyone,' said Caitlin, remembering what Zack had said.

The synthetic nodded. 'A winged serpent, the Goddess of Chaos.'

'Where was this battle supposed to take place?'

The synthetic nodded towards the broken dome of the Citadel. 'In the Court of the Four Winds.'

81

HIVE MIND

[Temple of the Sun, Aaru]

Out of habit, Zack found himself repeating the litany before entering the Temple of the Sun.

HAIL to thee, Amun-Ra, Lord of the thrones of the earth, the oldest existence, ancient of heaven, support of all things; Chief of the gods, lord of truth; father of the gods, maker of men and beasts and herbs; maker of all things above and below.

The statue of Amun-Ra glowered down at him with one eye. Half of its head had been blown away and was resting on its side in front of the main entrance. There were bodies too, priests pinned to the walls like notices on a door, their arms stretched out at right angles from their bodies in mocking crucifixion.

Holding his breath, he slipped behind the broken idol.

Inside the temple it was deathly silent. Instinctively, he took off his sandals and padded through the colonnaded courtyard in his bare feet, listening intently for any sound.

In the future, the entrance to the tunnels was situated

below the sanctuary and he prayed to the Seven that the architects had simply rebuilt on its original site.

As a novice, Zack had visited the temple every day. He'd always found a sense of peace within its walls, for some reason the building could quiet the storm in his mind, at least until they ripped the memory out of him. Nothing could heal that wound.

When he reached the Hypostyle Hall, the sound of the creature wallowing in the sacred pool stopped him in his tracks.

Zack studied it from behind one of the pillars. The head was crowned with an array of eyes that pivoted on fleshy stalks. The mouth was a long vertical slit lined with sharp rows of teeth, through which a series of tongues picked off the flesh from a wriggling fish.

Its body seemed to be fused with the armour, metal and bone protruding through its upper torso, while the lower half, though submerged in the pool, was mostly tentacles.

Closing his eyes, Zack reached out with his mind, as he'd done so many times before. Releasing his conscious-ness from his body he tentatively probed its thoughts.

Pain lanced through his mind, a searing, needle-like agony boring into his skull. He tried to pull away but the dark, evil thoughts were like black tar, clinging to him.

What have we here? The thing said in a chorus of a thou-sand voices inside his head.

Its mind was a mire, filled with visions of carnage. As the pain subsided Zack realised that it was not one mind, but many, the creatures were connected somehow — a collective mind of archaic hatred and despair that was so putrid it took every ounce of his willpower not to vomit.

A bright mind. Come to us little one. Sang the chorus of voices, although there were other thoughts below it, murmuring to each other like madmen.

Zack felt the pull of its will, creating an overwhelming urge to move from his hiding place. Blindly, he forced himself against the wall, feeling the smooth stone under his palms. He heard the sound of the water as the creature rose from the pool and slithered across the temple floor.

Where are you boy?

He tried to separate his mind, using all of his power to untangle himself from the black tendrils that wrapped around his mental probe. His heart hammered inside his chest and his breathing came in ragged gasps as the sweat ran down his face. Moments away from passing out under the strain, he felt the gentle touch of another mind.

Follow me. It said, in a girl's voice.

Focusing on her thoughts, he wove between the barbed strands of darkness, feeling their thorns prick at his soul, following the bright ball of light until finally he was free.

Who are you? He whispered, reaching out with his mind to the glowing sphere.

Her laugh was a bright, shining sound that filled him with joy. *You told me your name once? Don't you remember?*

He felt the memory surface, a vague recollection of her gentle mind touching his all those years ago, before Aaru, before he had been taken.

Lyra? He said softly, but the light was gone.

The creature was less than ten feet away, but was moving slowly now, disorientated as if searching for something, like a child that lost its mother.

Moving quietly along the opposite side of the hall Zack slipped through the door and into the sanctuary.

. . .

Lyra lifted her head from the table and smiled weakly at Juliana. 'I know where he is.'

'Well done,' said Juliana, patting her gently on the shoulder.

She went back to her chair and opened the speaking tube. 'Thomas, now we have his temporal location, prepare the tesseract.'

82

FACILITY

Detonations shook the crumbling walls as Zack sprinted through the waterlogged tunnel. He was directly below the river now, spurred on by the thought of how the next direct hit could flood the passageway in seconds.

Reaching the pressure door on the far side he placed his hand against the cold stone and felt the internal systems recognise his genetic code.

It was strange to think that somewhere in the passages on the other side of this door was a man that would one day become his grandfather. A so-called god who was currently trying to escape from the chaos with his family, leaving his people to fend for themselves.

He knew the stories of the Cataclysm as well as any child of Aaru: Tiamat, the Goddess of Chaos and her Djinn army came to punish the gods for their sins. Three of the Anunnaki: Anu, Enlil and Enki had fought valiantly but failed, while Thoth, Utu, Ishtar and Nergal had disappeared into other worlds, forsaking their children.

Nothing remained of them but the carvings on the walls of the temple, and half-remembered tales passed down through generations of survivors.

Their once great civilisation resorted to scrambling around in the dirt looking for clues as to what they had once been.

He looked down at the ring on his hand, feeling the power of the Anunnaki flowing within it. He would find the sword, he would use it to end the war, save his people and become one of the gods.

As the door slid away, he whispered another silent prayer to Amun-Ra.

83

TIAMAT

[Court of the Four Winds, Aaru]

The coils of the giant serpent were wrapped around the central dome of the Citadel. Its vast body covered in dark scales that glinted as if they were made of crystal. Black fire belched from its massive jaws, producing new forms of terrible creature with every breath.

In the Court of the Four Winds, the last of the guard formed a series of hollow squares making a valiant defensive formation around the remaining Anunnaki.

The three gods glowed in their brilliant armour.

The newly-born Djinn thrashed at the guard's shields with tentacles of spiny bone and arms carved into spears. They were a ghastly collection of nightmares, their bodies distorted and deformed by terrible experiments, nothing more than organic weapons.

Over the heads of the guards, the Anunnaki cast beams of light into the dark horde, cutting them down, only to have the fallen replaced by something equally terrible.

Josh and Rufius watched from the safety of a nearby

alley as the nightmare creatures slowly eroded the defensive lines. Their relentless attack was wearing down the guards who were slowly retreating inward.

'They've got less than twenty minutes before there'll be nothing left of them,' estimated the colonel. 'We need to get inside the Citadel.'

Josh didn't seem to hear him, he was too busy watching the dragon. 'We need to buy some time.'

'For what? If we don't get inside and stop Zack, there won't be anything left to save.'

'If we could stop the attack, he wouldn't have to use the weapon.'

Rufius scratched his beard as he considered the idea. 'What do you have in mind?'

'A diversion, something to give the Anunnaki time to regroup.'

The old man looked confused. 'And what exactly would this diversion consist of?'

Josh turned to Enkidu. 'How much damage can you do with those gauntlets?'

The synthetic raised his hands and tines of white energy arced between them. 'They are Enlil's, God of Storms.'

The colonel frowned, looking up into the clouds of dark terrors. 'I think we're going to need more than a strong wind to clear this.'

Suddenly, a loud boom rolled across the sky and the *Nautilus* burst through the dark clouds above the city, its hull shrouded in a halo of electrostatic energy.

Rufius cursed under his breath. 'Well now, that's a sight for sore eyes and no mistaking.'

Tiamat roared at the ship as it flew past, the forward

cannons blasting away everything in its path. Flexing dark, leathery wings, the serpent released her grip on the dome and launched herself in pursuit.

Josh tapped the synthetic on the shoulder and his eyes returned to normal. 'How on earth did they find us?'

Enkidu's eyes went white as he scanned the ship. 'I can detect four crew members, two share genetic signatures similar to those of Caitlin; another male who appears to be part Djinn and the last is a female with an aura similar to that of Zachary.'

'Lyra,' whispered Josh.

The colonel picked up his staff . 'Right, this is our best chance, you two make for the Citadel. Caitlin and I will keep them busy and try and get to the *Nautilus*.'

Josh turned to Caitlin. 'You going to be okay?'

She smiled and swung the staff under her arm. 'Let's face it, I was always the better shot.'

He kissed her and followed Enkidu towards the Citadel.

84

FLIGHT

[Nautilus]

'Can you handle their land forces?' Juliana's voice issued from the speaking tube.

Marcus swung the forward guns down, training them on the lines of dark creatures running across the square towards the guards.

'Yes,' he snarled through bared teeth. 'But I would be more useful on the ground.'

'Hold your horses big guy, there's going to be plenty of time for that.'

Juliana felt the shields take the full force of the dragon's fire as she banked around the dome.

'A couple more of those and we're going to need more than a refit,' she muttered to herself.

Lyra knelt with her hands pressed against the window, staring down at the square below.

'Tiamat, Goddess of Chaos,' she whispered.

'What?' said Juliana, struggling to keep the ship flying straight.

Lyra twisted around to face her. 'This is all I've dreamed of for weeks. They are all here, Zack, Caitlin all of them. To fight the dragon.'

'Great,' Juliana replied through gritted teeth. 'Now if you could possibly tell the goddess to get off my bloody rudder we might have a chance of rescuing them.'

85

BLOODLINE

[Research Facility, Aaru]

Z ack moved through the crowded corridors of the lower levels. The passages reeked of fear and desperation, the smell of frightened people exposed to their worst nightmares.

He ignored their pleading eyes, knowing that the best chance to save them was to reach the weapon.

The memory was still as vivid as the day the priests extracted it from him. They'd never realised how the images of the burned and dying haunted his dreams even after they had taken them.

Thoth's research facility was off limits to the civilians, hidden behind a steel door at the far end of the cavernous space of the central atrium. As Zack weaved between the huddled groups of refugees he wondered how long before the fire would come.

. . .

The door was secured by a genetic lock, fortunately his bloodline was a close enough match to allow him through. A crowd of bodies surged forward as the door slid shut behind him, severing more than one pair of hands as it slammed down.

Following the same path he'd seen in his dreams, he made his way through the labyrinth until he came to the tall doors of the vault.

Holding his breath, Zack placed his palm against the central symbol, the snake eating its own tail and waited. Tedious seconds passed before the sound of gears grinding into action resonated within the walls and the steel panels split in two and slowly moved apart.

'Hello son,' said his father.

86

GODS

'You think you can stop me?' threatened Zack, his mouth twisting into a cruel smile.

Josh shook his head. 'No, I know you'll just mess with my mind — but he might be able to.' He waved to something behind him.

'Hello Master,' said Enkidu, bowing as he stepped out of the shadows.

Zack's arrogant smirk fell away. 'Enkidu?' he said softly, his voice almost child-like. 'They told me you were destroyed.'

'Fate was kind,' the synthetic said, raising his eyes from the floor. 'We must leave this place Master. We do not belong here.'

'Abandon them? Just as they did?' Zack waved his hands around the room.

'It is not wise to change the past. I have seen what may come.'

Zack crossed his arms. 'So why did you take me? Why bring me to this god-forsaken world if not to change it?'

'It was never my intention to take a child, but you carried part of Thoth's pattern, without it we could not restore the timeless one.'

'And where is he now? Babbling in his tower? I've carried his guilt with me all these years, the pain and suffering of his failure. The sword can change all of that now. I have seen the way, it's my destiny.'

Josh looked down at the glowing sphere of Urshanabi below. 'The sword is dangerous. Thoth told me that it's unstable, there's not enough power to use it.'

'It has more than enough for what I need.'

Josh looked confused. 'What are you going to do?'

'Open the gates of the underworld, banish them to Duat.'

'And most of Aaru with it,' Josh added, assuming that Zack was planning to create a temporal breach into the Maelstrom by overloading the sword.

Zack waved his hand as if swatting a fly and started down the ramp towards the equipment. 'You forget father, I can see what is to come.'

Josh turned and followed him, motioning to the synthetic to wait.

'How can you be so sure? You never saw us did you? Rufius told me you didn't know we were coming.' Josh quickened his pace to keep up.

Zack reached one of the consoles and began to manipulate the controls. 'You were hidden from me, I cannot see beyond the borders of this continuum.'

The rotation of the sphere increased, and lines of energy streaked across its surface as the machinery shuddered to life.

Josh tried to ignore it. 'Exactly, no one can know everything. The future is too random to predict with any certainty. You never knew about this future until I gave you the ring.'

Zack laughed. 'I took the ring. It was part of my pattern. My inheritance.'

The sphere changed colour, shades of red and amber blossomed like ink in water over its surface.

'So you think this will save them?'

'I know it will,' his son said defiantly.

'It won't. I've fought the Nihil before, you don't have to be a god to beat them and you certainly don't need a machine.'

Frowning, Zack turned towards his father. 'You? How could you have stopped the Djinn?'

'Look in my head, it's all there.' Josh tapped his temple. 'Gods only have the power you give them, we're the ones with the ability to change the future.'

He felt his son's mind enter his memories, scanning through the events of the Eschaton Cascade and the battle with the Nihil, until he came to the final moment with Caitlin.

'She died?'

Josh nodded. 'Saving me.'

'And you changed everything to bring her back,' he said defiantly.

'I wanted to make it right, to find the perfect timeline. But it doesn't exist, and when I stopped trying to change the past, you came along.'

There was a high-pitched whine from the machinery, and the sphere began to collapse in on itself.

There were tears in Zack's eyes. 'You should leave now.'

Josh felt his son's will imposing itself, he found himself turning towards the ramp.

'You're still going to try?' he said as he began to walk away.

'I have to father, I can't let them die.'

'No,' said Enkidu, appearing from the shadows. His arms gently wrapping around Zack's chest, like a father embracing his child. He lifted him up and away from the controls. Zack struggled against the iron grip of the synthetic until his body went limp.

Urshanabi was becoming highly unstable, and Josh stared helplessly at the dials and screens unsure of what to try.

'Do you have any idea how to shut this off?' he shouted to Enkidu.

The synthetic laid Zack down gently on the floor, checking to see that he was still breathing and then calmly walked over to Josh.

'I observed Thoth during the preparation of our insertion,' he explained, his hands a blur as they moved quickly over the console. 'It seems he was attempting to override the containment fields. This should stabilise them.'

The sphere shimmered, losing cohesion for a second and then re-established itself, the patterns returning to normal.

'No shit,' said Josh under his breath, turning back to Zack, who was beginning to stir.

'Hey, do you mind if I borrow this?' asked Josh, taking Solomon's ring from his son's finger.

Zack looked up at Urshanabi and grimaced. 'You have condemned them all.'

Josh felt the strong grip of Zack's mind forming around his own. Felt the power of his rage enveloping him. He struggled to move, the coercion overriding his body's responses.

There's another way. I have seen it. Lyra's voice echoed through both their minds.

'Lyra?' Josh whispered, through clenched teeth.

'She's here,' said Zack, releasing his hold on his father's mind. 'And she's in great danger.'

Images of the battle flooded into their minds as Lyra shared her view from the *Nautilus*. The Djinn's horde were overwhelming the last of the Anunnaki.

'They all are,' said Josh, holding out his hand to help Zack to his feet. 'We can save them, if we work together.'

87

BATTLE

[Court of the Four Winds, Aaru]

Tiamat was wrapped around the *Nautilus*, her coils buckling the hull plating.

Inside the ship, Juliana was struggling to keep her in the air.

'I'm going to have to put her down,' she shouted to anyone who was listening. 'Prepare for a crash landing.'

Josh and Zack walked out of the Citadel. The *Nautilus* came in low overhead, its engines straining to control the descent. It glided across the plaza, trapping the dragon's body under the hull as it tore up the paving stones.

When the dust settled, Josh saw Caitlin and Rufius carving a line towards the ship. A hatch opened on one side and Marcus leapt out in full beast mode, ploughing into the surrounding Djinn with claws and teeth.

A scream echoed over the square as Tiamat writhed, trying to free herself from under the ship. The Djinn turned as one and swarmed like ants around the brass hull pushing themselves under the bow, trying to lift it to save their queen.

'We need to get them out, before she frees herself,' said Josh, pushing back his sleeves. 'Enkidu, you go and help Caitlin. Zack stay behind me.'

Enkidu nodded, powered up Enlil's gauntlets and ran down the steps into the fray.

When the first of the Djinn touched Josh, he felt the cold, empty void of its life leeching into him. The fire in the creature's eyes dimmed as its body crystallised, before shattering into a million pieces of black glass.

Zack look impressed, stepping back as two more creatures exploded before him.

'I'm like poison,' he explained, 'their timelines collapse when they connect to mine.'

His son followed him through the widening path of crumbling bodies towards the *Nautilus*.

Tiamat was hammering her head against the conning tower, her teeth tearing off the metal sheeting as she tried to free herself. The shaking of the ship roused Lyra. She found herself under a pile of cushions and books, and it took her a moment to orientate herself to the fact that the ship was lying on its side.

Juliana was still strapped in her chair, her head slumped down on her chest. The front of the ship shifted as if someone were lifting it, books and crockery rolled across the bulkhead that was now the floor. Lyra struggled to her feet and clambered over the pipework towards her.

'Juliana can you hear me?' Lyra whispered as she felt her neck for a pulse. There was a purpling bruise on the side of her face where she had hit her head in the crash, but she was still breathing and there was a strong heartbeat.

She came round with a jolt. 'What!'

Lyra fumbled with the harness, trying to loosen the buckle. 'It's all right. We've landed, but I think the dragon is going to break through any minute.'

Juliana blinked, raising her hand to touch the bruise. 'Where's Thomas?' she asked groggily.

'Here!' shouted her husband emerging from under a pile of debris at the other end of the bridge.

The ship shook once more.

'What was that?' asked Juliana as Lyra finally managed to unlock the harness.

'Tiamat,' replied Lyra, 'and her army.'

The dragon was thrashing its spiked tail like a massive mace at anything that got too close. The Anunnaki and their guards were firing the weapons at her head, but the bolts of energy were simply deflecting off the obsidian scales.

Tiamat roared and black fire spewed from her mouth, dark creatures twisted up out of the scorched ground.

Josh turned back to Zack, the path behind them was still clear, the Djinn too scared to cross the remains of their dead.

'Can you see how to save them?' he asked, stepping aside as another Djinn lunged at him.

Zack nodded.

. . .

Time slowed as he touched the hull of the ship, and Zack felt the future unfurl. The destiny of every person on board flooded into his mind. He saw the fate of his father, his grandparents and Lyra, who were all trapped inside the *Nautilus* when its tesseract imploded. The blast obliterated Tiamat and her army, but took all of them along with it.

'The tesseract is critically unstable,' he said, turning to Josh who was holding back the horde. 'It will destroy the dragon, but kill everyone inside.'

'Find a way to get them out,' shouted Josh.

Zack closed his eyes and looked for another path. Lyra and the grandparents would need more time to get free of the ship. The tesseract's decay could be slowed manually, but someone would need to sacrifice themselves to do it.

'There's a way,' he said. 'We need to reroute the power from the quantum capacitor. Can you get me inside.'

Josh nodded and grabbed his hand. The Ring of Solomon glowed as he drew on its power to move them inside the ship.

88

GAUNTLETS

[Court of the Four Winds, Aaru]

R ufius roared, driving back another Djinn attack with a spectacular sweeping arc of his staff. Caitlin stood pressed against his back, the unceasing wall of nightmare creatures looming up before her like a tsunami.

She fired randomly into them, they were packed so tightly together that there was no need to aim at anything in particular. But, no matter how many she took down, others replaced them instantly.

Marcus appeared from amongst the horde, his body raked with fresh wounds and his muzzle stained with black blood. He fell to his knees beside them.

They all knew it was a losing battle, but none was ready to admit defeat.

Suddenly a hole opened up in the front line and a silver-shielded form came striding through the masses.

'Enkidu!' shouted Caitlin, grateful for the distraction. The synthetic nodded, raising his gloved hand and loosing a series of powerful blasts into the Djinn.

The wall retreated and Enkidu increased the radius of his shield until it encompassed all of them. Any creature that came within two feet of the force field turned to ash.

'Where's Josh?' asked Caitlin.

Enkidu nodded towards the *Nautilus*. 'He is attempting to rescue your family.'

Caitlin frowned. 'And Zack?'

'They are together.'

She took some comfort from the thought of them working together. No matter how strange the situation was, at least they had each other.

'We need to help them,' she said.

'I'm not sure there's much we can do,' said Rufius, helping Marcus to his feet.

'I am here to keep you safe,' insisted the synthetic, his tone indicating he was not to be challenged.

89

SACRIFICE

[Nautilus]

The tesseract was fluctuating badly, the spinning cubes clearly losing cohesion.

Zack went to one of the dashboards and began to adjust the dials.

'How do you know what to do?' asked Josh.

'I can see the future remember? Everything I touch allows me to see the consequences.'

Instinctively, Josh put his hand on one of the levers.

'Don't move that!' snapped Zack. 'Lyra needs your help, they're on the bridge.'

Josh nodded and made his way through the topsy-turvy gangway that led to the forward section.

Lyra was sitting with Caitlin's parents, watching the battle through the window. Juliana was badly hurt, her face swollen with a large bruise on one side. Thomas looked dazed and confused.

Lyra jumped up, pointing an old army pistol at him. 'Josh!' she cried, lowering the weapon and stumbling over the floor to give him a hug. 'You got my message.'

Josh wanted to ask her how, but there wasn't time. 'Are you guys okay?'

'Fine,' said Juliana, 'looks worse than it is, which is more than I can say for my ship.'

'Where's Caitlin?' asked Lyra, stepping back and wiping her eyes.

Josh nodded towards the window. 'Out there, she's with Rufius and Marcus.'

The ship shuddered as the bow shifted again.

'We need to get off the ship,' continued Josh. 'Zack says the tesseract is unstable.'

Juliana struggled to get to her feet. 'We won't survive very long out there either,' she said, turning to help her husband to stand.

'I can get you to safety,' he said, holding out his hand, the ring of Solomon glowing faintly on his finger.

They reappeared in the atrium of the Citadel.

'Look after them,' Josh said to Lyra.

She nodded, kneeling down to examine Juliana's injury.

Thomas looked around the colonnaded walls of the building. 'Where's Zachary?'

'Still on the ship,' Josh said, turning back to the battle. 'I need to get him out.'

Suddenly time seemed to slow. A wave of energy rippled out from the *Nautilus*, flattening everything in the surrounding blast radius. The air around the hull distorted, a bubble of temporal energy enveloped the ship and Tiamat, twisting them in a thousand different directions at once.

'No!' screamed Josh, but it was too late.

A blinding light filled the plaza and then shrank to the size of a small sphere before disappearing completely.

With Tiamat gone, the Djinn disintegrated like smoke in the wind. Enkidu lowered the shield and Caitlin, Rufius and Marcus found themselves standing in a courtyard of ash.

She saw Josh running towards her, his face twisted and filled with agony and she knew something had happened to Zack.

90

FIFTEEN MINUTES

[Aaru]

They walked slowly back towards the Citadel, Josh holding Caitlin tightly around the waist to stop her from falling.

'I can't believe he's gone,' she repeated to herself, tears streaking her cheeks, emotion cracking her voice.

Josh tried to think of something to say, but there were no words. He was sure Zack knew what was going to happen before he entered the *Nautilus* — he'd seen his own death and went all the same.

One single, selfless act had saved an entire civilisation and changed the timelines of countless others. Now Enkidu would never come in search of his missing god, never steal their son only to have him become destroyer of a thousand worlds.

'He saved us all,' Josh said, feeling a strange moment of pride. He was their child, but also not. In Josh's mind, theirs was still a seven-week-old baby, not a man. It was hard to reconcile the two.

'I wish we'd got to know him better,' Caitlin said, wiping her tears away with her sleeve. She looked sad, even broken, Josh found it hard to look into her eyes.

Ahead of them, Rufius was virtually carrying Marcus up the steps into the building.

They followed, Josh stopping at the top to look out over the desolation. The citizens of Aaru were slowly emerging from the shadows, picking through the debris for what was left of their possessions.

'He lived with the memories of this day for most of his life,' said Josh, trying to imagine what it must have been like. 'It was always going to come back to this event.'

Caitlin sighed. 'So, what do we do now?'

Josh turned back to the Citadel. 'We need to talk to Enkidu.'

The synthetic was working on Urshanabi, manipulating one control after another, trying to stabilise the fields.

Standing behind him, they watched as the sphere separated the myriad timelines like a fraying rope, focussing onto one single continuum.

'Where do you want to intersect?' he asked calmly.

'I'm still not sure I understand the science of this?' said Rufius, scratching his beard.

Caitlin's mother sighed and tried to explain it once more, counting out the points on her fingers. 'One, the Cataclysm never happened. Two, the founder didn't abandoned them. Three, so he never came to our timeline and therefore Josh and the Order never existed.'

'And Zack was never stolen,' added Caitlin. 'Because he was never born.'

'So how come we're still here?' said Marcus, who had

transformed back into his human form.

Enkidu looked up from his console. 'Because when Urshanabi brought you here, it disconnected you from your original timeline.'

Rufius was still struggling with the concept. 'But won't our timeline have changed, because Thoth never left?'

'On the contrary,' said a deep booming voice. It was the founder, now dressed in the dark robes of Lord Dee. 'I have all of his memories. I will become the one you know as the founder. The Order will be restored.'

'How— '

Enkidu cut Josh off. 'I brought him here. It seemed such a waste to lose all of that knowledge.'

The founder walked up the steps towards the sphere. 'I will see you in two thousand years,' he said, before walking into the glowing light.

'Will we remember any of this?' asked Lyra.

The synthetic nodded his head. 'The sword will insert you into your own timeline at the point of your choosing, everything you have experienced will be retained, unless of course you wish it otherwise?'

Lyra shook her head. 'There are many things I wish I could unsee, but I want to remember Zack's sacrifice.'

They paused for a moment, each one of them reflecting on the last moments of the battle.

Caitlin took Josh by the hand. 'I think I would like to have a normal pregnancy this time, not one that involves shipping me out into the Maelstrom.'

'Not that we have a ship,' moaned Juliana.

'We'll build a new one,' said her husband reassuringly. 'With extra cabins for guests.'

'And a shower,' said Caitlin.

'Can we get going now?' interrupted Rufius. 'I've had

quite enough of this place.'

The synthetic nodded, he reset the coordinates and the sphere reestablished itself. Marcus, Rufius, Lyra and Caitlin's parents stepped up onto the platform, but Caitlin held back.

'You go, we'll be through in a sec.'

They waved and disappeared into the glowing ball of energy.

Josh turned to Enkidu. 'What will you do now?'

'After I have disassembled this machine, I will help to rebuild the city. There will be stories to tell of the new gods who helped save Aaru. Zachary will take his place in the pantheon of heroes. His sacrifice will not be forgotten.'

Josh smiled. 'So he becomes a god after all.'

Enkidu's face suddenly looked more human. 'I shall miss Zachary.'

'We all will,' agreed Caitlin sadly. 'But now we can give him the life he was supposed to have had.'

The synthetic bowed. 'It was an honour to meet you both. I will ensure that your names are written into our history.'

Josh looked at Caitlin. 'Actually, can you erase all references to our timeline? I think we've had enough contact with your continuum.'

The synthetic straightened. 'As you wish.'

'How precise can you be with this machine?' asked Caitlin, studying the control console.

He smiled, understanding the reason for her question. 'I can place you fifteen minutes after Zack's conception.'

Caitlin's cheeks reddened a little. 'Actually could you make it fifteen minutes before?'

Other books in the Infinity Engines universe.

The Infinity Engines

1. Anachronist

2. Maelstrom

3. Eschaton

4. Aeons

5. Tesseract

Infinity Engines Origins

Chimæra

Changeling

Infinity Engines Missions

1776

1888

You can download 1776 for FREE plus get updates and news by subscribing to my mailing list (simply scan the QR code below).

ACKNOWLEDGEMENTS

As ever, a big thank you to my family for supporting me. Without you, it would never have seen the light of day.

I would also like to thank the editorial team: Simon for the grammatical and fact checking, Karen for catching all the things he missed, and the members of the Infinity Engines group that continue to support my crazy ideas.

Most of all, thank you for reading my work, please feel free to join my community and let me know what you thought. And on that note, if you would be so kind as to leave a review on Amazon that would be most appreciated.

Cheers,
Andy x

ABOUT THE AUTHOR

For more information about The Infinity Engines series and other Here Be Dragons books please visit: <u>www. infinityengines.com</u>

Printed in Great Britain
by Amazon